GRIFFIN

HOPE CITY

MARYANN JORDAN

Griffin (Hope City) Copyright 2021 All rights reserved.

No part of this book may be reproduced or transmitted in any form or by any means, electronic or mechanical, including photocopying, recording, or by any information storage and retrieval system without the written permission of the author, except where permitted by law.

If you are reading this book and did not purchase it, then you are reading an illegal pirated copy. If you would be concerned about working for no pay, then please respect the author's work! Make sure that you are only reading a copy that has been officially released by the author.

This book is a work of fiction. Names, characters, places, and incidents either are products of the author's imagination or are used fictitiously. Any resemblance to actual persons, living or dead, events, or locales is entirely coincidental.

ISBN ebook: 978-1-947214-92-7

ISBN print: 978-1-947214-93-4

❦ Created with Vellum

1

"Stop! Stop right now!"

Damnit! Caitlyn raced out the door, turning at the last second to shout in her most authoritative voice to the others behind her, "Stay where you are!" She should have saved her breath for all the good it did as they crowded behind her, pushing through the doorway and out where the crowd was gathering.

The two boys in the hall were already throwing punches, fists hitting hard enough that blood spurted from one's cut lip and the other's nose was bleeding. Cringing at the sound, her stomach churned.

"Stop now!" she shouted again, her heart slamming against her ribs. More teenagers rushed into the hallway, and a brief image of the bloodlust from the ancient Romans watching the gladiators ran through her mind. Another hit knocked one of the boys backward as well as jolting her thoughts back to the happenings in front of her. Some spectators yelled, "Fight!" with exuberance while others shouted for whichever one they hoped was winning. *Where the hell are the other teachers?*

She moved closer to the action, trying to get them to stop as her adrenaline spiked. Shouting usually worked with guys. She found they were less likely to keep fighting with a female teacher intervening. *Now, girls fighting? Not so much. They'd keep punching, slapping, scratching, pulling hair, and whatever else they could do and never gave a damn about who was around!*

Having no recourse but to physically intervene, she saw her entry and darted. The two boys separated just long enough for her to place her hands on the chest of one, and she looked over her shoulder in gratitude to see one of her students, a huge football player, try to grab the other. The student she hoped was under her control lashed out one last time just as she attempted to move to the side. Her head snapped back as his fist connected with her face, and for a second, she felt nothing as she dropped like a stone, straight to the floor, landing on her ass. An exploding pain slammed into her, and the breath left her lungs. The world became black other than the dots of lights flashing in front of her. *Stars... fucking stars!*

Her hand clutched her face as she attempted to draw air into her lungs but found the pain kept her from doing anything other than gasp. Barely aware of the sounds around her, she caught lots of 'Shits', 'damns', and 'fucks' from the students, with a few voices chiming in with, "Oh, my God, you hit Ms. McBride!"

She no longer heard fists hitting flesh but no longer cared if the two boys pummeled each other into oblivion. She'd never been hit in the face before, and the pain sent nausea flooding over her. *Please, God, don't let me throw up.* Tears fell unbidden.

"Get back to your classes!"

Finally, the orders from more faculty could be heard through the cacophony of other sounds. Hands reached down to her, and with her one good eye opened, she managed to see a few of her students gathered close.

"Ms. McBride, you gotta breathe."

She recognized another student, concern plastered on his face, but couldn't focus through the pain. Turning her head slightly, she saw two male teachers with the fighters in tow, hauling them down the hall. One of the fighters looked over his shoulder and cried out, "I didn't mean to, Ms. McBride! Fuck, I'm sorry!"

"Someone get the nurse!"

She looked back at the student in front of her as he called for the nurse. He was shifted out of the way, and another face filled her vision.

"Hey, Caitlyn, let's see what we've got." A man squatted in front of her, and she stared at him from the one eye that still seemed to work. "How many fingers am I holding up?"

"Um... three..." she managed to grunt.

"Who am I?"

"Ja... Jamie."

"Good girl. Now, did we ever go out on a date?"

"Ugh..."

He laughed as he gently pulled her hand from her face, and she squinted before glancing around to see that the other teachers mostly had the students back in their classrooms. One of the administrators stood to the side, and the nurse hustled down the hall toward her.

"Gonna have a shiner there, Caitlyn. And for the record, I thought our date was good," Jamie said, bringing her attention back to him.

Not in the mood for anyone's humor, even a good friend who'd once been on a not-so-good date, she fought back the tears that were falling, afraid sobbing would hurt more. He was pushed aside as the nurse knelt in front of her.

"Oh, dear," the nurse muttered, holding Caitlyn's chin and turning her head from side to side. "Let's get you into the wheelchair."

"The boys... they were bleeding," Caitlyn mumbled.

"They'll live. The admins and security officers have them in the clinic right now. My assistant is checking them out before their parents are called."

"No wheelchair," she moaned, standing with the nurse and Jamie's assistance.

"Sorry, dearie, but school policy. You might have lost consciousness."

Her ass landed in the wheelchair, and she winced, both at the movement and seeing students still peering out of classroom doors to see what was happening. "My class—"

"Department chair will cover," Robert said. As one of the assistant principals, he was there to make sure the halls stayed cleared, her class was covered, and the nurse was getting her to the clinic. He placed his hand on her shoulder. "You know the drill, Caitlyn. You'll have to see a doctor per policy. And you'll have to write an incident report even though a review of the security cameras will take place."

"Um huh," she mumbled, pain and embarrassment vying for dominance. *Okay, seriously, it's the pain that's winning out.* Soon, they arrived in the clinic where the nurse followed the concussion protocol and gently probed her face before giving her an ice pack to hold on her eye.

"Well, the good news is that you don't seem to have a concussion—"

Caitlyn snorted, then winced again. "God, this sucks." Looking at the nurse, she sighed. "Okay, Louise, lay it on me. What's the bad news?"

"You're definitely going to have a black eye. Although the kids will just think you're even more badass."

Before she could respond, Frank, the school's security officer, came in, anger vibrating from him. "Their parents have been called. The admins have suspended both of them. The one that hit you probably won't be allowed back." He shook his finger toward her. "And you're gonna press charges, right?"

Not able to think past the pain, she attempted a glare in his direction but was sure it fell short if his grimace was anything to go by. "No, I'm not." She sighed. "It was an accident."

"An accident?" he shouted.

She sighed again. "Yes. He didn't try to hit me. I got in the way."

"Christ, you bleedin' heart teachers," he groused, stomping out of the clinic.

Watching him leave, she noticed her good friend, who was one of the teachers, standing in the doorway. "Hey," Barbara said softly. "How are you?"

"Peachy," she groaned. "My face hurts. I have to see a doctor. The kids in my class are probably freaked. And I'm no longer a favorite of our security officer."

Barbara looked at Louise. "Is she cleared to leave? I told the admins that I'd take her to the ER."

Sighing, Caitlyn wanted nothing more than to go home, take some pain medicine, and crawl into bed.

"Yeah, she's ready."

Thanking the nurse, she turned as one of her students ran into the clinic. "I've got your purse, Ms. McBride. Oh! That looks so bad! I mean, it looks like it hurts. I mean, you're still pretty, but... oh, my..."

"Thank you, Sidney," she mumbled.

Barbara walked her out to the teacher's parking lot. She climbed into the small car, and as they pulled onto the street, she chanced a peek at her face in the vanity mirror. *Shit!* Her cheek was already bruising, and the area around her eye was turning a deep purple. *It'll fade... eventually.* Tossing up thanks that her nose hadn't taken the brunt of the hit, she flipped the visor up and leaned her head back for the short ride. She closed her eyes, finding that it helped to keep the nausea at bay.

Thirty minutes later, she sat on the uncomfortable bed in an ER bay, fatigue weighing down her limbs as the adrenaline of the afternoon's excitement faded. Voices coming from the bay next to her caught her attention. At least eavesdropping gave her something to do besides concentrate on how much her face hurt.

"Fuckin' nail gun—"
"I told you to watch what Rodriguez was doing—"
"Only five stitches—"
"Better than my last trip to the ER—"

The curtain flung to the side when her doctor came back into her room, and she shifted her focus to him. "So, what's the verdict, Doc? Will I live?"

He chuckled and stepped closer. Her vision was still blurry in her good eye but her slightly jostled brain had no problem discerning the tall, blond, blue-eyed doctor with no wedding ring on his finger. Not that she was looking for Mr. Right, but she was tired of ending up with Mr. Wrongs. He patted her leg and then stood awkwardly as though he wanted to say more before moving to the computer. *Yeah, fat chance he'd ask me out looking like this.*

"You'll live. No concussion but I'll give you a prescription for pain meds. Just enough for three days, but you can come off them and use over-the-counter medicine as soon as possible. And my advice is to stay away from the guy that hit you."

As he pulled up her chart on the computer, she shifted her gaze to the hall where he'd left the curtain open. A man had left the room next to hers and was standing just outside her bay, his gaze on her face. One look at him caused all thoughts of the handsome doctor to disappear as all the oxygen around her seemed to dissipate. This guy was tall. A T-shirt fit tight across his chest, but it was his arms that sucked her in. Muscular, yet lean, as though he didn't just work out but actually worked. *What is it about arms?* Staring, she knew the answer... it was imagining those arms wrapped around her.

His hair was long and wavy, curling about his ears, and his sunglasses were shoved up on top of his head, not as a fashion statement but as a way to get them off his face when inside. His face was angular, chiseled, with lips pinched tight. Straight nose, high cheekbones.

The intensity of his stare made her feel naked, as though he could see straight into her... how her injury made her feel vulnerable. For a second, she wondered if he was going to come into her room, and while it made no sense that he would, she wanted to hold on to his attention. His gaze stayed pinned on her, and for a few seconds, she held her breath.

She'd forgotten the doctor was still in the room, tapping on the computer, until he said, "Yeah, being used as a punching bag is no fun, I'm sure."

Considering the doc knew the circumstances of her bruised and swollen face, she wanted to roll her eyes at his poor attempt at humor but knew that maneuver would be painful. Keeping her gaze on the hall, it was obvious the man heard the doctor's words. His eyes glittered, and his jaw tightened. She wanted to call out and explain that she'd broken up a fight between teenagers, not been abused. But then, he grimaced, and she stared, no words coming. Maybe it wasn't a true grimace, but the edge of his lip turned up. She'd only seen that look one other time, and that was when her mother had shown her a picture of Elvis Presley, and Caitlyn had been fascinated. But before she had a chance to say anything, the man turned and walked down the hall.

A strange sense of disappointment and loss moved through her. She'd never see him again and hated the idea that he thought she just let someone abuse her. The feeling that something special had just walked away moved over her. *How hard was I hit? Maybe I do have a concussion.*

The doctor turned his attention back to her and offered what she supposed was a sympathetic smile. But compared to the man she'd just ogled, the doctor no longer held the same appeal. Sucking in a quick breath, she asked, "When can I get out of here?"

A nurse came around the corner, pushing a wheelchair into her room. As though anxious to escape, the doctor said, "She'll go over your discharge papers. I hope you feel better."

Watching him leave as though his pants were on fire, Caitlyn sighed. Just as the nurse started to hand the discharge paperwork for her to sign, a much louder noise in the hall caught her attention. For a brief second, she wondered if the mystery man was going to come back, demand that she leave whoever was abusing her, and he'd carry her off on his white horse... *or black pickup truck,* which she felt sure he must have.

Instead, three men walked in, two with badges clipped to their belts and one in a paramedic uniform. All dark hair like hers. All piercing blue eyes like hers, their gazes locked on her face. And all looking extremely pissed. *Oh, fuck... just shoot me now.* "If someone from the school called one of you, I'm suing for breach of confidentiality."

"Shut it, Caitlyn."

She tossed a narrow-eyed glare toward Kyle, her second-oldest brother, the one with a trigger-temper, and she winced at the movement. Feeling the heat ratchet up in the room, she tried to settle her expression and her irritation.

"Hey, sis."

This came from Rory, the paramedic and third brother. He glanced toward the nurse and said, "Once she signs, I'll make sure she gets what she needs."

The nurse smiled, and Caitlyn managed a somewhat abbreviated eye roll as the older woman practically swooned at her brothers' feet. While Rory took charge of her paperwork, Sean and Kyle moved closer. She lifted her hand as their mouths opened and got there first. "Fight in the hallway at school. I intervened. Got clocked by a punch not intended for me. Fight stopped. Boys taken in by security and admin. I was brought here. Nothing more than a black eye. All good."

"Seriously?" Kyle bit out.

Sean shot his brother a hard stare, then smiled at Caitlyn and hefted his hip onto the bed next to her. "You sure? No concussion?"

Her shoulders slumped. "That's it, Sean. You can check the paperwork that Rory is so carefully scrutinizing." Now it was her turn to pin him with a stare out of her good eye. "So, what are you all doing here? Just happened to be in the neighborhood?"

"Rory was in the ER when he saw your name on the board. I'd already gotten a call from the deputy at your school, and I called Kyle in case he was closer."

As usual, the eldest of the six McBride siblings was

succinct and true to his take-charge nature. Sometimes, that was nice, and sometimes, it just chafed. "I'm surprised that Tara and Erin aren't here as well," she quipped, referring to her sisters.

"They've been notified," Rory said, turning from the nurse with paperwork in hand.

Swallowing, she leveled them with an incendiary glare that she hoped worked, but considering none of them disappeared in a poof of fire, she imagined that a one-eyed glare didn't have the same potency. "If any one of you have called Mom, I'll—"

Seeing their guilty faces, she cried, "Come on, guys. You know Mom's gonna freak! And there's no way she won't tell Dad."

"Yeah, well, they care. We all do. Your job is to teach, not get punched. I want to know where the other teachers were," Sean said.

"And security," Kyle added. "And why aren't you going to press charges?"

She was going to kill the school deputy. "Because, as you said, my job is to teach. It was two boys pissed at each other, probably over a girl. Neither are bad kids, and while I don't condone fighting to solve a problem, they weren't trying to hit me. And the one who did immediately apologized and, I'm sure, feels terrible. So, lesson learned to him without me needing to drag him to juvie court with an assault charge. It's over."

"Come on, let's get you out of here," Rory tossed out with a wink, giving her a hand into the wheelchair.

As they rolled her down the hall, she glanced around to see if the tall, gorgeous Mr. Gruffy was still around.

Not seeing him, she couldn't decide if that was good or bad. Noting her brothers staring, she quickly said, "My car is still at the school—"

"I'll get it," Kyle said. "I'll leave it at your place."

She dug out her keys and handed them to him as he kissed her forehead. "Thanks, bro. Give Kimberly my love." He offered a chin lift before turning to walk out the door.

Rory kissed her next. "Gotta get back to work."

Looking up, she offered a wan smile. "Tell Sandy I'll call her tomorrow. And thanks for checking on me."

Left alone with Sean, she climbed into his SUV. She started to close her eyes when he said, "Mom wants you to come to the house so she can see for herself that you're okay."

"Oh, Christ, Sean. No. No way, no how." He opened his mouth to protest, but she threw up her hand and pleaded, "I need some pain meds and my bed. That's it. Mom can come over tomorrow. Please…"

He twisted around to stare, then slowly nodded. "You got it. But I can only hold her and Dad off one day. Then they'll want to make sure you're really okay."

They drove the rest of the way in silence, but when he parked outside her house, he turned and said, "I know you're pissed we all showed, but you're our little sister. We have to look out for you."

Fatigue, frustration, and pain all warred within, bringing tears close to the surface. Swallowing hard as she nodded, she reached out and placed her hand over his. "I know, and I'm grateful. Honestly, I am. So many of the kids I teach don't have anyone at home who gives a shit, so I know I'm lucky."

He smiled and assisted her down from his SUV, walking her to the door of the large Victorian house. Kissing her forehead, he said goodbye, and she gratefully went inside. Bypassing her landlady's apartment door, she climbed up the stairs and into her apartment.

Usually, she loved stepping into her apartment, having created a space that was unique and beautiful, reveling in the fact that it was all hers. Now, ignoring everything around her, she headed straight into her bathroom and swallowed a pain pill. Stripping, she pulled on her camisole and sleep shorts before running a brush through her hair. Exhaustion pulled but she lifted her gaze to stare at her reflection in the mirror. Now seeing what her brothers saw, she was even more glad she didn't allow her parents to see her like this. Her left eye was almost shut, the purple all around giving her a decidedly prize-fighter-who-lost appearance. *One minute I'm teaching American Literature to a bunch of juniors and the next minute I'm on my ass. I wonder if there's a life lesson in that scenario?*

Refusing to think more about her day, she flipped off the light and climbed into bed. Pulling the covers up to her ear, she closed her eyes, but for a long time, the day's events continued to play on a loop in her mind. Angry shouts. The crowd. The hit. The pain. And the gorgeous man in the ER who looked disgusted when his gaze landed on her. *I have the worst luck.*

With that thought, she finally fell asleep, but strange dreams plagued her rest. Dreams of running through the dark halls of her school, the fear of an unknown someone racing behind her. Looking up, she spied a tall man with blue eyes at the end of the hall, light streaming in behind him. His hand extended toward her, beckoning. She reached out and… awoke, covered in sweat and shaking. Sitting up in bed, she blew out a long breath. *Damn, pain-pill-induced freaky dreams. God, I just want to sleep.*

2

"Hey, Griff! Where do you want this?"

Griffin Capella shook his head as he stood in the bed of the large pickup truck. One to always have his mind on work, he couldn't get the woman from the ER yesterday out of his mind. Unable to see much about her other than the horrifically bruising face, his thoughts had slammed back to years before when he'd felt so helpless, when his dad would come home from the bar, angry about something, anything.

"Griff!"

He jerked and glanced down at Nate, one of his workers. "Set it to the side, next to the house. We won't be here for another week, but the owner said we can go ahead and put the lumber at the back."

Nate and Andrew dropped the load of wood next to the brick house, the clatter resounding sharply in the early morning peace. Griffin pulled out his checklist and pencil, marking off what they were delivering. He'd never gotten used to using his phone or tablet for such a menial and yet necessary task. Pencil and paper always felt more organic. Sort of like the designs he created.

He'd always kept meticulous notes for his business, making sure to put them into spreadsheets when he got home each night so that Bette, his cousin and office manager, wouldn't lose her shit trying to decipher his handwriting. She could be a pain in his ass, just like when they were kids, but it was her eye for details that let him know about the thefts at a few of his worksites. And those thefts were more of a pain in his ass than she could ever be.

His true passion was restoring the intricate woodwork on the older homes in Hope City, specifically arches, lattices, decorative eaves, cornices, stairways, and porch spindles. While that kept him busy, to provide a steadier income, his contracting business handled numerous renovations on the older homes. Recently, a few thefts of building materials and tools from homes he was restoring had him on edge. He had talked to the owner of this home about the work she wanted to be completed, and because there wasn't space inside, he'd agreed to leave the wood on the outside but behind a locked fence. *God, let it stay safe!* His profit margin wasn't very high, and if he had to take another hit on replacing stolen materials, he'd have to raise his prices to include a large storage facility.

Wham! Another stack of wood landed on the pile. He glanced up then double-checked his list to make sure he'd brought everything he needed.

"What the hell is all that noise?"

The sound of a female's voice calling from above had

him lift his gaze to a balcony on the second floor near the back. The morning sun glistened behind her, and he squinted, unable to see her features clearly. Her dark, almost-black hair was a riot of waves around her head, shading her face, keeping her in the shadows. She had thrown on a long, multi-colored kimono-type robe, but it hung open in the front as though she'd raced outside, not bothering to tie the belt. Her sleep shorts were just that—*short*. He had no idea how tall she was, but her toned legs seemed to go on forever. Her tight top showed off a trim waist and the curve of her breasts, leaving little to the imagination.

She grabbed the sides of the kimono, jerking them together, now making his continued imagination go into overdrive. Sucking in a quick breath, he was struck by the statuesque woman on the balcony. Slammed with a bolt of lust, he wished he could see her face.

"It's too early in the morning to be disturbing other people's peace! Can't you do this later?" she called down.

It wasn't that her voice was strident or unpleasant, but considering he and his crew had been up before dawn, her complaint wasn't met with joy. His lust was now doused, and he growled, "Sorry about the noise, but some people have to work for a living, ma'am."

Her chin jerked back, and she huffed loud enough for him to hear her from the distance.

"Work for a living? I assure you, I work for a living, too!"

"Then you'll understand that not everyone can have a nine-to-five, Monday-to-Friday, right? So, pardon me if I don't care about your beauty sleep, and I'll get on with my job."

The sound of another huff and then a door slamming met his ears as he turned away to see Nate and Andrew grinning up at him.

"Damn, boss. You're gonna frighten off all the pretty customers like that!" Nate laughed.

"Just leaves more for us," Andrew threw out with a wink, rubbing his hands together.

"She's not the customer," Griffin groused. "Just a princess who thinks the world dances to her tune."

"Well, she can be my dance partner anytime," Nate said, picking up the last load of lumber and placing it gently onto the pile, making as little noise as possible.

Still grumbling, Griffin jumped down from the bed of his truck. "Cover it with a tarp and wrap a chain around it. Make sure to lock the gate behind you." Climbing behind the wheel, he waited until the others joined him then pulled onto the road, gunning his engine just a little more than necessary, ignoring the snickering coming from the passengers.

"If you two don't mind, we've got work to discuss."

"Sure, boss," Andrew replied.

As they drove several blocks to their current job, he reviewed the schedule for finishing the two houses they were working on. "We're down a man since Roscoe was in the ER, so there will be some overtime coming. I want everyone to make sure they take all their equipment with them each evening, and for fuck's sake, lock up all the materials. I'm sick and tired of having shit stolen."

"What was taken last time?" Nate asked.

"Two days ago. Tucker house. Jack called when he got there and said half the lumber was missing. When Bob got there, he realized two nail guns were gone also. I'm bleeding fuckin' money, so everyone has got to lock their shit up if they leave it and take with them what they can."

"Damn," Andrew cursed, his sigh matching Griffin's.

"I'm going to start putting in the new contracts that our materials and equipment can be left inside the home where possible, including the portable generator. If not, we'll have to carry it with us each day."

More grumbling came from the others until they reached their destination, a restored Victorian home in the heart of the city. Another contractor had installed new plumbing and electricity, and Capella Contracting was almost finished with the interior woodworking on the floors, stairs, mantles, and doorways. Now, they were on the last stages of the exterior. Arriving, he saw his other two employees, Bob and Jack, already at work.

Soon, the sound of the generator drowned out conversations as Griffin worked the lathe, turning the wood into spindles and balusters for the porch. His irritation over the woman from this morning eased as he settled into the rhythm of his work. He'd already created the smaller spindles and connected them in the intricate pattern to form the decorative eaves. Wiping the sweat from his brow, he stepped back and eyed the project as a whole.

He knew his crew thought he was just looking at the individual parts they had restored to the house, which was true, he was. But he also looked at the home. The home that had held families for numerous generations.

Before he started a project, he always did a historical search on the property. For one, it helped him know what architectural design would be in true keeping with the original. But the other, more private reason was it helped him imagine the original owners and subsequent families that called the property home.

Standing on the sidewalk, looking toward the front of their current restoration, he knew the original home was built in 1871, right after the Civil War. He took a moment to imagine the family and the excitement they must've felt when the house had been completed and they moved in. He knew the economy of the times, the education level of the patriarch, even the manner of dress the lady of the house would've worn.

Yeah, my crew would be shocked as shit if they knew everything I thought about when working on these homes. They simply knew he'd been in the Army as a carpenter, earned an associate degree in American history at the same time, and then worked as an apprentice for a custom home restorer when he returned, later taking over the business and making it his own. They had no idea he imagined the original owners, wondering if their spirits could see how the house was returned to its glory.

The vibration of his phone in his pocket jerked his thoughts back to the current century. Pulling it out, he shook his head as he answered. "Hey, Marcie. What's up besides all those kids of yours?"

"Very funny, brother dear, but I can't say you're wrong."

Hearing the shouts of kids in the background, there was no way she could deny that her kids were up and going strong on a Saturday morning.

"Bill is taking Bill, Jr. to soccer, and I'm trying to load up Tommy and Jenna for their game at a different park. I'm meeting Chelle there, also. I have no idea where Bert's kids are playing today. Anyway, the kids are clamoring to see their Uncle Griff, so stop being antisocial and come for dinner sometime."

"I'm not antisocial, I'm working!"

"Well, you don't work twenty-four-seven, so let's plan something soon. I'll see who else I can get. Mom'll love it. Oh, shit—Tommy, stop teasing your sister! Gotta go. Bye!"

She disconnected before he had a chance to say goodbye. Dropping his chin to his chest, he studied his boots for a moment. Griffin may have been the oldest sibling, but Marcie took her duties as the oldest girl in the family seriously. Only a year younger than he, she'd always assumed the role of big sister with ease, just like he'd become the man of the family at the age of twelve. A flash of the woman he'd seen in the ER the previous night ran through his mind. He knew many of the reasons why women stayed with a man who slapped them around. He'd seen the verbal abuse from his dad to his mother. But the instant their dad turned his anger physical, she'd found the courage to send him packing, even if that meant money to take care of five kids was tight. *Wonder if the lady in the ER will ever do that or if she'll keep being some man's punching bag?*

"Griff! You ready for us to paint these?" Bob called out.

With his attention dragged back to the job, he walked over to inspect the decorative eaves. *Perfect... fuckin' perfect.* Clapping Bob on the back, he nodded.

3

Caitlyn blinked awake for the second time that morning and spied the time on the clock sitting on her nightstand. The first time, she'd been rudely awakened from her fitful sleep by the sound of loud clanging just outside her apartment at an ungodly early hour. Sitting up, she winced as she lifted her fingers to her face, feeling the swelling. Glad it was Saturday, she looked forward to a restful weekend. *Well, restful if the loud noises won't occur again! At least my face will look better when I return to school on Monday morning.*

Thinking of her earlier interaction with the men outside, she sighed heavily. *Why did I bark at them? I never act that way!* She was determined to apologize the next time she saw them working. With her vision so blurry, she hadn't gotten a good look at the man in the back of the truck speaking to her. *Of course, he did call me a princess when he thought I couldn't hear him. Ugh!*

Not sure what to do, she fixed a bowl of cereal and cup of tea and sat on her balcony, glad to see the men from this morning had dropped off whatever they were leaving and had left. Now, the sun was shining in the blue sky, and she sucked in the fresh air, loving the view.

She loved her home, and even knowing it wasn't a forever place, she thought it was perfect. She'd never wanted a bland, typical apartment in a bland, typical apartment complex. What she'd found instead was a huge, old, red-brick, white-trim Victorian house that had been divided into four apartments. She loved living in a slice of history, feeling connected to all the people who'd ever lived in the house since it had been built over a hundred and fifty years ago.

The landlady and another couple lived in the two downstairs apartments. Caitlyn had one of the upstairs apartments, and the one across the hall was recently emptied. She'd hoped to entice her sister to consider the apartment, but Erin had moved in with her fiancé. So, Caitlyn had no idea who might be her neighbor soon.

The windows were tall and plentiful, allowing sunshine to pour into her apartment. The renovations included a wide living room facing the front corner with windows on two walls. The small dining room was just to the right of the door and it was separated from the large kitchen by a wide counter. A door led from the kitchen to a combination pantry and laundry room. A hall led to a guest bedroom and small bathroom, ending with a larger owner's bedroom and bathroom, including a claw-foot, soaker bathtub. And since her apartment covered half of the upstairs, she had views of both the front and back of the property. Her bedroom included a balcony deck with just enough room for two chairs and a small table, and it overlooked the park across the street.

Caitlyn's decorating was simple but kept with a green and burgundy theme for the curtains, sofa, and chairs in the living room. She'd created a warm, inviting space for her family and friends to visit but mostly for her to come home from a day of teaching and step back into her personal retreat.

A knock on the door caused a sigh to leave her lungs. *Bet I know who that is.* Peeking through the security hole, she chuckled. *Yep, right on cue.* Throwing open the door, she greeted, "Hey, Mom. Hey, Dad."

Her mother's lips were pinched tightly together as her gaze roamed over Caitlyn's face. "Well, I'd certainly like to kick some teenage boy's ass!" Sharon pushed her way into the apartment before pulling Caitlyn in for a mama-hug that felt just right no matter what age she was. As the youngest child, she'd always relished her mom's hugs, and that fact was just as prevalent right now. When Sharon finally let her go, she stepped aside and let Colm enter.

"Hey, baby girl," her dad said softly, as though her ears were injured and not just her eye. He tried but failed to smile, his eyes glittering as they roamed over her face.

She was about to offer them coffee when she saw what her father held in his other hand: a cardboard carrier of three large coffees and a pink bag with *Penelope's Bakery* on the outside. Her mother had her father on a short leash when it came to his treats ever since a mild heart attack led to his retirement a couple of years earlier than he had planned. So, coming with bakery treats was a good way for him to have a small indulgence as well—and she never begrudged her father an indulgence.

Squealing, she clapped her hands. "Penelope's! And coffee! Come on in!"

Sharon narrowed her eyes in a pretend glare as she glanced over her shoulder toward Colm. "Looks like our daughter's greeting gets more excited when we come bearing gifts."

Soon, Caitlyn was diving into a chocolate croissant, the flakey goodness going a long way to soothing her memories of yesterday. The hit of caffeine was welcome as well. It didn't take long to convince her parents that the black eye was the result of a misguided punch and that the miscreant felt terrible about the results. Licking her fingers, she also convinced her mother that all she wanted to do was rest and spend the whole long weekend doing very little. "I really don't want to go out with a black eye. So, I'll stay in, work on lesson plans, read some, and watch TV. Maybe Bekki or Erin can come over." Bekki King was her best friend since birth, and even though both her sister and friend were now engaged, the three still got together when they could.

Her father finished his decaf coffee and whole-grain bagel, only slightly grumbling at the healthy food. "I know Erin will be helping Torin at the pub this weekend. They expect a big crowd with the Tall Ships coming into the harbor."

"Oh... well, maybe..."

Sharon nodded as she finished her coffee. "Hannah mentioned that Bekki and Killian were going to a resort in the mountains this weekend for a getaway."

Sighing, Caitlyn buried her disappointment behind the cup she drank deeply from, letting the smooth-flavored coffee ease her disappointment. The King family lived next to the McBrides, and between them, eleven kids had grown up as best friends. Hannah, the King matriarch, was thick as thieves with her mom, and their dads had a special friendship as well. Now, all of Caitlyn's siblings and all the Kings were paired, having found their significant others. *All but me.*

She smiled but should have known it wouldn't fool her parents. Her father remained quiet as was his way, but his knowing smile reached her heart.

Her mother leaned over and took Caitlyn's hand in hers. "I know it's hard sometimes, sweetheart."

"It's not what you think, Mom. I'm glad everyone has their special someone. Really. But being the third wheel is a bit awkward at times. Anyway, for now, I'm more than content to stay at home for the weekend and get some rest. So, you don't have to worry about me."

Her parents sent furtive glances between each other, but before she could ask what was happening, her mother said, "I was talking to Father Martin, and he said that they are always looking for new teachers at St. Vincent's."

Shaking her head, she waggled her finger toward her mom. "Don't start on me. Anyway, if you think that teenage behavior is different at a private school, even if it is Catholic, then think again! Anyway, I love North Central High."

Her dad agreed. "She's right, Sharon. While some of the student population is different in the different schools, all schools have the same problems because all of society has those problems."

"Exactly!" she nodded. "Drugs, teen pregnancies, hormones, parties… all of these things are present throughout all of society, therefore are represented in the schools."

Her mother huffed. "I'm not saying they're not, but at least at St. Vincent's, the class sizes are smaller. They aren't overcrowded like at North Central."

"True, but I feel like I'm making a difference there and have no intention of jumping ship just because of a little incident."

Her mother opened her mouth, but Colm placed his hand on her arm. Sharon smiled and leaned over to hug Caitlyn. "Okay, dear. I know when I need to hush. Come on, Colm, we've got some shopping to do."

Saying goodbye, she leaned back against the solid wood after closing the door behind them. Sighing heavily, she pushed off and grabbed her coffee cup, taking another sip of the caffeine nectar. Her thoughts were in turmoil and the dull ache in her face didn't make her situation any better. A knock on her door startled her. Throwing it open, she smiled.

"Margaretha, good morning."

"Hmph, by the looks of you, it's not such a good morning!"

Margaretha Rossi, her landlady, pushed her way in.

At only a little over five feet tall, she was wiry and energetic. At eighty-two, she wore her white hair long, the waves hanging down her back, and colored a stripe in purple right next to her face. Her closet was full of velour athletic pants and matching zip-up hoodies, and today's ensemble included a fuschia set paired with a pale pink t-shirt. Her makeup was on, slashes of pink on her cheeks and lips. Despite her garments, she always wore a pair of pearl earrings given to her by her late husband, the explanation being, *"My mother always said a lady wore pearls."*

Her eyes narrowed as she peered at Caitlyn carefully then reached up to grab her chin, tilting her head to the left and right, inspecting the damage. "Quite a shiner, dearie."

"Yeah, well, you should see the other guy."

Margaretha laughed at Caitlyn's quip and shook her head. "Breaking up a fight at school?" At Caitlyn's nod, Margaretha nodded. "Hmph. Probably over a girl. Boys can be such dumbasses."

A snort of laughter erupted. "So, what brings you up here this morning?"

"Saw your parents come early. Saw your parents leave. And I may have had my window open and heard your mom grumbling. Figured something was up."

"You're quite the sneaky one, aren't you?"

"Nothing sneaky about it! Just sitting at my window, enjoying God's beautiful morning, and ascertained something was afoot at your place."

Caitlyn barked out a laugh. "Afoot? Who talks like that?"

"I do, for one. That's part of the problem today. Young people just use slang for everything." Margaretha sat down on Caitlyn's sofa, accepting the cup of tea brought to her. Nodding toward the Penelope's bag, she said, "My scones are better, you know. So is your baking."

"Yes, I know. But lacking your culinary delights and not feeling the energy to do anything myself, I had to make do with the next best thing."

Margaretha's face crinkled into a hundred creases as she laughed, and Caitlyn delighted in the sight and sound of her landlady's mirth.

Finally, Margaretha leaned forward and patted her leg. "You should take up kickboxing. Or some of that tai-kwan-doey stuff."

"I'm not sure I can use martial arts in school to break up a fight."

"Hmph," Margaretha huffed again, settling back on the sofa cushions. "Well, what are we doing today?"

Before she had a chance to tell her that resting was all she had planned, another knock on the door sounded. This time she opened it to Terri and Bjorn Sorensen, the downstairs renters. Stepping back to let them in, she was surprised when Terri pulled her into a hug. Terri was about the same height as Caitlyn while Bjorn towered over all of them. His white-blond hair hung to his shoulders, and he was wearing his typical tie-dyed t-shirt. He was only in his thirties, but she could have sworn his soul belonged to the hippies of the 1960s. Terri's long brown hair was braided and hung to her waist. She was much more casually dressed in jeans and a green T-shirt, but her wrists were decorated with bangles and leather bracelets, making noise as her hand patted Catilyn's back.

"I just knew something was wrong. Bjorn said he saw you come home late yesterday, and even though the hall was shadowed, he felt something was wrong with your aura."

"No, it's more like something was wrong with my face," Caitlyn said, grinning at Margaretha over Terri's shoulder.

Bjorn patted her shoulder and said, "We brought you some of our special tea. This will make you feel so much better." He hustled into her kitchen and, seeing the kettle already warm, looked up and smiled. "See, you knew tea was coming and your subconscious was ready."

"You two are nutty," Margaretha said, but her smile indicated she cared for her tenants.

Sitting down to Bjorn's tea, Caitlyn inclined her head toward the cup. "So, is this your new venture?"

He laughed and clapped his hands. "Of course! T&B tea to go along with our T&B candles, potpourri, incense, and jewelry!"

"I told him it was good we'd named our business T&B because to have B&T tea, would sound like we were selling piss!"

Caitlyn and Margaretha spit out their sips of tea at the same time, laughter filling the air. "You two really are nutty," she said, repeating Margaretha's description.

The foursome chatted about Terri and Bjorn's new line of tea to sell along with their other items. They sold online, went to a local market, and Caitlyn had taken some of the scented candles and potpourri to school to sell for them as well.

The conversation came around to the empty apartment, and Margaretha simply beamed. "I have someone in mind, but they haven't committed." She sat up straighter and glanced at her watch. "Oh, I hate to run, but RoseMarie is picking me up soon to take me to the golf course."

Caitlyn blinked, ignoring the pain in her eye at the motion. "I didn't know you golfed."

"I don't yet. But RoseMarie met two gentlemen that said they'd teach us."

Caitlyn's teeth worried her lip, but Margaretha smiled and patted her hand. "Stop fretting. It'll give you wrinkles before your time."

"I just don't want you to get fleeced by two men who prey on ol... um... more mature women."

Margaretha cackled. "Oh, honey. They're older than RoseMarie and me. But she said they still had some swing in their hips! I think that should help with their golf game, don't you?"

Having no response other than to offer wide eyes toward a giggling Terri and Bjorn, she nodded. Kissing the older woman's cheek before she left, Caitlyn then said goodbye to the others. "I'll come down sometime this weekend and help you pack up some of your candles and potpourri if you'd like." Between their online sales and direct deliveries, they stayed busy, and Caitlyn sometimes helped them box their products and they gave her free samples. Considering she loved the scents, now that they were adding tea, she was hoping to be a taste tester for them as well.

"Only if you feel up to it," Bjorn said, his gaze still moving over her face, concern filling his eyes.

Finally closing the door to the last of her morning visitors, she relaxed, allowing the soothing tea to ease her mind as well as the pain in her face. Despite the events of the previous day, she felt lucky. Blessed to have found a home that, while not a forever home, suited her for this time of her life. A delightful landlady and sweet neighbors. *Throw in a chance to sleep late tomorrow morning... perfect!*

4
───

"Ms. McBride, that was epic! You took that punch and managed to not get knocked out!"

"I thought it was horrible, Ms. McBride! I can't believe you jumped in between them!"

"He feels really bad, Ms. McBride. His parents are pissed as can be at him. His dad said it might cost him his football scholarship opportunities."

"Who cares! He should be more worried about almost going to jail!"

Clapping her hands, Caitlyn called the class to order. She grimaced but the simple movement pulled at her still-slightly swollen eye. Returning to work the following Monday, she discovered her *badass* reputation amongst the students had grown. She swallowed deeply, lowering her hands to hide the shaking from her students. What they considered badass had hurt so badly, she still had trouble sleeping at night. Finally, with another deep breath, she finally got her students settled into their seats.

As she'd stood in front of her mirror getting ready for the day, she'd applied her normal makeup, only adding a little extra cover over her still-bruised face. Caking on foundation would only look ridiculous considering everyone already knew she had a black eye. She'd been stopped by a number of the faculty wanting to see how she was, expressing concern, bemoaning the state of the world, or even chastising her for attempting to stop the fight. Tired of the attention and tired of feeling like crying every time she thought about it, all she wanted to do was get back to teaching.

"Okay, we've discussed the events of last Friday all we're going to. If I'm fine and moving forward, then you can, too. Now, we lost a day when I wasn't able to give you your weekend assignment, but you had your syllabus, so you should have gone over your notes. Let's jump into our discussion of *Number the Stars*. Your papers are due by the end of the week, but I want to know what you've divined from your reading. So, let's start with quotes that you've chosen."

The class was quiet for a moment, not unusual when teaching teens. Some know the answers and are loathe to begin a discussion, others haven't prepared, and some hate being in the spotlight. She'd learned that silence was a great motivator for someone to begin.

"I thought much of what she said was sad," one girl answered. Tonya's blonde ponytail swung over her shoulder as she crinkled her nose. "Why does *good* literature always have to be so sad?"

Caitlyn hid her smile as Tonya flipped through her notebook. Tonya would ace the test, but she wondered if the young woman would ever truly feel the story's words deep in her soul. "Okay, give me a sad quote."

Tonya found the page she was looking for. *"Mama was crying, and the rain made it seem as if the whole world was crying."* She looked up and huffed. "I mean, it's always horrible if someone's mother is crying. The only time I ever saw my mother cry was at my grandmother's funeral."

"Then she's very lucky," another girl said, her voice showing her irritation as she glared at Tonya.

"Why is that, Rashawn?"

"Annemarie's mama lost a daughter, and Ellen's mama had to tell her about Lise dying. That's reason enough to cry. I think if someone's mama hasn't cried then they ought to be happy."

Tonya turned around in her seat "I didn't say my mother hadn't cried. I just said that I hadn't seen her."

Before Caitlyn had a chance to redirect, another student piped up. "I think of you, Ms. McBride."

"Me? How so, Tad?"

He looked down at his notebook. *"It is much easier to be brave if you do not know everything."* Looking back up, he grinned. "You were brave when you jumped in to stop the fight. But if you knew you were going to get hit, would you have been so brave?"

Several students gasped, but she chuckled at his audacity. "You're absolutely correct. If I had known that I was going to get whacked, I would've been much more hesitant to jump in. But then, if I'd known that was going to happen, I might have ducked."

Laughter broke out in the classroom. While the

story they were discussing pulled many different heartstrings, she welcomed the levity.

Finally, one boy on the side raised his hand. Russ wore his hair long, half-falling over his face. Jeans, T-shirts, and heavy motorcycle boots made up his clothes. He didn't participate in afterschool activities or sports, but he worked at a local grocery every day when school let out. And as private as he was, just that tidbit had taken a while to learn from him. She had no idea what his home life was like, but she knew there was so much more to him than the persona he presented to others. He liked to pretend that he couldn't care less about literature but she always wanted to know his thoughts in particular. Much more perceptive than he let on, she found him brilliant.

"Russ, I'm curious to hear the quote you chose."

His hand lifted and he swiped the hair away from his face, only to have it drop back in place. With his gaze pinned on hers, he said, *"And they are beginning to realize that the world they live in is a place where the right thing is often hard, sometimes dangerous, and frequently unpopular."* He continued to hold her gaze unwaveringly. "I'm not saying that the lives we live can be compared to Nazi invasions during World War II like in this story, but I think it's a universal truth. Sometimes it's hard to tell what the right thing to do is. Sometimes you know what it is, but it's dangerous. And a lot of times, it's seriously unpopular."

Caitlyn blinked, feeling moisture gathering in her eyes, and she swallowed deeply, nodding slowly. "I think you're exactly right, Russ." She was impressed that he spoke from memory, not reading the quote from his notebook.

The class discussion continued, once again solidifying her decision to have gone into education. When the bell rang, she stood at the door saying goodbye, glad it was the end of the day. Turning, she was surprised when Russ was still in the room, standing nearby, his worn backpack slung casually over his shoulder. He tossed his head in another effort to move the hair from his eyes, and she waited. In his typical, no-nonsense manner, he didn't make her wait long.

"I was late to school this morning."

Not understanding his opening, she tilted her head to the side, continuing to wait.

"I was in the office since I had to sign in with attendance. I heard what the principal said to you."

She straightened her back, renewed irritation filling her. She'd been called into the principal's office first thing that morning so that he could cover his ass by telling her that teachers were required to only verbally instruct fighting students to separate but they weren't to intervene physically. In doing so, she put not only herself but other teachers, students, and the school at risk. When she'd argued that standing to the side was simply being a spectator, he waved her concerns with a flip of his hand. "I expect my teachers to be smart. Not unnecessarily brave."

Doubting he'd ever been smart or brave, she stormed out of his office, swallowing back her retort. Now, knowing his comments had been overheard by a student, she pinched her lips together.

"He was berating you for doing the right thing, for being brave. I marked a lot of quotes from *Number the Stars*. Another one was this. *'That's all that brave means—not thinking about the dangers. Just thinking about what you must do.'* I know my opinion doesn't mean shit, Ms. McBride, but there's no such thing as unnecessarily brave. You were just brave. He's wrong. You did the right thing."

As tears threatened again, she sucked in another deep breath, inclining her head slightly. "Thank you. That means a lot to me."

He offered a chin lift and passed her on his way out the door. Just before he disappeared into the hallway, she called out, "Russ." When he looked over his shoulder toward her, she added, "Never think your opinion doesn't mean shit. Sometimes, it means everything."

She watched his lips quirk upward before he ducked his head and joined the masses of students walking down the hall.

Packing up, she was more tired than usual. Her face ached from the movements of often smiling as she taught. She loved having juniors. They were old enough to handle discussions on American Literature… *usually*. They came to her with their thoughts, problems, hopes, dreams, and plans. She still had time to have an influence on their lives, and in turn, they on hers.

Reaching up, her fingers gently ran over her puffy eye. Her vision was still a bit blurry although better than over the weekend. She hadn't been able to clearly see the men making such a racket with their lumber when she had been so rudely awakened. Margaretha said she was having some work done and had told the contractor he could leave the wood on her property until he started working. *I wonder when the work will start. And how long it will last. And how much noise they'll make.*

"Hey, lady."

She startled as she looked up, then smiled as her teacher friends walked into her classroom, Barbara, Suzette, and Renée. "Hey."

Renée, a chemistry teacher, plopped down into one of the chairs. "How'd you do today?"

"Not too bad. My face is a little stiff, and I'm ready to head home."

"I heard about your chat with Mr. Carswell this morning," Suzette, an art teacher, said, her eyes flashing. "I swear, if you hadn't stepped in and one of those boys' parents complained to the School Board Office that no teacher intervened, then he'd be on your case for not doing anything."

Renée nodded in sympathy, pushing her blonde curls back from her face. "You can't win with that man. I've heard he's looking to get booted up to a School Board position. I wish he'd leave the area altogether. He's just not a supportive principal."

"I suppose I was the talk of the faculty lounge on Friday?" Caitlyn grimaced, already knowing the answer to the question.

"Most of the faculty supported you, of course," Barbara said. "There's always a few old biddies that clucked about you putting yourself in danger needlessly. And, of course, a few other teachers that claim it was reckless, mostly because it would never dawn on them to intervene at all."

"Other than that, everybody thinks you did the right thing. And the kids think you're awesome!" Renée said, her expression full of sympathy.

Caitlyn sighed and shook her head, slinging her purse and school bag over her shoulder, tired of having her motives dissected. "I'm ready to head home. Are you guys leaving now?"

"I told Jamie I'd help out with track practice," Barbara said. She cast her eyes to the side before looking back at Caitlyn. "Are you sure you don't mind if I go out with him?"

Waving her hand in front of her, Caitlyn shook her head. "Absolutely! He's a nice guy but there was no spark between us. He likes to joke about it, but honestly, we're just friends."

She caught Barbara's smile and hoped that if Jamie did ask her out, he'd be a better date with Barbara than he had been with her. His conversation had bordered on the monotonous when the only thing he talked about was the track team's performances, running, and his low body fat count.

"What about you? Any hot dates recently?"

She glanced back to Renée and shrugged. "I got asked out for this next weekend. It's a blind date, a friend of a friend."

"Oooh, then you'll have to fill us in on how it goes." She and Renée waved goodbye to the others then headed out to the teachers' parking lot.

"You weren't able to be at the faculty meeting on

Friday afternoon, but Mr. Carswell talked about the tight budget, as usual. He said the teachers are welcome to do fundraisers, but we have to fill out all the paperwork ahead of time with the bookkeeper."

"What kind of fundraisers?" Caitlyn asked, stopping when she got to her car.

"One suggestion was that we have booths at the sports activities where people in the community can sell their crafts and the school would get a percentage. I don't know how that would work, and the only person I know who might participate is my grandmother who still crochets winter caps."

Waving goodbye, Caitlyn sighed as she started her car and pulled out of the parking lot. *Low school budgets, principals that only cared about what the SBO bought, struggling students, a blind date Friday night, and a work crew that left more materials behind the house again early yesterday morning... no wonder I'm exhausted!*

5

"And then I got to visit the CEO in his corner office that overlooks the harbor. He's telling me that he's impressed with my record, and if I keep it up, one day I could work on that floor as well. That's the executive floor, you understand."

Caitlyn plastered on a smile to cover a yawn. She'd heard the cheerleading coach say numerous times to the girls and guys with the pom-poms. *"Smile, even when the team is losing. You have to keep up everyone's spirits, especially when you don't feel like smiling!"*

The blind date was going... Well, it was going, just not fast enough. The restaurant was great—casual with a bar to the side. The food was prepared perfectly, and her drink was excellent. The music was also good. But the man? She wanted to bang her head on the table.

He droned on about the company he worked for, his rising in the ranks, his sales record, his condo, and the new car he was test-driving tomorrow. He'd even asked if she wanted to go on a test drive with him, which she turned down due to a fictional previous engagement.

A group of men had come in and settled at the far end of the bar, their laughter sounding real, making her wish she was there instead of at the table pretending interest in her date's career. Her vision was still a bit blurry in her injured eye, but she could see well enough to know they were casually dressed, relaxed, not for show. Good-looking in their jeans and work shirts compared to her date's white button-up and red tie.

Why is dating so hard? She had given in to accepting a date with Jamie, the physical education teacher and track coach at school. She enjoyed his company other than his unwavering dedication to exercise and diet. At the restaurant, when he announced the calorie and carb count of the lasagna on her plate that she was in the middle of scarfing, she knew they had no future other than friendship.

Next were a couple of dates with the FBI agent that had interviewed her and her sister, Erin, after the Hope City Marathon bombing. Her father, a former FBI agent until his retirement, had beamed when she'd told him they were going out. He was handsome and didn't act like God's gift to women, well-built but didn't talk about it, a great conversationalist… but, alas, no spark. They also parted as friends.

Lots of friends, but no sparks. And she wanted sparks. She wanted someone that would make it hard to breathe when he walked into a room. She wanted someone whose eyes would find only her in a crowd. She wanted someone who'd tell her she was brave while dashing off to slay her dragons. She wanted someone who made her long to kiss him just because he was there and not because he thought he'd earned it. *Yeah, I want sparks.*

Another flash of the man she'd seen in the hospital the week before ran through her mind. *Jesus, he was tall. And gorgeous. Like, movie-star gorgeous. A working-man movie star. Not on the red carpet in a tux although that would be nice, too. But the kind of man who looked like he could take care of himself, his buds, and his woman. Holy hell, he looked like he could take care of a woman.* She hated to admit how much her brief eye-catching moment with him had stayed with her, fueling her fantasies.

"I have to admit that I've got my eye on the office I'd like to have. Give me about another year or so, and it should be mine."

Caitlyn's forced smile finally came to an end when the bill arrived, and she knew honesty was the only way she could extricate herself. She reached into her purse and pulled out several twenties. "Tom, I believe that we should split the check. It's been lovely, but to be completely honest, I don't feel a connection. I prefer we share a Dutch-treat meal."

He blinked, his surprise obvious. "Oh… well, oh. Um… no, I insist on paying. Really. Um… well, hopefully, we can do this again sometime."

Smiling, she said, "I think we're better as friends and not as a date. Since we came separately, I'll say goodnight now and then head to the ladies' room before leaving. Thank you, and good luck with your corner office aspirations." She meant those final words; after all, he should pursue whatever dreams suited him. They just weren't important to her.

She rose from her seat, lifted her purse onto her shoulder, and weaved through the tables. Her smile felt less forced as she walked away, and the tension she'd held in her shoulders relaxed. By the time she passed the end of the bar leading to the hallway where the bathrooms were located, she heaved a huge sigh of relief.

"You really should dump someone who does that to you, you know?"

Hearing the male voice growling just behind her, she turned around. Facing a broad, black T-shirt-covered chest, she startled, leaned her head back, and peered into the intense stare of blue eyes that didn't waver from hers. Blinking at the gorgeous man in front of her, she gasped. "You?"

His chin jerked back slightly but he kept his gaze on her.

The air felt thick between them. She licked her dry lips, swallowing deeply. Seeing him again didn't diminish her fantasy at all. In fact, it flamed higher. Realizing he was still staring as though waiting for her to speak again, she felt the air rush from her lungs. "Um... I saw you at the hospital... in the ER... um... but what did you say to me? Dump who?"

He inclined his head back toward the table she came from. "Him. The one who gave you the shiner that your makeup still can't cover completely."

Her mouth dropped open as she shook her head slowly, hating the cold finger of reality that started to douse the fire she felt between them. "He didn't... no one gave me—"

His rough voice cut through her explanation. "It was obvious from where I sat at the bar that you weren't even talking to him. You just let that guy run all over you, and when he's had enough, he hits you?"

The fantasy she'd imagined had now completely disappeared, replaced with white-hot anger. "What the hell are you talking about?" She glanced furtively around, realizing her voice had risen with each word, hating that her voice shook.

His eyes narrowed, his gaze still intense. "I heard the doctor give you good advice. Stop letting him use you as a punching bag."

Straightening her spine, she clamped her lips together for a moment as incredulity slid over her. "Listen, mister. I don't know who you are, but you couldn't be more wrong about me."

He stepped closer, his gaze still boring into hers, making it hard to think, much less breathe. He was much taller than she, and as he leaned over, she felt surrounded but not crowded.

"A girl as pretty as you could have any man. Putting up with one that hits you is tragic. No woman should endure that." With those words, he turned and walked back to his friends at the bar.

Caitlyn stood for a few seconds, so stunned by the brief conversation that her feet didn't move. When she finally became unstuck, she quickly headed into the ladies' room. Taking care of business, she stood at the sink, washed her hands, then stared into the mirror, her insides quaking. He was right, the makeup didn't cover the bruises still fading around her eye. But he was very wrong—she would never allow someone to hit her.

Filled with fury that he'd been so presumptuous, she still couldn't forget the way her body naturally leaned toward him, the desire to be tucked into his embrace almost overriding her good sense. *"A girl as pretty as you could have any man." He'd noticed me.* It dawned on her that Tom's gaze had lingered for a few seconds on the slight bruising around her eye but he hadn't appeared concerned. *Ugh, get a grip, girl!* She threw open the door and marched out of the restaurant, refusing to see if either Tom or Gruff were still inside.

Caitlyn opened her eyes, blinking several times to clear her vision as well as her sleep-fogged brain. The sound of boots on stairs resounded throughout her apartment. Glancing at the clock on her nightstand, while still early, she'd slept later than normal.

The clomping continued, retreating this time before coming closer again. Tossing back the covers, she slid from the bed and ran to her door to peek through the security hole. She always wondered about the tiny magnifying circles that were supposed to provide security. Often too blurry to discern a person clearly, she supposed it at least gave her an inkling of what lay on the other side of the door.

From what she could ascertain, several men were going in and out of the apartment across the hall.

Jerking back, she tried to remember if Margaretha told her that someone was moving today. Wincing, she had to admit that whereas she normally checked in with her landlady multiple times during the week, she'd seen her rarely in the past few days. Peering through the hole again, she had no idea which man was moving in. *Could be a couple.*

Feeling better than she had in a week, she touched her face, glad to discover the swelling down. Wandering into the kitchen, she started her coffeemaker. After pouring a cup, the idea of muffins hit her. *The perfect welcome gift for a new neighbor. And Margaretha. And Terri and Bjorn. And for me.* Realizing she needed to double her usual amount, she hastily mixed the batter and poured it into an extra-large muffin pan. She hoped whoever moved into the apartment was nice—and had good taste in music if they played it too loud.

Popping the pan into the oven, she set the timer and raced into her bedroom to take a shower, having just enough time to get cleaned up before the muffins were baked.

She belted her robe after drying and wrapped a towel around her long, wet hair, piling it on top of her head. Leaning forward to wipe the condensation off her mirror, she jolted when the blast of her smoke detector screeched throughout her apartment.

"Jesus!" She careened out of her bedroom just in time to see smoke curling from her oven and the sound of pounding on her door barely heard over the screaming alarm. She raced to the kitchen and turned off the oven, throwing open the door and letting more smoke escape. Glancing down to the black, charred muffins, she cursed again before screaming, "Hold on!"

Sprinting to the apartment door, she tried to jerk the towel from her head to wave it toward the oven but it was stuck in her hair. Throwing open the door with her free hand, she expected to see Bjorn or Terri. She stared dumbly, not believing her sight. "You? Again?"

6

Griffin had climbed the stairs numerous times already that morning, glad his crew volunteered to help him move into his new apartment. Excitement vibrated through him. He'd lived in the same crappy apartment building for the past several years, saving money to eventually buy his own house. But when the owner of this Victorian home hired him to complete renovations, she'd eyed him carefully. He'd thought at the time that she just wanted to size him up for the job. But then, she'd smiled widely and leaned forward to pat his arm.

"*Mr. Capella. Do you own your own home?*"

"*No, ma'am. I rent while saving to buy a house like this one day.*"

"*Ah,*" *she smiled.* "*You want to own a piece of history, too.*"

Nodding, he agreed. "*Absolutely. But until then, I work on these great houses and save my money.*"

"*How would you like to live in this house while you work on it? And longer, if you like?*"

He blinked. "*I don't understand.*"

She smiled, her eyes twinkling. "Well, there are two upstairs apartments, and one is empty. Let's take a look at it, shall we?"

He'd seen the upstairs when he first came to look at the restoration projects she had in mind. Now, he followed her upstairs with the idea of looking at a space to live in. It seemed nuts to consider her proposal, but the timing was perfect. One of his crew was recently divorced and needed a place to live. He could sublet to his employee and take this apartment as his own.

Just as he remembered, the door opened into a large living room with bay windows at the front of the house. Wooden floors, wainscoting, tall windows, high ceilings. In need of refurbishing, but gorgeous. A dining room opened into a well-appointed kitchen. A hall led to the back where a small guest bedroom and bathroom were on one side and the larger owner's suite on the other.

They chatted about what was covered in the lease and the rent, and his excitement grew as he decided to move. As they stepped back to the stairway, he inclined his head to the apartment across the hall. "I assume you have a renter over there."

"Oh, yes! A lovely lady, very quiet. You'll find her to be such an accommodating neighbor, no bother at all."

Of course, that had been before he'd had words with the woman complaining about the noise. Now, a month later, he was ready to begin work on the house and move in. He'd just made it up the stairs with a load of boxes when suddenly a fire alarm sounded, the screech reverberating off the wooden walls. Jolting, he dropped the boxes to the floor and bolted out into the hallway where the scent of something burning hit him.

Racing to the door opposite his, he tried the knob but it was locked. Pounding on the wooden door, he heard others racing up the stairs behind him. Looking at some of his crew, he yelled, "Bob! Go to the landlady and see if she's got a spare key!"

Continuing to pound, he finally heard a female voice on the other side calling, "Hold on!" It took a few more seconds before the door swung open. The barefoot woman wasn't short, but still, her head would tuck under his chin. A towel was falling from her wet hair, and a familiar, bright, multi-colored silky robe that hit her mid-thigh wasn't tightly belted and gaped at the chest, showing a delectable amount of cleavage. His eyes stayed glued to her as she battled the towel on her head, finally jerking it off and waving it toward the smoke detector as smoke drifted from her oven. He wasn't sure the robe would contain her modesty.

She finally got her hair pushed back from her face, grabbed her robe with her other hand, and stared wide-eyed. "You? Again?"

His gaze jumped from the smoking oven, which was the only reason he'd been able to drag his eyes from her cleavage. Now, he twisted his head to see the woman standing in front of him, her wide, clear blue eyes staring at him. Gut punched, he fought to catch his breath as he stared at the beauty in front of him. Truth be known, he hadn't been able to get her out of his mind since he'd seen her in the ER and then again in the restaurant. Even with a black eye, it was obvious she was gorgeous. And now she was standing in front of him, once more, unable to believe his eyes. "You live here?"

He didn't wait for an answer as the alarm continued to assault his ears. He pushed past her and headed into her kitchen. Grabbing a potholder from the counter, he snagged the blackened pan from the oven, tossed it into the sink, and turned on the water. The pan sizzled as the cold liquid hit its overheated metal, but at least the smoking ebbed.

"Boss, you okay?"

Turning, he looked over his shoulder as Bob, Nate, and Andrew crowded just inside her doorway, their gazes locked on the woman still standing in a too-short robe looking both bedraggled and like a wet dream. Growling, he shot them a glare. "Yeah, yeah, go on and get the next load up. I'll make sure everything here is okay."

He didn't miss their lingering gazes on the woman as they backed out the door and down the stairs. Turning around, he rubbed his chin as he eyed her gaze moving between him and her smoking pan. Not giving her a chance to complain about the mess in her sink, he asked, "You trying to burn the place down?"

Her lips pinched together tightly as she clutched the front of her robe. "I was making muffins to bring over to the new neighbor."

"For me?"

"You?" she sputtered, her clear blue eyes widening even more. "You're my new neighbor?"

He blew out a long breath. "One and the same," he

nodded, flipping off the water, staring down at the blackened lumps that he now knew were supposed to be muffins. Nodding toward them. "You always try to impress with culinary disaster when someone new moves in?"

His effort at mirth fell short as she flinched. "I was trying to be nice! I turned on the oven then went to take a shower—"

"You walked away from a hot oven?"

"I thought I'd have plenty of time."

"So, what happened?" he asked, crossing his arms over his chest. Slammed with the idea that she could have started a fire in the old house had his words rushing out.

A crease settled between her brows as she stared at the oven. Finally, a gasp slipped from her lips. "Oh, my God. I had the temperature way too high. Damn."

It was on the tip of his tongue to comment on kitchen safety, but the crestfallen expression on her face halted his words. Sighing, he planted his hands on his hips and held her gaze for a moment, noting the bruising around her eye was almost gone. "Does he live here?"

Her mouth opened then snapped shut, her brow lowering. "Who?"

"The guy who did that to you?" he grumbled, inclining his head toward her face. It dawned on him that there was no way he could live across the hall from a couple where a guy took out his anger on a woman.

He watched as her blue eyes chilled and felt the temperature drop in the apartment as she lifted her chin to glare. She might be a foot shorter but she sure as hell was looking down at him.

"No one lives here but me," she bit out, turning to march to the open door. Standing with her hand on the door and the other hand making a sweeping motion, she continued to glare.

He took the cue and walked out of her apartment, but just as he was about to thank her for the thought of making muffins, the door slammed behind him.

After saying goodbye to his crew, he stood inside his apartment and looked around. His furniture wasn't a perfect fit for the place, but it would work for now. He had a sofa, chair, console with a TV, coffee table, small dining table with four chairs, a bed, and dresser. His kitchenware didn't nearly fill the cabinets, so he had lots of extra space.

His old apartment offered little direct sunlight. Standing in the living room with the sun pouring in through the tall windows, he sighed in relief. Closing his eyes for a moment, he let the feel of home settle over him. A knock on the door jolted him from his enjoyment, and he winced at the thought that the beautiful yet angry neighbor might be on the other side, ready to hurl a charcoal muffin at his head.

Peeking out the security hole, he spied the landlady. Light blue shirt with pants and a zip-up jacket that looked like velvet paired with a wide smile on her face.

Opening the door, he ushered her in. "Welcome, Mrs. Rossi. As you can see, I'm moved in."

"Call me Margaretha," she said, her hands fluttering in front of her as she sat down on his sofa. A satisfied grin graced her face as she looked around the space. "It looks good here. A house like this should always have people living in it that appreciate its uniqueness."

"Well, my crew will be back on Monday, ready to start some of the restorations."

"Good, good." She leaned forward, her eyes twinkling again. "I hear there was some excitement earlier."

He dropped his chin, shaking his head before looking back at her. "Um... yes, ma'am—Margaretha. It seems the neighbor across the hall was baking and set the temperature much higher than she meant."

Her face crinkled as her delight shone through. "Such a surprise! Our Caitlyn is an excellent cook and always provides treats for us. I'm sure she must have been in a hurry or her mind somewhere else. Poor thing! She always has so much going on."

He sucked in his lips, rubbing them together for a moment, wondering what the landlady would tell him. While he decided, she chuckled, drawing his gaze back to her.

"You look like a man who has something to ask. Just go ahead, Griffin. No sense in twiddling your thumbs when you want to know something."

Now it was his turn to chuckle. Nodding, he said, "Okay. I actually met her a couple of weeks ago. Right after she... um... was..." He waved his hand around his eye, uncertain what to say to the elderly lady now that he'd opened his mouth.

"After she got whacked in the face?"

He blinked in surprise, his chin jerking back slightly. "Uh... yeah. I wondered if the person who hit her was still around."

"Oh, my, yes! She didn't press charges, so while they had to be suspended for a few days, I'm sure they're back. But she assures me that they feel really terrible about what happened."

His chest depressed as the air rushed out of his lungs. "*They*? There was more than *one*?"

The purple strand near her face bobbed with the force of her nod. "Technically, she was only hit by one of them, but there were two fighting."

"Two men fighting?"

"Well, I'm sure they'd like to think they're men, but they're nothing but boys."

"Ma'am—Margaretha, I'm afraid I don't understand."

"Well, it's just an example of our Caitlyn, isn't it? Selfless. Jumping in to help without worrying about herself. She tells me that it's not an everyday occurrence, but it does happen."

"She was helping?" he prodded, now wondering what had happened and if he would ever get the story out of Margaretha about *our Caitlyn*.

"I suppose teachers these days have to deal with so much more than teaching. Certainly not like in my day, I can tell you that! If we crossed our eyes, our hands were slapped by the nuns!"

Scrubbing his hand over his face, a clearer picture

was now forming. "She got hit in the face by two guys fighting at school?"

Margaretha laughed delicately and patted his arm again. "You do seem to be having trouble following, Griffin. But yes, our Caitlyn jumped in between two teenage boys fighting, and one of them accidentally punched her in the face. I know she said that he didn't mean to hit her, but still…" She tsked, shaking her head, then sighed heavily as she stood. "I wouldn't worry about it, though. If she burned the first batch, I'm sure she's baking another treat to bring to you. She's such a sweetie."

His mind was still whirling when she took to her feet and said, "Well, I'm off. It's bowling night." She started for the door then turned. "Do you bowl?"

"Um, no, I don't."

"Pity. You and Caitlyn could make a foursome with me and a friend. Oh, well, maybe you'll learn."

Walking her out, he watched as she descended the stairs back to her apartment, then stood and stared at the closed door of the now-silent apartment across the hall. *She was the woman complaining about the early morning noise… the day after I saw her in the ER. She was the one I told should dump the guy using her as a punching bag. She was the one I just insulted when she was baking something to welcome a new neighbor.*

Blowing out his breath, he was positive *our Caitlyn* was not inside baking another treat for him.

7

The next morning, Caitlyn wandered from the bedroom into the kitchen and flipped on the coffeemaker. She'd managed to get through the rest of yesterday without hearing any noise in the hall or outside. As though her feet had a will of their own, she'd constantly walked to the door and peered through the security hole out of curiosity, but her gruff neighbor was either gone or inside his apartment.

Now, it was Sunday morning, and she was still moping around her apartment. *Only I could end up with a drop-dead gorgeous neighbor with the personality of a grump. And I was baking him muffins!* At that thought, she cringed. She loved to cook, but baking sweets was second to her heart besides teaching English. She loved to create new culinary delights as well as pore through old cookbooks to find tried and true desserts from the past, and neighbors and coworkers received the benefits of her endeavors considering her curves would keep expanding if she ate everything she baked.

She walked away from the door and stood in front of her oven, shaking her head. When she'd set the timer, she had been in such a rush and managed to have the temperature much higher than intended. A mistake that she never made... until yesterday morning.

Sighing heavily, she thought about her new neighbor, the one Margaretha had said would be working on the house. And living here. Right across the hall. And he'd seen her practically naked.

Grimacing, she tried to push that mortifying thought from her head. *He thinks the worst of me. That's so like my older brothers. Always jumping to conclusions when it comes to me!*

She glanced toward her sliding glass door. His balcony was on the back of the property also, which meant every time she was out there, she'd be on edge, wondering if he was going to come out, also. And when she left her apartment each day, she'd wonder if he was going to be in the hallway.

Argh... stop! Watching the coffee drip into the carafe, she wondered what to fix for breakfast. Standing and staring into the refrigerator, her attention was diverted by a knock on the door. Peeking out, she gasped at the sight of her neighbor. His head was down, but she had no trouble recognizing his broad shoulders and muscular chest pulling at the material of his T-shirt. She glanced down at her attire, glad that she was at least clothed even though the worn and faded leggings and slouchy T-shirt were hardly flattering.

Throwing open the door, she settled her face into

the blankest expression possible, faltering only when he lifted his head and his blue eyes met hers. His hair was slightly damp, the length curling at top of his T-shirt, and the desire was strong to reach up to see if it was as soft as it looked... and that wasn't the only desire running through her. Clearing her throat, she tilted her head to the side. "Yes? Can I help you?"

"Um... we didn't get a chance to properly meet yesterday," he began.

"Oh, really? I thought on the several occasions we've run into each other, we've had a chance to already get to know each other." His brow lifted in confusion, and she continued, "You're a grouchy, growly, grumpy Mr. Gruff. You make assumptions about strangers and then proceed to voice your opinion to that stranger. Instead of thanking someone for the idea of a gift, even if that gift turned out to be burned, you make another grumpy comment. So, Mr. Gruff, I'd say I already know you fairly well."

He dropped his chin and appeared to study his boots for a moment, a heavy sigh leaving his lips. Caitlyn pressed her lips together, and her irritation slowly ebbed. She felt her indignation was appropriate, and yet, her parents had always taught her to take the high road.

Her sigh joined his in the silence now lying awkwardly between them. He lifted his head, his eyes holding an emotion she couldn't define.

"I'm sorry." "I'm sorry."

They spoke at the same time, and his lips lifted on

one side. What had seemed like a sneer the other day now appeared more as a quirk. A cute quirk. An endearing quirk. The distinction might be small, but a quirk was definitely more acceptable in her book.

"Look, I'm not usually such a raving lunatic," she said, one hand on the door and the other fiddling with the frayed hem of her shirt.

"And I'm not usually such a judgmental dick."

A snort emitted before she blushed and slapped her hand over her mouth. "Sorry," she mumbled. "I didn't expect that." Cocking her head to the side, she asked, "So, why the apology? What brought that on?"

"I talked to Margaretha," he admitted.

Nodding her head slowly, she sighed. "And she filled you in, I'm sure."

His hand lifted, and as his arm muscles flexed to squeeze the back of his neck, her gaze stayed snagged on the way his T-shirt stretched impossibly tight over his biceps.

"Yeah, she did. She corrected the assumptions I'd made."

She sighed. "You know, if I was in an abusive relationship, your condemnation would probably have had little effect on me other than to make me continue to feel bad about myself."

Now it was his time to sigh. "You're right, and I should know that."

Something flashed through his eyes, and she sucked in a quick breath. But before she could ask, his face cleared while still holding on to regret.

"I saw you in the hospital, beautiful even with a

black eye, and hearing the doctor comment about not letting the guy use you as a punching bag, all I could think of was that you needed to get away. Then, seeing you in the restaurant where you obviously were not having a good time, I continued to think the same thing. I really am sorry, Caitlyn."

"Thank you, and I accept your— Wait, how did you know my name?" Before he had a chance to answer, she chuckled. "Margaretha."

He smiled and nodded. "She kept calling you, '*Our* Caitlyn.' I almost thought that might be your name. I'm Griffin, by the way."

Mesmerized by his smile, she stared. *Holy moly, he really is gorgeous.* Seeing his head tilt to the side, she realized he'd spoken. "Oh, yes. Um... Griffin?"

"Griffin Capella. My friends call me Griff, not Gruff."

Eyes widening, her face heated. "Oh. Sorry. That was rude—"

"Nope, under the circumstances, I'd say you were spot on."

Still standing in the doorway, she was struck with indecision, uncertain if he'd come just to apologize. He lifted his hand, the pink bag in his hand a tell-tale sign of a peace offering she wasn't about to turn down. "Penelope's Bakery?"

"Well, you were nice enough to bake muffins, and since I owe you a thank you for the thought as well as an apology, and since I don't bake, I thought this might be a good substitution."

Swinging the door open wider, she waved him in.

"Penelope's is a sure way to get into my good graces."

He handed the bag to her as he entered, and his gaze moved around the room. She glanced around, suddenly wondering what he thought of her décor.

"This is nice, Caitlyn." He swung his head back around, capturing her gaze, a smile on his lips. "I'm afraid my furniture just takes up space but yours makes it look comfortable."

"I like color but understated, I suppose." She shrugged, then smiled. "You should see the downstairs apartment. Terri and Bjorn have decorated in complete bohemian hippie, and yet, it so works for them."

"I haven't met them yet."

"Oh, you will. They're super-friendly and you won't be able to resist their sales pitch on why you need candles, incense, potpourri, and even their special blend of tea."

"Is that why the hallway downstairs always smells so… uh… interesting when I first come in? It's coming from their place?"

Nodding, she laughed. "They run a small business out of their home, making all those items."

He chuckled, shook his head, and rolled his eyes. Uncertain about the eye roll, she tilted her head to the side and waited to see if he would explain.

"I'm sorry, it's just that I assumed somebody was burning candles to try to cover up their pot smoking. I didn't know if it came from the downstairs apartment or up here."

She plopped the Penelope's Bakery bag onto the counter and faced him with her fists planted on her hips. "You do realize you're making more assumptions again, right?" He opened his mouth, then snapped it closed, dropping his chin for a moment. She winced, shaking her head. "Griff, I'm sorry."

His head lifted quickly. "What are you sorry for? I'm the one who can't keep his big foot out of his mouth when I'm around you."

"I really shouldn't have accused you." Crinkling her nose, she added, "To be honest, some strange smells can come from their apartment. They do have a business from their home, and I'm sure it's just a mixture of oils they use in their products that make it seem like they're trying to cover up other odors." She turned her attention to the pink bag and peeked inside, seeing an assortment of pastries.

"Well, I should be going."

At his words, she twisted her head around. "Um... hungry?"

"I'm sorry?"

She hesitated for a second then shrugged. "There's quite a bit here, and Lord knows my hips don't need all of these, or I'll be running extra miles, and honestly, I hate running. So, maybe you'd like to join me?" She held her breath, waiting for his response, not knowing if the gift was just a peace offering to a neighbor he'd been a dick to or if he'd like more of her company.

He squeezed the back of his neck again, but this time, his lips curved upward and the air rushed from her lungs. He was good-looking even when pissed off, but with a smile, he was devastatingly gorgeous.

Dropping his hand, he nodded. "Sure, I'd love to join you."

Standing straighter, she grinned. "Good. I'll make more coffee and you can pick out your favorites. Believe me, with Penelope's, you can't go wrong with any of their choices."

She poured two mugs of coffee, doctored hers with flavored creamer and sweetener, asking, "How do you take yours?"

"Splash of milk," he said, pulling out the pastries and putting them onto the plate she'd set on the counter.

"That's boring. Here, I'll rock your world." She poured salted caramel creamer into his mug and set it before him. He met her offering with a lifted brow. "Oh, come on," she cajoled. "Take a walk on the wild side."

He laughed but lifted the hot brew to his lips and took a sip. Nodding, he smiled wider, and she sucked in a quick breath. It wasn't lost on her that a smiling Griffin first thing in the morning was beautiful. She started to speak but all that came out was mostly a croak. Clearing her throat, she asked, "Good?"

"Good," he agreed, taking another sip.

His lips continued to quirk upward. *Yeah... definitely a cute quirk.* They stood at her counter drinking coffee and munching on pastries, and she wondered how such a dull Sunday morning had turned into something so different.

As he wiped the crumbs from his lips, he turned his gaze to her and asked, "So, what made you jump between two teenage boys and take an unnecessary hit to the face?"

She blinked as she finished chewing and swallowing in an attempt to not choke. Licking her lips to catch the stray crumbs, she noted his gaze dropped to her mouth, which in turn made her think of his mouth.

"Caitlyn?"

At his prodding, her head jerked slightly, bringing her attention back to his question and off his mouth. "Unnecessary? I don't know what you mean."

"I can't imagine you were the only adult around. And I know there's got to be rules for the staff to follow. So, with male teachers and administrators, some who had to be bigger than the guys, why didn't you let someone else handle it?"

She wouldn't have thought a Penelope's pastry could taste like sawdust, but that was all she tasted right now. Taking a huge swig of coffee, she tried to tamp down her anger but found her mouth wasn't ready to listen to her brain. "You're determined to just be condescending, aren't you?"

He straightened from the counter, his brows lifted to hide underneath the hair that dropped over his forehead. "No! That's not what I meant. I just wanted to know what happened, that's all."

"Well, you've got a dumbass way of asking that implies I didn't follow rules or was too hasty in intervening."

Once again, his hand lifted over his head to squeeze the back of his neck. "Caitlyn, if there are rules, then they're there for a reason."

She stared at the man on the other side of the kitchen counter, so tall she had to lean her head back to hold his gaze, and wondered if it was worth missing out on Penelope's if she threw the last bite of her pastry at his head. Deciding nothing was worth that travesty, she shoved the last bit into her mouth at one time, hoping the sugary confection would soothe her ruffled feathers.

8

Griffin looked down at the pissed-off woman, and the image of his younger sisters ran through his mind. Well, not completely. The angry expression that came from him questioning what they were doing certainly looked familiar. But all other thoughts about Caitlyn were definitely un-sister-like.

He'd seen her with flawless date-night makeup and her hair flowing over her shoulders, dressed in a cocktail dress that managed to be non-slutty and yet fuck-me at the same time. He'd seen her fresh out of bed, standing on her balcony, her hair wild about her face and her simple sleepwear the kind that made a man want to take her right back to that bed—but not for sleeping. He'd seen her in the ER, her face bruised and swollen, and while he might have had her situation pegged wrong, he wished he'd known her then so that he could have entered the room, sat on the bed with her, and wrapped his arms around her. Yesterday, he'd seen her straight out of the shower, barely dressed with wet hair in her face and in a panic to get to the stove. This morning, he'd finally managed to see her smile, and that was the expression that punched him in the gut more than any other.

And now? He'd managed to piss her off—again. With both hands on the top of the counter, he leaned his weight on them, wanting to drop his chin but refusing to give up holding her eyes. "You're right."

Her eyes widened and her brows lifted but she remained silent.

"I do have a way of asking a question that implies the other person did something wrong."

"That sounds like you have previous experience."

With no trace of humor, her voice sounded haughty, but he could hardly blame her. Nodding slowly, he agreed. "Yes. If you asked any of my younger siblings, they would tell you that it's one of my faults."

He kept his gaze on her, noting as she dropped her chin and stared at her empty plate, dragging her forefinger through the powdered sugar before popping the tip into her mouth. That small, innocent motion had his blood run south, and he was glad the counter hid everything from his waist down. He wasn't sure that the tenuous conversation would proceed positively if she noticed the swelling behind his zipper.

She lifted her clear-eyed gaze and said, "Faculty and staff are required to verbally attempt to dissuade student altercations. Sometimes, that works. If you have two students that are mouthing off to each other, a forceful, '*Stop,*' will do the trick. Things become murkier when you have students engaged in a physical altercation. That's when decisions are often made in an instant, but my goal is always to try to protect the students."

Fascinated with both her and what she was relating, he knew his best bet for keeping her talking was to stay quiet, so he simply nodded.

"Certainly, some of the younger male teachers and staff will be quick to jump in to physically restrain and protect. But, sometimes, the situation requires quick action."

He leaned closer, his weight now on his forearms resting on top of the counter, his hands close to hers. "And that's what happened to you?"

"Boys are usually easier to deal with in a fight."

His chin jerked back slightly, his head tilted to the side. "I don't understand."

"Boys are often trained to stand up for themselves but not to hit a female. I'm not saying that happens for all of them, but while our society might cheer on two men fighting, there's generally societal condemnation for hitting a female. Boys also will generally fight when angry, then turn it off. I've seen two boys whaling on each other, and by the end of the day, they're friends again."

"And I take it this doesn't happen with girls?"

Her lips curved, and it hit him how in those few minutes where he'd lost her smile, he craved to have it back. Determined to not fuck up again, he remained silent but smiled his encouragement.

"Girls in a fight don't mind getting dirty. Slapping, scratching, biting, pulling hair, and they don't care who gets in the way. If I hear a ruckus in the hallway, I always feel better if it's two boys instead of two girls."

"So, you intervened thinking it was safe?"

Nodding, she chuckled. "I got between them and had my hand on the chest of one and was looking toward the other. The first guy was trying to take one last shot to the other guy right when I turned into the path of his fist."

"Jesus, Caitlyn. I haven't been in a lot of fights, but unlike on TV and the movies where you get hit, shake it off, and keep going, a punch to the face is going to hurt like hell."

"Oh yeah, it did! Dropped me straight to my ass! Of course, the kids went wild, the guy who hit me felt horrible, and by then, we had a hall full of kids, teachers, staff, and I was still on my ass."

His jaw tightened just thinking of her landing on the hard floor after taking a full fist to the face by an angry, testosterone-overloaded, adolescent male, even if his intended target was the other guy.

"The principal was irritated that I didn't just stand to the side, and the security officer is pissed because I didn't press charges, and the kids think I'm badass, which I'm not sure is a good thing or not."

His irritation fled with the warmth of her smile and the realization that she didn't take herself too seriously. The first time he saw her on the balcony demanding they stop working so she could sleep, he categorized her as a princess and dreaded renting the apartment because of having to live across from her. His sisters certainly hadn't been raised as princesses. He'd never dated one and had no time to coddle one where he lived and worked.

Now, he thanked his lucky stars that they were going to share the upstairs. The gorgeous woman sent a jolt of lust through him, but Caitlyn was turning out to be so much more than he'd thought. An intriguing enigma, one he hoped to spend more time getting to know.

Glancing at the clock on her microwave, he pushed upward and away from the counter. "I hate to leave, but I need to go. I've got a couple of men who are working overtime hours, and we're going to get started on the renovations on the back porch first."

She mimicked his actions and pushed away from her side of the counter, then walked toward the door. "Thanks for the goodies. I'll make some again and promise to not burn them next time."

He walked to the door, hesitating just as he was next to her, so close their bodies were only a few inches apart. Looking down, he held her gaze. "I'll look forward to that." Stepping into the hall, he heard the door click behind him as he rounded the top of the stairs. As he jogged down to the first floor, he had a smile on his face.

He met Bob coming in the front door. Bob smiled, dipping his chin. "Hey, boss, everyone is here. Where do you want us to start?"

"Let's work on the back today. Tell Andrew to get up the cones and signs to keep everyone off the back porch while we redo the flooring."

For the next hour, his crew worked seamlessly

together to dismantle the flooring on one side of the wraparound porch that abutted the side of the house where Terri and Bjorn lived. While they replaced worn and rotted floorboards, he removed a few porch rail balusters and spindles, carefully measuring them. Making drawings of their decorative shapes, he determined they were a combination of Revival and Victorian.

As his hands smoothed over the wood, his mind drifted to the original craftsman who wouldn't have had the fast, electric lathe to turn the wood stick into spindles. The thoughts of children playing on the porch over the years filled his mind along with the idea of adults gathering on the wide space to visit, keep an eye on each other, or just to enjoy.

"Hello!"

Startled out of his musing, he looked over to see a downstairs window open and a woman with her head stuck out watching the proceedings. Her long, brown hair was braided, falling over her shoulder.

"I've got some tea if you'd like a drink. It can be served hot or cold, but we figured you'd prefer cold since you're working outside."

Before he had a chance to reply, a man in a khadi shirt that hung to his knees and harem pants came from around the corner, carrying a tray in his hands. "Here! Don't be shy, gentlemen. It's the most refreshing drink you can enjoy on a day like this."

His men immediately stopped what they were doing and reached for the cups. Grinning, he stepped forward, offering his thanks. "You must be Bjorn."

The man looked at him through round, wire-framed glasses and grinned. "Margaretha told us someone who was working on the house would be living here. Is that you?"

Sticking his hand out, he nodded. "Griffin Capella. Griff to my friends."

"Griff. I like that! Hey, Terri, this is Griff, our new neighbor!"

She leaned out the window again and waved enthusiastically as though she'd been stuck on a desert island and he was the first to arrive with the boat. "Griff! Hi! Nice to meet you! I'm Terri!"

Chuckling, he threw up his hand and returned her wave. Turning back to Bjorn, he accepted the tea, but before taking a sip said, "We'll be working here for a while and will get started around eight in the morning. I hope that's not going to be a problem."

"No, no!" Bjorn waved his hand dismissively. "Terri and I are always up early. At that time, we are usually doing our yoga and meditation in the backyard." His eyes widened as well as his smile. "Since you live here now, you should join us!"

Catching the grins coming from his crew, he shook his head. "Thanks, but not really my thing."

"That's cool, man. We celebrate all things here. You just be you."

The others handed their cups back to Bjorn, stifling their laughter but offering sincere thanks. "Yeah, man, we'll make sure the boss here is keeping it real."

Throwing a glare toward Bob, he finished the iced tea and gave his cup back as well. "Get to work," he groused to his crew, turning back to what he needed to do. Walking around, he snapped more pictures with his phone of the various decorative architecture of the house. He'd taken many when he first accepted the job from Margaretha but now wanted to focus on the details.

Making his way to the back, he noted Terri and Bjorn's porch door was standing open. Coming out was Caitlyn, her arms full with a large box. "I've got these!" she called over her shoulder, looking back into their apartment.

Just as he was getting ready to let his presence be known, she turned and startled, her foot missing the next step. "Shit!" she yelled as her body pitched forward.

Griff leaped forward, his hands shooting out, latching on to both Caitlyn and the box she juggled in an attempt to keep it from falling. The box wasn't heavy, and he easily shifted it to the back deck, his left arm still firmly wrapped around Caitlyn's waist. Her chin lifted and her wide eyes looked up at him.

"Oh, I didn't see you! Lordy, that could have been a disaster," she gushed.

Grinning with her still in his arms, not embarrassed to admit he loved the feel of her pressed against him, "Disaster averted," he quipped. He shifted, making sure her feet were steady underneath her, and regretfully loosened his grip.

Terri rushed out, her eyes darting between Caitlyn, Griff, and the box on the porch. "Are you okay?"

Strangely, her gaze was on the box when she spoke, but obviously, it was Caitlyn that replied. "Yes, I'm fine.

Thankfully, Griffin was here to keep me from tumbling off the porch."

Terri's concern melted from her features as her face relaxed. Walking over, she picked up the box and said, "I'll reopen this just to make sure everything's okay."

"Oh, I'm sure it is. Griffin retrieved that as well, and he's the one who set it on the porch. It would have more shaking in the mail truck."

Terri hesitated, then smiled again. "You're right. That's why we pack things so tightly before they go into the mail." She walked down the porch steps and placed the box into the back of a pickup truck parked on the side street.

During this, Griff stayed right next to Caitlyn with no excuse other than he wanted to be near her. Now in shorts that showed off a great length of tanned legs, with her feet encased in red sneakers that matched her red T-shirt, showcasing her curves without being skintight, it was hard to keep his mind on his original task.

As she looked up, her smile beamed at him. "I should get back to work."

"Work?" He cocked his head to the side as he glanced behind her toward the door she'd come through.

"I had some free time, so I'm helping Bjorn and Terri pack up some of the items they sell." Her nose crinkled. "Well, sometimes I pack, and sometimes I do labels. It all depends on what they need."

"I'd think after a week of wrangling teenagers, you'd be ready to relax and kick back with your friends."

Her nose crinkled again, but instead of saying

anything, she simply sucked in her lips, pressing them together for a moment before sighing then offering a smile. Stepping back, she glanced to the side to see his crew peeking around the side of the porch and grinned, tossing a little finger wave before turning and walking back inside the house.

With his hands on his hips, he glared at his crew again. "You all gonna work or gawk?"

"I don't know, boss," Andrew tossed out. "With those legs that just disappeared back into the house, I'd rather gawk."

Stomping closer to the side of the house so that his words wouldn't be heard, he shook his head. "Cut that shit out. No talking about clients or residents. And anyway, she's off-limits."

Jack's brows lifted as his smile widened. "You claiming, Griff?"

"I live here, man. She's a neighbor, and the last thing I want is trouble where I live." He wasn't surprised when the crew kept their smiles on their faces as they got back to work. They were good men, and he knew they might privately enjoy looking at Caitlyn when she was around, but they'd never disrespect her. Continuing around the house, he snapped more pictures, but his mind drifted to the woman living across from him.

Living near the gorgeous woman was either going to be torture or heaven… right now, he wasn't sure which.

9

"He's so virile!"

Caitlyn snickered at Terri's description. "Virile?"

Terri looked over, a crinkle between her brows. "Yes. Virile. Manly, masculine, sexy—"

Laughing, she said, "I know what virile means. What I don't know is anyone else who uses that word!"

Caitlyn had stepped back into the bohemian-decorated apartment, something Terri called creative chaos. Now, hearing Terri's description of Griffin, she glanced over her shoulder to see that her friend's face was even more illuminated than before. Terri's glee at the looks of their new neighbor caused Caitlyn to grin in return. Nodding, she looked down at the label she was currently working on. "But then, I guess virile is as good as any other word to describe him."

"So, he'll be living right across from you."

"Uh-huh."

Huffing, Terri walked over and plopped onto the silk patchwork cushioned chair at the table where Caitlyn was working. "You can't tell me you're not interested." Bjorn walked over and sat down as well, his attention focused on her.

Looking into her friends' faces, she rolled her eyes. "I'd have to be dead to not notice that he's exceptionally gorgeous, but interested? Come on, guys. Seriously? He lives right across from me."

"Yes!" Bjorn exclaimed. "Think how easy it would be to date someone that lives so close."

"Date?" Shaking her head, she said, "You two are delusional. I think you've been smoking your incense!"

Terri's brow lowered. "And just why would we be delusional? You're gorgeous and single. He's gorgeous and single—"

"You don't know that," she retorted.

Terri's mouth opened and closed. "Well, easy enough to find out." She stood and started to the door.

"No!" Caitlyn rushed forward and grabbed Terri's arm. "You can't go out there and ask."

"Why not?"

"Because he'll know you're not asking for you since you're with Bjorn. He'll know you're asking for me."

"What's wrong with that?" Bjorn asked.

If there was one thing she'd learned from getting to know them during the past year that she'd lived over them, they were almost innocently honest. Drawing a deep breath into her lungs, she let it out slowly. "First of all, Griffin and I got off on the wrong foot and we've just now straightened out an earlier misconception. Second of all, while he's certainly eye candy, I don't know anything about him. And thirdly, even if he was

Mr. Perfect, dating someone in the building could have disaster written all over it."

Seeing Bjorn's crinkled brow, she elucidated, "If it ended badly, I'd have to run into him all the time. How awkward."

"Oh, yeah, I see what you mean," Terri said, her hound-dog expression holding sympathy. "He'd bring his dates over, and you'd be right across the hall seeing the parade of women come and go."

Caitlyn sucked in a quick breath, hating the idea of seeing a parade of women going in and out of Griffin's apartment... *even if we never go on a date first.* But she knew it was inevitable. She may have given up on dating for the foreseeable future, tired of being disappointed, but there was no way a man as breathtaking as Griffin would not have lots of women interested if he wasn't already seeing someone.

Glancing at Terri and Bjorn, she saw the disappointment on their faces. "Come on, guys. I'm fine being single. And right now, we need to get these packages labeled and sent out or you're not going to make any money this week."

That seemed to do the trick as the couple jumped from their seats, and with the three of them working, they soon had the task completed. Just as she was ready to leave, she turned quickly. "Oh, I forgot to ask about selling some of your items at the teachers' fundraiser this next Saturday. I don't know how we would work it because some of the money would have to go to the school, but it would get you more local exposure."

"At your high school?" Bjorn asked, his brows raised, shooting glances between her and Terri.

"Yeah, uh... but you don't have to. It was just an idea."

"No, no. I think it's a good idea," he enthused. "What do you think Terri? A fifty-fifty split of profits?"

"Sure, babe. That'd be fine."

Now it was Caitlyn's turn to lift her brows. "Wow, a fifty-fifty split of profits? Are you sure? That's more than I was thinking."

"It'll be good for business. You come by on Friday evening, and we can give you stuff to load in your car."

"Great! I was trying to figure out what to take, so that'll be perfect." As Caitlyn said her goodbyes, Terri pressed a small box of candles, potpourri, and tea into her hand. "Here, this is for helping us."

Caitlyn thanked her, knowing her protest would fall on deaf ears. She never expected payment for helping them out but knew it made them feel better to give her something. With her box of delicious scents in her hands, she climbed the steps and went back into her apartment. Peeking out her window, she could see that Griffin's crew had left but she had no idea where he was. No sounds were coming from his apartment, but since she had lesson plans to prepare, it was just as well. Her mom was expecting her for dinner, so she wouldn't be alone.

The image of taking Griffin with her to a family dinner flew through her mind, but she quickly dismissed it as she shook her head. *Good God, I just met the man. Surely, I'm not that desperate or lonely.* Refusing to answer her own question, she plopped the box onto her counter, pulled out a candle, and lit it. Settling at her table with her lesson plan book and the floral scent drifting over her apartment, she got to work.

"Essays on an American novelist from the early 1800s are due on Friday. Not next Monday. Friday." Caitlyn looked over her advanced English class of juniors, watching their faces carefully as the groans and cries of, "Ms. McBride," filled the air. Waving her hand, she arched a brow, calling for silence. "This assignment has been on your calendar since the beginning of the year. Most of you will be going to college after high school and need to get used to having deadlines and due dates. So, no excuses. On my desk Friday."

"We've got extra practices this week, Ms. McBride! Athletes should get an extension."

She shot Devon a hard look, but it was Russ that replied.

"Jocks aren't the only ones with things to do, so quit your bitchin' and man up."

Devon's lip curled, and Caitlyn recognized a true sneer. "Just cause you gotta bag groceries for a living—"

"Shut up, Devon," Angelique said, turning around in her seat, her eyes narrowed on him.

Clapping her hands again, Caitlyn regained control of her class before they devolved into what she hoped would only be mild chaos, but with teens, she never knew what might happen. Devon was a good student, an excellent athlete, and his parents had money, something he hadn't flaunted in the past, but she knew his cockiness was growing as his athletic scholarship opportunities increased. Angelique was independent-minded and a staunch defender of anyone she viewed as an underdog. One look at Russ' face and it was clear he wasn't happy, whether from Devon's taunts or Angelique's defense, Caitlyn wasn't sure.

"Again, essays due next Friday. We'll use the last few minutes of class today discussing topics if anyone wants to run their idea past me."

Caitlyn spent the last fifteen minutes of the class moving amongst the students as they bounced their essay topics off her and she offered suggestions. She loved all her classes but particularly appreciated having this advanced class at the end of the day. The students were motivated, interested, excited about learning, and even if literature wasn't a great love of theirs yet, she always hoped she could impart an appreciation for the written word.

As the bell rang, she walked to the door, saying goodbye and answering a few more questions. The hall was crowded, a sea of teens filling the space as they moved, generally on the right side of the hall with a few like salmon swimming against the stream. As the sound of lockers slamming shut mixed with the cacophony of other sounds, she stayed at her door, supervising along with the other teachers. Slowly, the sounds receded as students rushed to their buses, the parking lot, or after-school practices.

Walking back into her class, she was surprised when Russ reappeared.

"Ms. McBride?"

Turning, she smiled. "Hey, what's up? Did you forget something?"

His head hung down for a moment as though finding his boots the most fascinating item in the room. She rested her ass against her desk, crossing her legs at the ankles, and waited patiently.

"Not going to college." She remained quiet, and he finally lifted his head to hold her gaze. "I know most in this advanced class are, but not me."

"Okay, Russ. Is there a reason you want me to know this now?" she asked, keeping her voice soft and steady, wanting him to keep talking.

His wide shoulders hefted, and she wondered what all he carried on them. "Family's got no money, and it's just not what interests me. I prefer working with my hands. I like this class, though. English and math are the only advanced classes I take."

"Math and English. Interesting combination."

He snorted, his lips curving upward. "Yeah, well, math just comes easy to me, and English… well, um… I'd heard about your class." At her lifted brow, he continued, "Everyone says you're the sh—um… you're the best. You care about students, and you teach literature in a way that makes it about real life. I wanted to know about that."

"It's nice to know that's my reputation because I do care about my students." Silence ensued for another moment.

"So, tell me what you'd like to do with your life, Russ, because I definitely don't think that college is for everyone. My brothers and one of my sisters joined the military after high school. They didn't get their advanced education until they were a bit older. And not all of it was through college."

Her words appeared to surprise him as he continued to hold her gaze. He'd adopted her pose, his hips resting against a nearby table, his arms now unfurling from having been crossed over his chest as his breath released.

"I don't know. I know I don't want to work in a grocery. I know I like working with my hands, but other than that, I have no idea. I just hate… hate…"

She waited as he struggled, then asked softly, "What do you hate, Russ?"

"I hate feeling helpless, like I've got no choices. I'm not like that prick, Devon, who wouldn't know work other than to catch a football."

"But you're not helpless, Russ. You're young, intelligent, hard-working. You have a future that is yours to grasp."

He held her gaze again, swallowing deeply. "Society possesses a conventional standard whereby it judges all things."

Her quick inhalation sounded out in the room. "Theodore Dreiser's *'Sister Carrie'*." Shaking her head, she added, "We don't study that novel until the next grading period."

"I've already read all the novels for the year," he said, a blush tinging his cheeks.

"I see…" She tried to steady her breathing, not

wanting to embarrass him by gushing over how impressed she was and yet so moved by his quote. "So, tell me about how you feel judged by society?"

Shoving his hands into his jeans pockets, he looked to the side, shaking his head slowly. "Not all of society. Just people like Devon... those who feel that daddy's money makes it okay for them to look down on others. People who see someone bagging groceries and think they're better." His cheeks puffed out as he heaved a sigh. "Sometimes, not having money makes it hard. Makes it hard to know what the right thing to do is."

His sudden change from a literature quote to wondering how to do the right thing had her zero in on his face, seeing conflict in his eyes. The last thing she wanted was for him to feel pushed into the wrong choices because it was too hard to do the right thing. She now remembered the quote he'd given in a previous class about doing the right thing. "Do you sometimes feel that it would be better to take an easier route to success, especially if we define success by money?"

"It's hard, Ms. McBride. My dad left years ago. Mom works as a cleaner for one of the big hotels. My older sister just got on there as well, but she's making minimum wage. I get the younger kids home from school and settled, then head to the grocery to work." He grimaced. "I know there's easier money out there... I just..." Another heavy sigh left his lips.

"You don't have to go to college to be what you'd like to be, Russ." She straightened and walked toward him, patted his arm, then stepped back. "But you just need to stay true to yourself."

He swallowed hard again, nodding slowly. Startling, he looked at the clock on the wall. "I gotta go, Ms. McBride." He pushed off from the table edge, swung his backpack over his shoulder, and walked to the door. Looking over his shoulder, he held her gaze then offered a chin lift before disappearing through the door.

She remained locked in place for a long moment, his situation filling her thoughts. She had many students from economically disadvantaged families in her classes and wondered how they would resist the temptation for easy money. Whether drugs, thefts, moving stolen property, gambling, just to name a few of the reasons teens were arrested, she prayed he would be able to rise above and keep working.

Shaking off the maudlin feelings, she walked to the teachers' lounge and quickly visited the ladies' room. Stepping out, she listened to several teachers discussing the teachers' fundraising fair that they were all expected to participate in.

"I have no idea what to bring," one of the older teachers said. "I don't bake. I don't knit. I don't make jewelry on the side. And yet, the principal wants us all to bring something to sell at the Saturday event."

"What are you bringing, Caitlyn?" Barbara asked. "Cookies?"

Shaking her head, she replied, "I figure there will be lots of baked goodies. But my neighbors make potpourri, candles, and tea. They're going to let me bring some to sell and have said that they'll split the profits fifty-fifty with the school."

"Oooh, like that great scented potpourri you have in your classroom?" another teacher asked.

She smiled and nodded. "Hopefully, they'll sell well, and it'll be a win-win for the school as well as my friends."

As the conversation droned on, she excused herself and walked back to her classroom. Once at her desk, she graded papers, tests, and assignments. The soft click of a locker closing gently sounded, and she glanced at the clock on the wall. Students should have left the building unless they had stayed late with a teacher. Standing, she walked to the door and pulled it open, leaning her head out. A few students were at the end of the hall, but it appeared one of the coaches was with them. Moving back to her desk, she gathered her purse and bag, glanced around at her room, and then walked out.

The place was deserted until she came to the hall by the PE locker rooms that led to the teachers' parking lot. A lone student headed toward the locker room door when they looked up sharply. Ducking their head, they barely lifted their hand toward her as they pushed their way into the locker room. Students were supposed to be accompanied, but she assumed Renée or Jamie were inside, both being PE teachers and coaches.

She hesitated, then pushed open the outside door. Glancing over her shoulder, she spied Russ and the other student leave the locker room at the same time.

His gaze landed on her, and she could have sworn his eyes widened for a second before he and the other student half-heartedly threw up their hands in another wave before turning to go out a different door.

She hesitated, wondering what they were doing. She probably should go back to the office on the other side of the building to report that she'd seen them. *Damnit!* Standing with her hand on the door, she sighed heavily. *It's Russ... I know him... I trust him. Ugh!* Forcing suspicions to the side, she continued outside. Weaving through the cars, she finally came to her small car. Not sorry she'd chosen to give the boys the benefit of the doubt, their actions niggled.

Needing a distraction, she detoured and stopped by her parents' house. The streets of the old neighborhood were so calming. Large brick homes, each different. No modern McMansions in sight. Tall oak trees bordered the sidewalks that had cracks and bumps in them from the roots. Near the end of the street, she came to the two houses, both as familiar as the other. One, the McBride family home where she and her five older siblings were raised, now where just her parents lived. The other, owned by the King family where they raised their five children along with her siblings. They, like her parents, now lived in the home alone, but with the multitude of adult children, significant others, and grandchildren coming along, the houses were often filled.

The backyards, which had remained open to each other and still had a worn path between the two, often held picnics and gatherings of whoever could come at the time. Seeing no other cars, she wasn't surprised to walk into the kitchen and see Hannah King sitting at her parents' table, sharing tea with her mom. Looking through the sliding glass door, she spied Chauncey King with her dad in the backyard, sharing a beer as they sat in the Adirondack chairs. Greeting her mom and Hannah, she sat down and accepted the cup of tea offered.

"Oh, my, your face looks so much better!"

Smiling at her mom, she nodded. "Yeah, there's just a bit of yellow bruising which I can cover up with makeup."

"I hope they threw the book at that kid!" Hannah exclaimed, then tossed her hand up. "I know, I know, it was an accident. But still, that's no excuse. Between the two of us, we had six boys, and while they were testosterone monsters as teenagers, none of them ever got into a fight in high school that would've involved hitting a teacher!"

Before she had a chance to retort, the sliding glass door opened, and Chauncey and her dad walked in. Greeting both of them, she listened once again as they all clucked over her previous injury. Wanting to take the focus off past events, she reminded them of the school's fundraising event that weekend. "My neighbors have agreed to split the profits, so I'll have a booth with their creations to sell. I hope you guys can come. Lord knows the school needs as much help as it can get."

"It's nice of your neighbors to do that," her dad said. "Your mom and I will stop by and support the fundraiser. Put out a call to your brothers and sisters, and I'm sure if they're available, they'll stop by, too."

"I'll let my brood know," Hannah said with a smile.

"There'll be some police presence at the event," Chauncey said. As the head of the Hope City Police Department, Chauncey managed to have his finger on the pulse of everything going on in the city, which, considering the size of Hope City, was a feat. "We've seen a significant increase in the drug traffic amongst teenagers around many of the high schools."

Caitlyn sighed, hating to hear his words even though she knew they were true. "I know our security officer is overworked with trying to keep up with everything."

"We'll probably send the dogs in twice this year instead of once," he added.

When the drug-sniffing dogs were brought in by the police department, the whole school went into a lockdown where the halls were cleared and the students stayed in their classrooms. The police dogs didn't go into individual classes, so she'd heard that the students suspecting the dogs were coming simply kept their drugs in their backpacks and not in the lockers. She sighed again, hating the measures needed to try to keep the drugs out of the schools, but for some students, it was a big business.

"How's the work going on the house?"

Recognizing her mother's tactic of changing the subject to one she was more comfortable with, Caitlyn grinned. "I think it's going well although from what Margaretha has told me, it's gonna take a long time. The person she hired will rebuild the elements so that they look like the original. I don't know if I mentioned it, but he's moved in across the hall from me. I guess he needed a place to live, and she needed a renter, so it works for both of them." She dropped her gaze to her teacup, suddenly finding the pattern fascinating as she felt her mother and Hannah's gazes boring into her. She now wished she hadn't mentioned anything, knowing their ability to ferret out secrets.

"Oh, so he lives right there?" Hannah asked, a sharpness underlying each word. "Have you had a chance to get to know him?"

This question came from her mom, and she shook her head. "We've chatted a couple of times, that's all. I'm sure I'll run into him occasionally."

Hannah opened her mouth to ask another question, but Chauncey's phone alarm vibrated, and he looked at his wife. "We've got to go. Brock and Brody are stopping by to pick up one of the dressers in the spare room."

Caitlyn breathed a sigh of relief from getting out of the inquisition. Deciding to leave at the same time, goodbyes were offered all around, and promises to come to the next big family gathering were made.

Once home, she spied Margaretha through her living room window watching TV. Entering the front door, she could smell the sweet scent of candles emanating from Terri and Bjorn's apartment. Climbing the stairs, her heart rate increased as it did every day, wondering if she would run into Griffin. She hadn't seen him close-up since their interaction the other day when she'd spectacularly tripped outside and he caught her. Her face heated at the memory, the embarrassment still vivid. And yet, for the moment she was held in his arms, something felt so right. So real. So much more than she'd felt on any of her last dates where all she wanted to do was get away. With Griffin, she would have happily set up residence in his arms. *Yeah, if that doesn't make me sound like a loser.*

Her phone rang just as she entered her apartment and was attempting to let the disappointment of not seeing Griffin overtake her. Seeing the caller ID, she grinned. "Hey, Bekki!"

"I miss you, bestie!" Bekki called out. "Mom said she ran into you today."

Laughing, Caitlyn shook her head. "That was about half an hour ago. How quick is your mom's phone tree finger for letting everyone know what's going on?"

"You know Mom," Bekki said in an exaggerated long-suffering voice. "Anyway, I've got tomorrow night free. How about meeting at the Celtic Cock? Erin is sure to be there, and I'll see if Sandy wants to come also."

Agreeing, Caitlyn thought a night out at her soon-to-be brother-in-law's pub would be the perfect antidote to sitting in her apartment listening for any comings or goings from Griffin's apartment and pretending that wasn't what she was doing.

10

"You fuckin' moron! You should have kept your head down, but instead, you fuckin' smiled at Ms. McBride at the locker room."

The three people gathered in the room lit only by a small lamp looked at each other, a combination of irritation, anger, frustration, and defensiveness painted on their faces. Brought together by a common goal, they each had much to lose.

"It would look bad if I didn't. She doesn't suspect anything. Why would she?"

"Because she's smart. Because she might put two and two together."

"Ignoring her woulda made me look suspicious. I didn't know what to do. Anyway, you decided on the locker room because there are no cameras there. Where the fuck am I supposed to get the stash?"

"We gotta look for an alternative place. One that isn't so visible and yet accessible."

"Fine, do it, but stop fuckin' around with me until you do."

Another voice entered the conversation. "We still have our backup location. We need to keep the carriers rotating. Enough to keep the heat off but not confuse the ones dropping off or picking up,"

"You want to start using the locker rooms down on the practice field?"

"Let's see how the next week goes. No more recruiting. We use the carriers we have for now, but they'll be busier. That's fine. Keeps them under wraps and quiet."

"Dogs'll come in some time."

"Won't matter if it's in a neutral location that doesn't have eyes on it and there's nothing there."

"Dogs only come in during school hours. After hours, it won't matter."

"We can cover and confuse. That's the smart play."

All three nodded as the leader agreed. "Keep the course." Pinning the other two with a hard glare, they added, "And keep the carriers in line. I hear one word that someone is skimming, hell's gonna rain down on everyone."

"No worries, I've got them in line."

"Good." The leader turned and walked out of the room, no words or waving goodbye, just the click of the door closing behind them making the only sound.

The other two blew out simultaneous breaths, looking at each other.

"Things are getting complicated."

A snort erupted. "You thought this shit would be

easy? Just remember what you've got going into the bank."

When finally alone, the last one in the room sighed heavily. *Bank account won't mean shit if my ass is dead or in jail.*

11

It wasn't as though the Celtic Cock was the best bar near the Inner Harbor, but as Caitlyn walked down the sidewalk toward the iconic pub, she was struck with how many good times she'd had in the old establishment. Owned by siblings Torin and Maeve Flanigan, it was one of the favorite haunts of many first responders, including her three brothers, her brothers-in-law, and the Kings. Of course, that was why she'd avoided it during college, but now, the Celtic Cock felt like family, even more so since her sister, Erin, and Torin were engaged.

As her heels clicked on the sidewalk, she glanced up at the iconic wooden sign that swung over the doorway. The carved relief of a rooster inside a Celtic circle called like a beacon. Pulling open the heavy wooden door, she was immediately met with sounds of friends mingling, music, the clink of glasses, and laughter. Smiling at some familiar faces, she weaved through the crowd to the high-top table where her friends waited.

Before hefting her booty onto a bar chair, she moved first to Erin, offering a heartfelt hug. Next, she greeted Sandy, a friend and now sister-in-law. Last but certainly not least, she wrapped her arms around Bekki. Once seated, she gave her drink order before turning back to the others. "What have I missed?"

"Not much," Erin said. "We've only been here a few minutes."

Taking a sip of her vodka and cranberry, she glanced at the glass of water sitting in front of Sandy. Her gaze jumped up to the beautiful blonde sitting across next to her, discovering a smile playing about her lips. "Sandy, where is your Lemon Drop Martini?" In all the years she'd known the beautiful blonde who was now Rory's wife, she'd never seen Sandy just stick to water.

Sandy continued to grin as the others stared, then gasped.

"Oh, my God! You're pregnant!" Caitlyn gushed. When Sandy nodded, the four women became a tangle of arms as they all rushed to hug her.

Once seated again, Sandy pinned them with a hard stare. "But you *cannot* say anything to anyone! Rory and I haven't told the parents yet."

"Please, tell me you're not going to wait long," Erin begged. "If Mom finds out that we knew and she didn't, there'll be hell to pay!"

Caitlyn nodded emphatically. "Yes, please, tell us that you're going to let them know soon."

"We're going over tomorrow to tell your parents. Then we'll announce it at the next family meeting." She reached over and clutched Erin's hand. "Considering

I'm married to your twin, I know Rory wanted to be the one to tell you. But as soon as he looks at you, he's going to know that I've already let the cat out of the bag."

Erin waved Sandy's concerns away. "Don't worry about it. Rory and I ran into each other earlier today, and he told me. I just didn't want to let anyone else know until you were ready."

Caitlyn looked at the three women sharing her table, her heart full. She was lucky, she knew it, and she never took it for granted. Her family was large, loud, in your business, and some of the most wonderful people she'd ever met. The Kings next door were the same.

For the next few minutes, the conversation rolled around to who was expecting, due dates, husbands, soulmates, and future plans. It wasn't hard for Caitlyn to keep the smile on her face. She loved these women, and their happiness meant the world to her. She just hoped that one day there'd be someone out there for her to feel the same about.

"So, Caitlyn..."

Sandy's singsong voice caught her attention. "Yeah?"

"I've been designing the offices for a new law firm, and one of the lawyers is gorgeous, funny, does not take himself too seriously, and believe it or not, is single. I happened to mention that I had a friend—"

"No, no blind dates." As the other three women blinked in surprise, Caitlyn realized her voice was harsher than she'd intended. Blushing, she shook her head. "Sorry, it's just that I've been on so many first dates lately that turned out to be un-fun. I think I'd just rather meet someone organically."

"I get it," Bekki said, nodding. "But you could be missing out on someone amazing just because you haven't run into them yet but one of us thought of you."

Her brow scrunched as she nibbled on her bottom lip, Bekki's explanation making sense.

"I think it's important to respect whatever Caitlyn wants to do. If she's not into a blind date now, that's fine. And if she decides later that she'd like to try it again, that's fine, also." Erin reached over and placed her hand on Caitlyn's arm, squeezing it.

Caitlyn held her sister's gaze, gratitude filling her smile. In many ways, they were such opposites. Erin had come back from her time in the Army a haunted woman, brought back to embracing life by Torin, while Caitlyn had always been taken care of by all the older siblings. Bekki was the most like her, carefree and fun-loving. But now that she was with Killian, Caitlyn could see his calming influence on her friend.

"Thank you, Erin. You put it perfectly." Looking back at Sandy, she continued, "And I might take you up on some date set-ups later, but for now, I think I'd like to just see what comes my way."

"So, what's up in the world of teenagers?" Erin asked. "No more fights to break up?"

"No," she laughed. "It's a good year. My classes are fun, the students are really into what we're learning. Out of seven, I've got four that are advanced, more than last year. Probably why my principal mostly stays out of my business."

"More kids are interested in you than in literature," Bekki grinned. "You're smart, funny, a great teacher, and let's face it, you're a dream come true for those adolescent hormones."

"Ugh, please," she groaned, taking a sip of wine. "Believe me, those hormones are not aimed at me, but some days, trying to keep everyone on task and not looking at each other is hard!"

"I happened to drive by your place the other day and saw some scaffolding materials on the outside. Is your landlady having work done?" Sandy asked.

She nodded. "She's hired a contractor who's going to be doing some historical refurbishing of the outside. I think he'll also do some work on the inside as well."

Sandy's eyes sparkled and she grinned, her decorator instincts showing. "Ooh, that sounds delightful." She then crinkled her nose. "Although, the noise and mess can be a problem while the work is being accomplished."

"What about that empty apartment across from you that I'd looked at before moving in with Torin?" Erin asked. "Is it still empty?"

Shaking her head, she looked down at her wine, pretending great interest in the half-filled glass. "No, someone has just moved in. It's the contractor who's doing the work."

She continued to stare at her drink until realizing the table had gone completely silent. Lifting her chin, her gaze bounced between the other three women, noting their smiles. "What?"

"Nothing," Bekki said, her smile widening. "It's just

that you adopted such a forced nonchalant attitude when you answered, it immediately made my antenna go up."

Sandy nodded, her smile just as wide. "So, is he handsome?"

"Yes," she admitted, rolling her eyes. "There's nothing wrong with a little eye candy in the building."

"Not at all. But why does he have to just be eye candy?" Bekki asked, leaning closer. "I mean, what good is candy if you don't have a little taste?"

"Oh, my God. I thought I left the adolescents back at school!"

The others laughed, but before they had a chance to pump for more information about her new neighbor, Sandy checked her phone and grinned. "I hate to call it an early night, but that's one thing about being pregnant, I get tired easily. Rory just got off work and he's almost here to pick me up. I'll talk to you all soon." She slid from her seat and offered hugs before making her way toward the door.

Caitlyn watched her, always amazed that even though Sandy was petite with her thick, long blonde hair and fairy princess face, the crowds in the bar seemed to part for her and she made it to the door easily. Movement next to her caught her attention, and Bekki was sliding from her chair as well.

"Killian's back from his meeting, so I'm gonna head home." She hugged Caitlyn and whispered in her ear, "Don't wait too long for Prince Charming to walk through the door. Killian's brothers are gorgeous!"

Laughing, she nodded. "I promise, I'll let you know if I decide I'm desperate for a blind date!"

Now that it was just her and Erin, she looked toward the bar and realized only Maeve was there. "Isn't Torin working tonight?" As part owner, Torin was almost always at the pub.

Shaking her head, Erin said, "He came in early today to meet with the accountants so they could get ready for tax time."

"Then you need to get home. Anyway, one drink is enough for me, so I'll walk out with you."

The two sisters walked out of the pub arm in arm. She stopped at Erin's car and nodded toward hers just across the street. "I'm over there." They hugged goodbye again, and while friend hugs were amazing, it was the feel of her sister's arms around her that caused tears to threaten. Swallowing deeply, she plastered on a smile as she leaned back and watched as Erin climbed into her car. Knowing that Erin wouldn't leave until she was across the street at her vehicle, she jogged over, then turned and waved.

The night was warm, and a gentle breeze blew down the street from the harbor. Her family used to come to the Inner Harbor when she was younger, and she loved it. A ride on one of the boats, a hotdog at a street vendor, a chance to watch the fishermen come in.

With her hand resting on the handle of her car door, she lifted her chin, lost in thought as she breathed in the salty air. Only the muffled sounds of the pub when the door opened could be heard in the background. Until heavy footsteps came closer.

Whirling around, she gasped as a tall figure stepped into the light from the lamppost near her. *Griffin!* "Oh, God, Griffin, you scared me!"

"I'm glad," he bit out, not stopping until he was directly in front of her. His gaze glanced around then settled back on her face. "What the hell are you doing out here?"

Surprised at his tone, she tilted her head to the side and her chin jerked out. "What does it look like I'm doing? I'm getting into my car."

"That's not what it looked like from where I was standing."

"What are you talking about? And why are you here, anyway?"

He leaned against her car, his arms crossed over his impressive chest. His stance may have seemed casual, but energy vibrated from him, which she found strange given the circumstances and yet a real turn on. The breeze had caught his long hair, ruffling the curls the way she wished her fingers could do.

"I just happened to be in the neighborhood."

Lifting a brow, she decided to adopt his pose. Crossing her arms, she leaned her back against the door of her vehicle. "That's a line as old as time."

"It's true. I'd come with some friends to the pub. We were in the back playing pool. I saw you when you came in and noticed when you left. Since I was getting ready to leave anyway, I thought I'd make sure you got to your car safely. It's a good thing I did since you were standing here, your mind on God knows what while you weren't paying any attention to your surroundings."

"Arrogant," she grumbled, hating that he was right. With as many family members in law enforcement as she had, she knew the cardinal rule of a woman by herself needing to always be aware of their surroundings.

"I might be arrogant, but I'm right, aren't I?"

By now, he'd straightened from her car, his arms no longer crossed. Staring up into his face, she saw no smugness, only what looked like concern. She sighed heavily and nodded. "Yes, you are. I know I should always be aware of what's going on when I'm by myself at night, but... Well, I guess I just have a lot on my mind."

He appeared to measure her words, his silence almost as disconcerting as his perusal. A strange sense of vulnerability moved over her. Not from fear of him but from fear of what he was seeing when he looked at her. With every encounter they'd had since first seeing each other in the ER, she'd felt lacking. Now, staring up at his face, so handsome in the shadows of the evening, she wanted him to see her differently. Not as a mess but as a woman.

His gaze moved from her face to over her shoulder and back again. "You were looking toward the harbor. If you'd like to take a walk, I'd be happy to accompany you."

Her eyes widened in delight, and she let out a breath she hadn't realized she'd been holding. "I'd like that." Then, glancing toward the pub, she looked back up at him. "But I don't want to take you away from whatever you had planned."

"Didn't have anything planned. It's been a while since I walked around the harbor in the evening, so this would be nice." He dragged his fingers through his hair before continuing. "A friend drove me here. Would you mind if I bummed a ride home after our walk?"

With her hand clasped against her chest, she moaned with great exaggeration, "Oh, it would be so out of my way."

"You're a goof," he laughed, rolling his eyes. He pulled out his phone and mumbled, "Let me shoot my friend a text letting him know I've got a ride." Shoving his phone back into his pocket, he nodded.

They left her car on the street and walked along the sidewalk leading toward the harbor. Several bars and restaurants were still open, and the streetlamps provided plenty of illumination.

They continued walking, side-by-side but not touching. Her mind wandered to her younger days and she inwardly winced at what she knew she would have done: pretend to stumble over a crack in the sidewalk so that he would reach out and take her hand. Find a way to joke with him so that she could shoulder bump him, which almost always led to hand holding as well. She would have giggled and flirted, excited to maintain his attention.

Glancing to the side, it wasn't as though she didn't want to hold his hand but wanted it to happen only if he really wanted it.

After a moment of silence, he was the first to break it. "So, hanging about streets alone outside of bars at night isn't typical for you?"

"With my family? That's what's so crazy about what I was doing. Believe me, safety has been drilled into me since I was very young."

"From your family?"

Nodding, she rolled her eyes. With her hands in front of her, she ticked off her fingers one by one. "Let's see, my father is a former FBI investigator. My oldest brother, *Detective* Sean. My next oldest brother, *Detective* Kyle. My next brother, *Paramedic* Rory. My brother-in-law, *Detective* Carter." Looking up at him she laughed. "Getting the picture?"

"Oh, hell yeah."

Shaking her head, she added, "That's not all." Continuing to tick off her fingers, she said, "Our closest family friends and nextdoor neighbors are Hope City Police Commissioner Chauncey King, and his sons and a few daughters-in-law are all in law enforcement as well. Believe me, as the baby of the group, I've had all the lectures and all the warnings."

"So, you're the baby. That's why you remind me of my youngest sister."

Reminding him of his sister was hardly the effect she'd hoped to have on him. The last thing she wanted him to feel for her was brotherly.

12

As soon as the words *"you remind me of my youngest sister"* left his mouth, Griffin winced. His attraction to Caitlyn was definitely not sisterly. Quite the contrary. Even in the crowded pub, it was as though an electrical vibration moved through him that caused him to search the crowd for its source. When his gaze had landed on the dark-haired, blue-eyed beauty, he couldn't believe his eyes.

The Celtic Cock was not a bar he generally frequented, but when Andrew had asked him to join a game of pool before taking them home, he'd discovered the pub vibe to be welcoming. A great number of patrons appeared to be first responders, something that boded well for the pub being able to handle the crowd and keep everyone orderly.

A tingle hit the back of his neck, and he'd turned to discern the cause. As soon as he'd spied Caitlyn, his attention was no longer on the pool game but riveted on her. He'd noted she was with friends, not a date. He'd watched the four women catch the eyes of many men, but no one approached. Now that he knew her connection to the Hope City law enforcement, he could easily assume she was well known amongst the patrons.

He couldn't tell if her blue silky blouse was the same color as her eyes or if her eyes reflected the color perfectly. Either way, he was mesmerized. He watched her smile, her eyes warm on her friends. She'd laugh, throwing her head back with enjoyment. Her dark hair swung about her shoulders with the movement.

The stylish blonde at her table left first, shortly followed by another. As Caitlyn and the last woman left, he imagined they were related considering they looked so much alike.

No longer interested in the pool game, he told Andrew that he was going to step outside, wanting to make sure she made it to her car safely. When he did, he watched Caitlyn walk the other woman to her car before she crossed the street. But instead of getting in immediately, she stood and stared into the distance. The expression on her face, illuminated by the streetlight, made him think that she was miles away. He couldn't believe that she was so lost in thought that she barely heard him approach. He hated that she thought he was a grouch, but the idea of who might have caught her unaware and vulnerable... His jaw clenched tight at the thought. If that had been his sister... *Shit...*

Caitlyn was now staring up at him, disappointment moving through her eyes, and he quickly amended his last statement. "It's just that my youngest sister often gets lost in her imagination and sometimes doesn't notice what's going on around her. I never knew if that was just her personality or if she was always so sure that one of us would be around to help her out if needed." With his hands jammed into his pockets, he sighed. "I suppose I used to always fuss at her to make sure she stayed alert. "

A smile had replaced Caitlyn's disappointment. "Oh, I see. You're an older brother. Yep, I can definitely understand that now. Do you just have one sister?"

Laughing, he shook his head. "No, there were five of us."

Now it was her turn to laugh, and he loved the sound. Realizing that so many of their previous conversations had not included any laughter, he hoped it was something that would change.

"I told you about my three brothers and the detective brother-in-law who's married to my oldest sister. The woman that I walked out with is my other sister. So, yep, that makes six of us. And I was the baby."

"I was going to ask if you were spoiled, but for once, I thought about my words before I said them."

Still laughing, she said, "I'm glad. I would've been horribly offended. But while I don't think I was spoiled, I was the youngest. Growing up, either everyone had already done something before me, or they were watching me closely *because* they'd done something before me."

They stepped off the curb, and he reached out to take her arm until they crossed. The material of her blouse was silky underneath his fingertips, and he reluctantly let her go as they reached the other side.

The Inner Harbor was bordered by the water on one side and shops and restaurants on the other with a wide walkway in between. The shops were closed but the restaurants were still open, lively music and conversations drifting over the area. He looked around, making sure they were still in the light and scoping out the people walking around.

"Oh, don't you just love the harbor at night? The twinkling lights on the water. The sound of the waves hitting the edge. It's been ages since I've been here," she enthused.

Her expression matched the tenor of her words as she looked around, her smile wide. He tried to look at the scenery through her vision. The streetlights were close enough together that their path was easily illuminated. Concrete pylons lined the harbor, and the dark water slapped against their sides. The undulating water captured the lights from the lamps as well as lights from the boats twinkling in the distance.

They walked close to the edge, and as they stood there looking out over the harbor, she moved a little closer to his side. "My brother Kyle married one of my college friends, Kimberly. She and I used to come out here at night just because we both loved it so much. Then, one night, we saw the biggest rat in the world. Scared us silly!"

"I've seen some big rats, but I can't swear that they were the biggest in the world," he quipped, grinning as she laughed. He reached down and took her hand in his, leading her over to one of the unoccupied benches. Quite a few people were strolling along the Inner

Harbor, and they saw the occasional police officer on patrol. Giving his attention to the beautiful woman at his side, he slid his arm around her shoulders, wanting to know more about her. "With your siblings all around, I take it you were raised in Hope City?"

"Born and raised here. My parents still live in the big house in the north part of the city, still next door to the King family. What about you?"

"Yeah, me too. Not quite so idyllic, but my family is still close."

She twisted around toward him, her eyes pinned on his face. "Not idyllic?" Her voice was soft, and he found that he wanted to take the look of concern from her.

His throat worked, uncertainty filling him. He wasn't used to talking about his family, at least, not with someone he just met. And yet, with Caitlyn's big, blue eyes on him, he opened his mouth and the words began to flow.

"My mom is great… funny, loving. My dad, not so much. He drank too much, and my early memories were of him yelling a lot. Mostly at Mom, but sometimes at me or my sister, Marcie, or brother, Gary. But, over time, he became physical. I think Mom tried to hide some of his crazy from us, but eventually, I was old enough to notice. By then, Bert and Chelle had come along. When I was about twelve, he came home drunk one night and started to get physical with anyone in his path. Mom had had it by then and kicked his ass out."

"Oh, my goodness! Good for her!" Caitlyn's gaze snapped with indignation, then suddenly she grabbed his arm. "But I shouldn't have said that. I mean, I'm sure it was hard on everyone."

He shrugged. "Mom worked during the days, and I managed to get the other kids ready in the mornings and took care of them after school. We didn't have a lot, but home became a place of calm."

She sighed and added, "That's why you were so upset when you thought my injury was from someone who had hit me."

"I only saw my mom with a black eye one time. One time was enough." His voice was soft as he gave more than he'd meant to. Looking at her, he added, "I didn't realize the doctor was making a poor joke when he said for you to not be a punching bag."

He felt her shoulders sag as she nodded. It struck him that she wasn't just an impartial listener but seemed to ooze empathy with what he'd gone through. Staring at her, he wondered how he had ever thought she wasn't as strong as he was beginning to see that she was.

"Tell me more... I'd really like to know," she prodded, squeezing his arm.

"When I graduated from high school, Mom got remarried to a good man, and I joined the Army. Can't say it was due to patriotism or a grand plan on being a soldier, but I needed a steady job. And, in truth, I needed to figure out who I was. Mom and Joe—that's her husband—encouraged me, giving me the freedom to finally take off the mantle of caretaker of the younger ones."

"My brothers and sister, Erin, served also, but Sean

never lost his oldest brother vibes. I love him, but I swear, sometimes, I think he has a knack for getting on my case or getting on my nerves!"

Griffin smiled, slowly shaking his head. "If you asked Chelle, she'd tell you that I'm the same."

"Chelle... that's such a pretty name. Is she the youngest?"

"Yeah. There's me, then Marcie, who's an accountant, married, and has a few kids. Then there's Gary. He joined the Army also but has made a career out of it. He's in California now. Bert is in Richmond and works for a building supply company. And Chelle's the baby. She's an art teacher in a school in the county and makes jewelry on the side that she sells with her online store."

Caitlyn squeezed his arm, her gaze never wavering. "I can tell how proud you are of them. And just think, older brother, you had a hand in making each of them what they are as adults. You stepped up to be the father figure they needed."

He'd never had anyone say that to him other than knowing he had their mother's gratitude. The air seemed thick as he breathed in, her words moving through him, finding a corner to take up residence.

They were silent for a moment before she sighed and leaned a little closer. "Where did you learn to work on old houses?"

By now, she'd turned so that they were facing each other on the bench. His arm rested on the back, his fingers now gently rubbing her shoulder.

"I got an associate's degree in American history while I was stationed in Germany. I was a builder and combined my two favorite things when I came back home. I hadn't spent hardly any pay in my four years, so I had enough to start my own business after working for a brilliant contractor in town who specialized in mid-1800s houses."

"Does that include the jillions of townhomes built then?"

"No, actually, the Victorian homes are my specialty. And believe me, there are plenty of those although I'm a general contractor, so I can take any work to make sure my workers stay employed."

He couldn't remember the last time he'd talked so much about himself and wanted to turn the conversation back to her.

Just as he opened his mouth, the breeze picked up and Caitlyn shivered. "Come on, let's get home." She looked up and grinned. "Weird, isn't it?"

"What is?"

"Home. It's the same for you and me."

Keeping her fingers linked with his, he grinned. As they walked, he was aware that she'd managed to find out more about him than he'd given to anyone—ever. Wanting to balance the scales, he jiggled their connected hands and asked, "Besides what your siblings do, what about you?"

"I teach American Literature at North Central High School."

"No shit? Really?"

Her brow lowered as her face turned up toward him. "Um... no shit. I really teach there. Why the shock?"

"You probably won't believe it, but that's where I

went to high school. I sure as hell didn't have an English teacher that looked like you."

Rolling her eyes, she said, "As serious as you were, you probably did and didn't notice."

"Oh, Caitlyn, I would have noticed anyone as beautiful as you."

The breath left her lungs in a rush, and she looked straight ahead as they continued down the sidewalk.

"Why American Lit?"

She continued staring ahead and he couldn't get a good look at her face in the shadows all around. He jiggled their hands, and she looked up with wide eyes. "Oh, what? I'm sorry, did you say something?"

A deep-chested chuckle erupted as he lifted a finger to ease the crinkle that had settled between her brows. "I asked why American Literature?"

"You said you studied American History, so you must be aware of the link. It's through the writings of a time that we can see into the souls of those before us, not just the facts of events."

"Is that what you do? Want to see inside the souls?"

She pressed her lips together, the crinkled between her brow deepening as she kept her gaze on him. *Sucked in.* That's what struck him. He was completely sucked into her and waited to see what she would say.

Swallowing audibly, she nodded. "Everyone so often thinks the youngest child is… well, impulsive, flighty. So used to others telling them what to do. But, for me as the youngest of six, and if you throw in the Kings next door, Bekki and I were the youngest of eleven kids, I watched. I listened. I absorbed the actions of others.

Their words. Their mannerisms. I took in all that my family was, each as individuals. I'm not sure the older kids in the family can do that because there's so much on them to help out. My brother, Sean, is such a good, responsible man. The best. Honest to God, the absolute best. But, sometimes, I think he was so used to making sure we were behaving, getting ready for school to help out Mom and Dad, checking our homework because Dad was working and Mom was trying to run the house, I don't know that he had the time to really *see* us as individuals. He didn't have the time to sit and observe." She shrugged. "But I did. So, yes, I love literature. When I was younger, I could fall into a book or a character and disappear. I wasn't the baby anymore. I wasn't the pesky little sister. And as I grew older, I fell in love with all literature, but American is my favorite."

Griffin hadn't realized they'd stopped on the sidewalk while her passioned explanation caused his chest to depress as he exhaled and his heartbeat pounded. Her face was turned up toward his, her blue eyes twinkling underneath the streetlamp's illumination. Her cheeks held a hint of blush, and her mouth was moist, and her lips parted slightly.

"I want to kiss you." As the words left his mouth, she blinked, and he had no idea how to pull them back even if he wanted to, which he didn't.

"Okay," she whispered, her voice barely more than a breath. Stepping closer so that her front was pressed to his, her head tilted back to maintain eye contact.

"I don't know if it's a good idea," he admitted, the words rough and choked.

"I'm not sure I care." Her tongue darted out, licking her bottom lip, and his resolve snapped.

He let their linked fingers go to lift both hands, wrapping his palms around the sides of her neck, his fingers tangling with the silky softness of her hair and his thumbs gently sweeping over her cheeks. Her hands lifted to his waist, and she clutched his shirt. Her lips parted as he moved closer, his mouth sealing over hers.

The instant her tongue reached out to barely touch his, a groan resounded from deep inside. He slid his hand into her hair to grasp the strands, tilt her head slightly to the side, and thrust his tongue into her warmth, finding and losing himself at the same time.

She lifted onto her toes, and he slid one arm to band around her waist to take some of her weight, loving the feel as she melted into him. Her soft body pressed against the hard planes of his, her fingers digging into his waist. It had been a while since he'd been out with a woman, but he usually didn't go so fast. With Caitlyn, they weren't even on a date, but damn if he didn't care. In his arms, she felt as though she belonged.

The sound of laughter came from across the street, and he shifted them around so that when he lifted his head from her mouth, he could see the noise came from inside the pub. A hasty glance to the side revealed they were standing next to her car. His gaze dropped to her face, her half-lidded eyes still shining in the light of the lamp and her tongue sweeping over her kiss-swollen lips. *Shit... what the fuck am I doing?*

She breathed heavily, her sweet breath puffing

across his face, a smile playing on her lips. "Are you still uncertain if this is a good idea?"

It seemed she was holding her breath waiting for his answer, but honesty was all he could afford. All he knew was that he had no clue what he was doing with the beautiful, bewitching neighbor. Nodding slowly, he replied, "Yeah. I'm completely uncertain."

As soon as the confession of doubt left his lips, he winced.

13

Dragging her lips from the best kiss she'd ever had, bar none, Caitlyn stared dumbly. As soon as the words fell between them from Griffin's lips, she inhaled quickly, unable to stop the gasp from slipping out. She'd asked the question hoping he'd tell her that there was no uncertainty. In fact, she'd been sure he was going to push aside all doubts. *But no.* Settling her heels back onto the sidewalk, she loosened her grip on his shirt, her hand flat on his abs, smoothing over the now-wrinkled material. Her face felt hot, and she was glad for the darkness to keep her heated blush from his eyes.

Sucking in her lips, she tried to think of something to say, but the awkward silence filled the air, threatening to choke her breath. Finally, she reached into her purse and pulled out her car keys. Forcing a smile onto her face, she inclined her head toward the vehicle behind him. "We should get home."

"Caitlyn, I'm sorry. That's not… I didn't mean—"

Stepping back, she darted around him and threw open the driver's door. Once behind the wheel, she started the car as he climbed into the passenger side. Pulling out onto the almost empty street, she desperately tried to think of something to ease the awkward silence. Alighting on something he'd said earlier that would be a safe subject, she said, "If you went to North Central High, then you probably remember Mr. Aylesford."

Keeping her eyes on the road, she felt Griffin's stare against the side of her head. Her fingers gripped the steering wheel a little tighter until he spoke, allowing the change of subject to ease the tension.

"I can't believe he's still there. He was the English teacher everyone dreaded to have. I was never sure he even liked literature."

Still trying to fill the void, she kept going. "I've heard the rumor that this is going to be his last year. He's way past retirement, and it's not that he doesn't have anything else to do. He's got family in Florida and his wife has been after him to retire so they can move. I think to help that along, the principal gave him all ninth-grade English classes, the bane of every teacher's existence. I know they are making him crazy, so I'm pretty sure he'll finally leave." Realizing she was blabbing, she snapped her mouth closed.

"I'm over there fairly often. Well, not at the high school, but right behind it, near the stadium. There are several older houses that I've been working on. One is finished, and they were so happy with the work that the neighbors want me to do some work there as well."

"Oh, I know the ones you're talking about. The street that curves around behind the stadium that has that gorgeous blue house?"

Clearing his throat, he nodded. "Yes. I'm going to start reworking that porch. The one next to it, the brick one, is what we just finished."

By the time they'd arrived at their home, the tension she hoped would have eased was still just as choking. Embarrassed heat still moved through her, making her stomach churn. *How did I read his signals so wrong?* She couldn't remember the last time she'd enjoyed a kiss so much and could have sworn he enjoyed it, too. Parking in front, she felt his hesitation but threw open her door and hopped out quickly. The last thing she wanted to hear was an *'it's me, not you'* excuse. By the time she'd stepped onto the sidewalk, he joined her there, keeping up as she walked briskly to the front porch. He pulled out his keys and unlocked the front door before stepping back and allowing her to go in first.

When the house was divided into four apartments, the architect and contractor kept the original wide, wooden staircase that led from the entry foyer to the second floor. The hallway narrowed beyond the stairs, ending in the door that led to the back porch. Margaretha lived in the left apartment with Terri and Bjorn occupying the right. The light in the hallway always stayed on so the stairs were well illuminated. Tiptoeing so that her shoes did not make excessive noise, Caitlyn immediately moved up the stairway, her hand lightly gliding along the polished banister.

She wished she didn't feel his presence right behind

her, but Griffin was a hard man to ignore. The ceilings in the house were tall, and there were sixteen steps to get to the second floor. Not that Caitlyn needed to count them, considering she'd already done that when she moved in and had memorized each step as she and her siblings lugged furniture to the second floor. But now, with him directly behind her, each one seemed to multiply as she walked up the stairs, ready for the evening to be over.

Rounding the top, she took a step toward her door, then turned. "I had a nice time getting to know you better tonight, Griffin."

"Caitlyn, please…" He stepped closer, conflict written across his face. Finally, swallowing deeply, he nodded. "I enjoyed getting to know more about you, as well."

Unwilling to prolong the awkwardness, she jerked her head toward her door and said, "It's late, and I need to get to bed. Work tomorrow, you know. But thank you for making sure I left the pub and got home safely." He opened his mouth again, but she turned and quickly inserted her key into the lock and swung the door open. Stepping through, she turned and saw him still standing at the top of the stairs, staring at her. Lifting her hand to wave, she barely whispered, "Goodnight, Griffin." As the door closed, she leaned her back against the wood, torn between wishing he'd pound on the wood as he cried what a fool he'd been and beg her to let him in, or he'd leave quietly and disappear back into his own apartment.

It only took a few seconds for her to hear the click of

his door shutting and knew that he'd made his decision. Letting out a shaky breath, she stayed against the door for another moment, playing the evening over in her mind. The surprise at seeing him. His irritation that she'd been neglectful of her surroundings on a dark street. The offer to walk to the harbor. Their conversations. The easy laughter and interest. And the kiss. The kiss that shattered her imagination, making her want to stay up all night just to keep experiencing the way her lips tingled and her core tightened in anticipation.

Then... nothing. An uncertain shutdown. A step back.

Sighing, she pushed off the door and tossed her purse and keys onto the kitchen counter. Not turning on any lights, she headed into the main bathroom and flipped on the water. Stripping, she pulled her hair up into a large clip and stepped underneath the spray, wincing as the hot water hit her sensitive skin. Rinsing off the day, she wished it was as easy to rinse off the disappointment.

She snorted as she flipped off the water. *Hell, my feelings about Griffin have bounced between irritation and lust ever since I first saw him.* As she dried off, still processing the tumultuous thoughts moving through her head, she had to accept that getting to know him this evening had been a turning point for her. No more seeing him as Gruff... just a man she wanted to get to know more. And if that kiss was any indication of the electricity between the two of them, she really wanted to explore it more.

Pulling on her sleep shorts and a soft, faded T-shirt,

she climbed into bed and tried to put Griffin Capella out of her mind.

Another snort erupted in the dark night. *Yeah, right.*

Rushing the next morning, Caitlyn ran a brush through her long hair, deciding that hitting the snooze button had been a mistake. Pulling her hair back into a low ponytail, she slid her feet into low-heeled boots and grabbed her purse and bag. She hesitated with her hand on the doorknob, leaning forward to place her ear against the door, breathing a sigh of relief when she didn't hear any noise coming from Griffin's apartment.

Stepping out into the hall, she quickly locked her door and hurried down the stairs. Before she was able to make it outside, Terri popped her head out of their door.

"Caitlyn! I'm glad I caught you. I've got some things for you to take to school. I know you said you'd take some samples before the fundraiser and could get some preorders, perhaps."

Nodding, she walked down the hall behind the main staircase and accepted the small cardboard box from Terri. "This will be great," she said. "I'll put these in the teacher's lounge along with the little placard you made with your online store website."

Just then, she heard the front door open and the sound of heavy boots. Sighing, she'd hoped to make it to her car unobserved by Griffin this morning. She had no plans of avoiding him for long, just wanting a day or so to get over the embarrassment of practically throwing herself at him. Pressing a little closer to Terri's doorway, she remained hidden, not intending to eavesdrop.

"Griff, do you want the portable generator around back?"

"Probably, but why don't you ask Bob? He's the one who's going to be using it today."

"Gotcha. Andrew said you got a ride home last night from the hot girl that lives upstairs. You makin' a move, boss?"

"Shut the fuck up, Nate. Don't talk about her that way. Anyway, you know I'm not about to shit where I live."

At those words, Caitlyn gasped, her gaze jumping up toward Terri, whose eyes filled with sympathy, the last thing Caitlyn wanted. Giving a little shake of her head, she said, "I've got to get to work. Hopefully, you get some sales from this."

With her head held high, she walked straight toward the front, seeing Griffin and his employee's eyes widened and mouths dropped open at the sight of her. "Good morning, gentlemen." As she walked to the front door toward her car, she was proud that she'd managed to greet them without her voice betraying how shaken she was at Griffin's description that being with her would be the same as *shitting where he lived*. She knew what he meant, and truthfully, he was right. Starting a relationship with someone that lived in her building could be fraught with peril. Climbing into her car, she rolled her eyes at her dramatic turn of phrase. As she pulled into traffic, she glanced into her rearview mirror and could see him standing on the front porch, his sunglasses shoved on top of his head, his hands planted on his hips, and an undefinable expression on his face.

14

Griffin stood on the porch, a full day's work ahead of him, his crew waiting for instructions, and all he could think of was the woman who'd been in his thoughts for days. The woman who'd been so honest and free, ready to take on new experiences without fear. The woman who'd looked like an angel, kissed like a goddess, and whose body tempted his like no other. The woman he'd had an amazing evening with last night until he let his doubt get in the way.

Doubts about trying to date while spending so much time growing his business. Doubts about trying to date someone who lived across the hall from him. Doubts about trying to build a relationship when his past ones hadn't ended well. *Fuck, why is this so hard?*

She'd filled his thoughts for most of the night as he tried to rationalize why he shouldn't have a relationship with a neighbor. And all he'd managed to do was piss himself off. And now, she was the woman who'd heard ing." Once the work site was taken care of, he offered goodbyes as his crew left, and he walked around the porch to the front door.

Not seeing Caitlyn's car back from school yet, he sighed then climbed into his truck. Pretending he wanted to check on the house near the high school, he drove past the teachers' parking lot seeing her vehicle still there. Wondering if she was working or just avoiding going home because he was there. Turning onto the street behind the stadium, he parked and walked around the house, pleased to see that it appeared everything was on schedule. He'd already turned the balusters and spindles and Nate would be there the next day to supervise the rail replacements. *Maybe I should start coming over here—no, that'd be a chickenshit way to avoid Caitlyn.* Squeezing the back of his neck, he hated the way she avoided his gaze this morning.

Climbing back into his car, he drove to one of the close neighborhoods, parking in front of an older, midsize house. Red brick, white trim, and a hunter green door to match the shutters. The flowerbeds along the front walk had been mulched, ready for the winter. The leaves had turned on the trees, and he remembered years gone by when he would rake leaves from the tall oak that stood in the front yard. The tree had been taken down, and smaller trees planted in its place. He walked around toward the back, not surprised to see his mother in the kitchen. Her face brightened when she spied him through the window and met him at the back door.

"Griffin! What a nice surprise!"

14

Griffin stood on the porch, a full day's work ahead of him, his crew waiting for instructions, and all he could think of was the woman who'd been in his thoughts for days. The woman who'd been so honest and free, ready to take on new experiences without fear. The woman who'd looked like an angel, kissed like a goddess, and whose body tempted his like no other. The woman he'd had an amazing evening with last night until he let his doubt get in the way.

Doubts about trying to date while spending so much time growing his business. Doubts about trying to date someone who lived across the hall from him. Doubts about trying to build a relationship when his past ones hadn't ended well. *Fuck, why is this so hard?*

She'd filled his thoughts for most of the night as he tried to rationalize why he shouldn't have a relationship with a neighbor. And all he'd managed to do was piss himself off. And now, she was the woman who'd heard him use vulgar slang to falsely describe what being with her would be like.

Christ, I'm a dick.

Andrew called out, and he turned toward the other end of the wrap-around porch. With a chin lift, he called out, "Be right there." He stared down the street for another few seconds even though Caitlyn was long gone. Knowing that she wasn't going to drive back just because he was staring, he scrubbed his hand over his face and walked toward the side of the house where his crew was now working.

By the time they stopped for lunch, most of his crew hustled off, more to get away from him than to take care of their hunger. He'd barked instructions, snapped orders, and complained about work he didn't consider to be up to par.

Bob hung back and leaned his hip against the railing that they had not disassembled yet. Rubbing the whiskers on his chin, he looked over at Griffin. "Boss, you want to tell me what the hell is going on today?"

Biting back the rude retort that jumped into his mind, Griffin clamped his mouth shut while shaking his head slowly.

"Heard about what was said this morning," Bob pushed. Bob had been his first hire when he'd created Capella Construction. Bob had experience with older houses, had been in construction for years, had a work ethic that rivaled Griffin's but had no desire to run his own business.

A heavy sigh did little to ease the weight that was

piled on his shoulders. "Can't believe I said something so rude."

"Have to admit, I was surprised. That's not like you at all, Griff."

Unused to discussing feelings, and certainly not with a crewmember, he held the older man's gaze and nodded.

"Look, I'm no good at all this psychology shit... my wife's the one who can set a person straight in no time. But, to me, you got a great girl living across from you. No one's got a crystal ball, but then, if we all held back because of the idea that something could go wrong, then none of us would be with a partner." He hefted his shoulders and grinned. "Well, there's my two-cents worth and that's probably all it's worth. Gonna go eat now and hope my grouchy-ass boss is better this afternoon than he was this morning."

The afternoon went quickly as he settled in with the lathe, turning spindles for the porch, losing himself in the creative process of taking wood and shaping the exact spindles that were on the original house. He always told his crew to focus when using machines, and he wasn't about to fuck that up himself. Even as the pile of spindles grew, he was surprised when Bob called out, "Quittin' time, boys."

They worked seamlessly as they cleaned up their work area, waited as Griffin inspected the work for the day, and gave out assignments for the next day. "Nate, I'm going to have you go to the house behind the high school tomorrow to oversee what they're doing. I'll stop by in the afternoon, but I'd like you on-site in the morning." Once the work site was taken care of, he offered goodbyes as his crew left, and he walked around the porch to the front door.

Not seeing Caitlyn's car back from school yet, he sighed then climbed into his truck. Pretending he wanted to check on the house near the high school, he drove past the teachers' parking lot seeing her vehicle still there. Wondering if she was working or just avoiding going home because he was there. Turning onto the street behind the stadium, he parked and walked around the house, pleased to see that it appeared everything was on schedule. He'd already turned the balusters and spindles and Nate would be there the next day to supervise the rail replacements. *Maybe I should start coming over here—no, that'd be a chickenshit way to avoid Caitlyn.* Squeezing the back of his neck, he hated the way she avoided his gaze this morning.

Climbing back into his car, he drove to one of the close neighborhoods, parking in front of an older, midsize house. Red brick, white trim, and a hunter green door to match the shutters. The flowerbeds along the front walk had been mulched, ready for the winter. The leaves had turned on the trees, and he remembered years gone by when he would rake leaves from the tall oak that stood in the front yard. The tree had been taken down, and smaller trees planted in its place. He walked around toward the back, not surprised to see his mother in the kitchen. Her face brightened when she spied him through the window and met him at the back door.

"Griffin! What a nice surprise!"

He wrapped his arms around her, catching a scent of apple cinnamon coming from the kitchen that blended well with the vanilla of her perfume. "It always smells so good in here."

"Are you working at the house near here today?"

His mom had leaned back, and even though it had only been a few weeks, his gaze roved over her, assessing. Her dark hair, now streaked with silver, lay in waves over her shoulders. Her smooth complexion and twinkling blue eyes gave evidence that his sisters gained their genetics from her.

"I haven't been working there but I wanted to come by and check on things. Since I was in the neighborhood, thought I'd pop in and see you. Is Joe home from work yet?"

"He'll be along soon, so it's my lucky day that I get to visit with you before. Sit down, and I'll get you a slice of apple crisp."

Not about to turn down that offer, he watched as she bustled around the kitchen plating her delicious dessert, and pouring a glass of milk. It didn't seem to matter how old he got, his mother was determined that he'd drink milk with his sweets.

Finishing the dessert, he pushed the plate back and looked up, seeing his mom eyeing him carefully. She somehow had a way of making him feel as though he was under a microscope and could never figure out if it was just her or was a mama-thing. Finally, he said, "You're staring."

"Well, as much as I like you trying out my dessert, your face tells me you have something on your mind, so

I'm just wondering when you're gonna bring up whatever it is that's bothering you."

He couldn't keep the smile off his face as he shook his head. "You're good, you know that, don't you?"

She shrugged. "I'm a mom."

"I've met someone," he blurted.

She propped her elbow on the table, rested her chin on her palm, and grinned. "It's about time! But, then, from the look on your face, you seem a bit conflicted. Tell me about this special someone."

"She's smart, funny, beautiful, and manages to enjoy life no matter what comes at her."

"So far, she sounds delightful."

"We're such opposites, though."

"You know what they say about opposites… they attract!" she laughed.

Shaking his head, he retorted, "That's just a saying, mom, not a basis for a relationship. I'm a planner and she's spontaneous. I like to know what's going to happen, and she goes with the flow. I weigh the risks, and she jumps in feet first."

"I think that sounds perfect." He startled, but his mom continued, "Life is about finding balance, Griffin. Work with play. Responsibility with freedom. Time with others and time alone. The same thing can be said for relationships. You can learn to loosen up with someone like this woman. And, perhaps, she would learn from you, as well."

"Do you speak from experience?"

She snorted indelicately. "I was very young when I married your father, and truthfully, had not spent enough time around him before we became serious. And my youth also played a part in my not seeing the warning signs. But then, considering I gained five beautiful children from him, I focus on that. But with Joe, I speak from experience. I was wary, and he was what pulled me out of my self-doubt. Together, we work."

His brow furrowed as he pondered her words. Still in the mood to debate, he continued, "And, on top of everything else she lives right across the hall from me."

She dropped her hand so that her arms were now crossed on the table, and continued to hold his gaze. "Okay..." she said, dragging out the word.

"That's the problem. She lives right across the hall in the new house I've moved into."

Brow scrunched, his mom shook her head slightly. "Griffin, honey, I'm sorry, I'm not seeing the problem."

"I just don't know if it's smart to try to date someone who lives right across the hall. I mean what if it goes bad? And then you're right there with that person. Running into them all the time. Seeing who else she might be going out with. She's gorgeous, mom. There's no way she wouldn't have a new boyfriend that I'd have to battle the desire to punch them every time I opened my door."

His mother's lips quirked upward. "Okay, and what if it goes good?"

His brows lifted. "Goes good?"

"Sweetheart, if you really like this girl, not taking a chance on a relationship because you're afraid it might go wrong down the road could make you miss something amazing. You know that Joe and I met at a group at church for divorced singles. Talk about pressure! If we started dating, everyone was going to know it. And if we failed at staying together, everyone was going to witness. But we both knew that life was precious and the opportunity to find that special someone wasn't easy. Best decision I ever made."

"Okay," he nodded. "But what if it hadn't lasted?"

Shrugging, she smiled. "It would've hurt. And it would've made it difficult in the group to have to admit that we tried and failed. But the most important thing is that we tried with the absolute hope that we'd succeed." They sat quietly for a moment until they heard Joe's truck pulling into the driveway.

"I should get back to the house after I say hello to Joe," he said. They stood and he embraced her once again

She leaned her head back and looked up, smiling. "You were the oldest, the most responsible. You're so used to taking care of everyone, but I've always hoped you'd find someone who wanted to take care of you. The problem is, Griffin, when you find that someone, you need to allow them to do so. But please, don't turn away from possibilities just because you think they might not work out in the end." Hearing the back door open and Joe's boots on the floor, she squeezed him before letting go. "Remember, life is always about possibilities. You just have to be willing to embrace them."

Joe walked in, his gaze soft as he greeted his wife, then smiled widely as he saw Griffin. Offering a back-slapping hug, the two men embraced. "You're leaving? You don't want to stay for dinner?" Joe asked.

"I've got to get home, but I've had some of the apple crisp. Gotta tell you, you're in for a treat." Waving goodbye, he headed out to his truck. Once inside, he glanced through the window where he could see Joe and his mom embracing. Glad that she'd found happiness after years of unhappiness and then loneliness, her words resounded in his head. *Life is always about possibilities. You just have to be willing to embrace them.*

Pulling up to the house, he now saw Caitlyn's car parked on the side of the road. Glancing up to the second floor, he could see a light on in her apartment. As soon as he walked through the front door, Margaretha's door opened.

"Good afternoon, Griffin."

At the sound of his landlady's voice, he forced a smile onto his face as he turned. "Good afternoon, Margaretha. How are you?"

"Oh, it's a lovely day. I've had some delectable man-candy to watch as they worked on my house, and Bjorn brought over some tea. I'd say I'm doing just fine."

At that, his smile was no longer forced. "I'm glad," he said with sincerity.

Her wrinkles deepened. "I know you're not here to do general maintenance, but could I prevail upon you to take a look at my hall closet door? It's stuck and I can't pull it open."

"Of course," he replied easily, stepping through the front door and into her apartment. It didn't take long to realign the latch bolt of the door that looked like it had been misaligned for years. "This should make it open easier." Stepping back, he opened and closed the door several times.

"Oh, you are so clever!" She sat on her sofa, sipping her tea. "My Harvey was also clever with his hands. He was a watch and clock repairer. He could work for hours over the tiny, intricate workings of a watch and always find a way to repair it. To relax, he created jewelry. We used to have a little shop on the east side of town. We worked so well together. I was his sales clerk and did the books for the business. Our kids were practically raised in that shop."

She waved her hand toward the opposite chair, and he sat to listen even if his mind was on Caitlyn and not on Harvey's watches and clocks.

"I was watching you turn the wood today," she continued, drawing his attention. "It was fascinating. I haven't seen someone work a lathe in many years and had forgotten how intricate the work was. It was intriguing to watch you take a long, rectangular stick of wood and create patterns on spindles that are things of beauty. And it got me thinking. You're not changing the wood. Oak is still oak. Maple is still maple. You're not even changing the functionality. A rectangle spindle would hold up the railing just as well as a decorative one. But just by being in your hands, the wood is simply enhanced."

"You're right, Margaretha. I guess I never thought of it like that, but yes, the wood and functionality are the same."

"Unless, of course, you use too much pressure and

make the spindle too narrow. Then, it becomes weak, doesn't it?"

He chuckled, nodding. "Oh, yeah. I've done that before, especially when I was first learning. I'd try to get too creative and end up making the spindle very narrow, especially in the middle of the wood. Then it'll snap if there's too much pressure put on it."

She sipped her tea and smiled. "You know, you and Caitlyn have a lot in common."

At that pronouncement, his chin jerked back slightly. Having no clue what to say, he waited to see what else she would say.

"You handle wood with care, bringing out the best in it. She does the same with the young people she teaches." She set her teacup onto the table and continued. "You know, my husband and I bought this house after it had already been divided, wanting just an apartment and the opportunity to have rent income after he retired. I was afraid when he passed that I might not be able to handle it by myself, but I've had such luck with lovely renters. I think my favorite renter of all would be our Caitlyn. I've never met anyone so generous with her time or her talents."

His chest squeezed as he wondered if she had overheard his words from that morning. The last thing he wanted her to have heard was something vulgar in reference to Caitlyn. Sitting up straighter, he swallowed deeply. "Margaretha, I know. Believe me, I'm well aware of her qualities."

"It'll take a special man to be with her. The kind of man who knows how to handle her carefully, always bringing out her beauty without changing her or breaking her." She held his gaze, her grey eyes pinned on him. "Someone… well, someone like you."

His chest depressed, but it was hard to drag more oxygen back inside. "I… I've… I'm not sure that's me…"

"Nonsense," she declared. "If you give up at the first knothole you come to when making a spindle, I can't imagine you're the right man for the job."

Leaving her apartment, he knew no matter what happened, he owed Caitlyn an apology. Climbing the stairs, he walked directly to her door and knocked. He wondered if she was going to answer, but after a moment, her door opened. His gaze was filled with the shadows in her blue eyes that were no longer twinkling, and she crossed her arms around her middle as though protecting herself for whatever might come.

"Caitlyn, I'm so sorry about this morning—"

"It's fine," she threw out, her chin jutting up slightly.

"No, it's not. It was a rude thing to say, and I have no excuse. It wasn't like me. That wasn't the way I was raised, and I can't even imagine what my mom would say if she knew. What's more, it was me taking the chicken way out."

She tilted her head to the side but remained quiet. He'd hoped she would give a small sign that she accepted his apology or that she understood, but her silence was thick between them.

Squeezing the back of his neck, he continued. "I let my concerns about becoming involved with someone who lives near me overtake everything else. So, I'm not only sorry for what I said this morning that you overheard, I'm sorry that I even had those thoughts. I'd like it if we can go back to getting to know each other again."

Her spine stiffened, and she shook her head. "I don't think so, Griffin. This morning really was strike three. I'm sure living across from each other, we can be amiable neighbors. But anything else would risk my heart, and I'm just not willing to do that while you decide what's important to you. But I do appreciate the apology."

Before he had a chance to say anything else, she stepped back and closed her door. The click of the lock snapping in place echoed in the empty hallway.

Dropping his chin, he stared at his boots for a moment before turning and heading into his apartment, heart heavy with regrets.

15

"Russ, if you have time after school, I need to see you," Caitlyn said as her students were filing out the door.

With his backpack on his shoulder, he nodded but held her gaze. "I've got some time before my brothers and sisters get off the bus. Is everything okay?"

"I hope so." Wanting him to be comfortable, she waved him toward a desk while she sat in one close by. "The other day, I saw you coming out of the gym locker room quite a bit after the last bell had rung. Technically, students are not supposed to be in there unless they are with a teacher or coach, which you and the other student were not. As a junior, you don't take PE anymore. And you said you don't play sports because you have to work after school. I just wanted to know why you were there."

He glanced away, and she wondered if it was to come up with a plausible excuse. After what was probably only a few seconds but felt much longer, he sighed.

"Marcus lives close to me. He'd missed the bus and

asked for a ride home. My mom lets me drive her car twice a week. We got about halfway home, and he said he left something in the locker room. I didn't think I'd have time to come back, but he was begging me, saying he had a big project that was due today and he needed to get his work. So, I turned around and we came back."

"And... you needed to go into the locker room with him because..." she prodded.

"He said he didn't want to go into the locker room by himself. Marcus is kind of scrawny. He said the last time some of the jocks were near him after school, they pushed him around. He knew I wouldn't let that happen, so I went with him."

She continued to hold his unwavering gaze, and while she couldn't swear he was telling the truth, she had no reason not to believe him. Finally nodding, she said, "Thank you for telling me that."

"Are you going to report me and Marcus?"

She'd battled back and forth on what to do since seeing them. She didn't know the other boy but knew Russ... or liked to think she knew him. The principal would probably suspend him just for being in the locker room unaccompanied after school just because he preferred to suspend easily when he had a student whose parents weren't liable to push back. Staring into Russ' face, she saw nothing that made her think he was lying.

Clearing her throat, she sucked in a deep breath. "Other than seeing you come out of the locker room, I would have nothing else to report. I haven't heard any reports of anything being stolen. I'm going to trust you, and I hope you value that trust."

"I do, Ms. McBride."

She nodded, then tilted her head to the side. "When you think about life after high school, what have you thought about doing?"

He barked out a laugh, shaking his head. "Sure as hell don't want to keep working at the grocery store." He leaned forward, his forearms resting on his knees, his hands clasped together. "The only way to get ahead is to have some kind of training, but that all takes money."

"What would you love to do?" He looked up, doubt moving over his face, but she rushed to continue. "What sparks your imagination?"

"You're going to think it's stupid."

Rearing back, she narrowed her eyes. "Russ, have you ever known me to think any answer a student gave me was stupid? What am I always telling my students?"

Snorting, one side of his mouth curved up. "Everyone's dream has value."

"Right! So, what is your dream?"

"You ever see those home shows on television? The ones where they're fixing up old homes?"

Nodding, she leaned forward slightly, giving him her full attention.

"I like that stuff. Fixing up homes. Sometimes, I watch those shows at night before I go to bed, and I think about what I would do if I was the person working on it."

"Russ, there's no reason that dream can't come true.

You could apprentice with someone after high school and learn how to do everything you need to do."

He hefted his shoulders. "Yeah, maybe. But you gotta know somebody. I mean who's gonna take on a kid right out of high school?"

Nibbling on one side of her bottom lip, her mind raced. While things had blown up between her and Griffin, she wondered if he'd be willing to take on a student wanting to learn more about the business. Uncertain what to say to Russ in case Griffin couldn't because of the teenager's age or wouldn't because he had no interest, she remained quiet. Finally, she said, "Well, if I hear of any possibilities, I'll let you know. But, until then, keep working at the grocery store, doing the best you can in school, and staying out of trouble. Then, when an opportunity comes along, you've got nothing standing in your way."

He stood and swung his backpack onto his shoulder and offered a chin lift as well as his thanks before walking out of her classroom.

Ready to go home, she packed up her bags and had just closed her classroom door when Barbara and Suzette walked around the corner, smiling when they saw her. "Hey, what's up?"

"One of the PE teachers caught a student trying to sneak into the locker rooms after school. She called the security officer, and he had some baggies of drugs shoved in his pockets. They're wondering if the locker rooms had been used for drop-offs."

She turned to walk with them down the hall, glad they could not see her face. The memory of Marcus and

Russ coming out of the locker rooms the previous week slammed into her. *Shit! Please, let it be as simple as Russ' explanation.* He'd never given her a reason to doubt him, and she didn't want to now. *Maybe if he had more future to look forward to, it would keep him on the straight and narrow path.*

Keeping her face blank, she waved goodbye once they were in the parking lot. Arriving home, she noted that Griffin and his crew were working on the far side of the porch closest to Margaretha's apartment. She had no intention of trying to avoid Griffin, but neither was she ready to search him out.

As she climbed the stairs, a flash of color near her door caught her eye. Jogging up the last few steps, she saw a bouquet sitting by her door. Stooping, she plucked the embossed florist's card from the plastic stick inserted amongst the flowers. **Ben Franklin said, "Never ruin an apology with an excuse." So, no excuse... I'm sorry. Truly sorry. Griffin**

She knew he was still outside but couldn't help looking over her shoulder toward his apartment door. Smiling, she stood with the flowers in her hand and went inside her apartment. She looked around, then set them in the middle of her kitchen table. The bouquet was so large and her table so small that they took up most of the space, but she didn't care. Their bright colors fit perfectly in her apartment.

She knew it didn't change anything between her and Griffin but was glad they could be cordial. Her chest squeezed slightly, and she sighed. *Okay, I wish we could have been more. Why are relationships so difficult?*

A knock on the door had her bounding over, hoping the giver of the flowers would be standing on the other side. Throwing open her door, it was hard not to drop the smile from her face as she saw Terri standing there with a small box in her hand. A broomstick skirt swept almost to the floor, its bright colors reminding her of the bouquet she'd just received. Dangling, silver earrings graced her ears, and her typical long braid hung over one shoulder. Greeting her, she welcomed Terri inside, surprised as the box was immediately thrust into her hands.

"Here's some of that special blend of tea that I know you like so well."

"Oh, okay. Let me get my wallet—"

Terri laughed and waved her hands in front of her. "Nope, these are a gift from a secret admirer."

"Huh?" She looked down at the box in her hand, her brow crinkled.

"Well, okay, not so secret. But an admirer, nonetheless."

"Terri, who are you talking about?"

Now it was Terri's turn to scrunch her forehead as she thought. "Well, he didn't say I couldn't tell you. And he didn't say it was a secret. And if I'm truthful, he didn't actually say he was an admirer, either."

"Terri! Who sent the tea?"

"Oh, it was Griffin. He ran into Bjorn this morning and asked what your favorite tea was. Bjorn couldn't remember, so he came to me. When I told them, he went back out to talk to Griffin. And then Griffin told him to pack up a box and deliver it to you. Then Bjorn asked him if he wanted to give it to you himself. But then, Griffin said he wasn't sure he'd see you, and so he told Bjorn he could deliver it."

By now, Caitlyn was laughing. "Terri, you do have a gift with words. You could have just said that Griffin wanted to give me some tea."

Huffing, Terri shook her head. "Abbreviated versions of people's interactions are so boring!"

Still laughing, Caitlyn nodded. "I think I'm going to have to write that down and tell my students. I'll give you full credit for that quote!"

Terri's eyes widened and she gave a little hop as she clapped. "That's exciting! To think that I can be famous." Throwing her arms around Caitlyn, she gave her a quick hug. "I've got to go. Bjorn is cooking up some more of his scented candles, and he'll need my help. Bye!"

Before she could blink, Terri had darted out of her apartment. Looking down at the box in her hand, she recognized her favorite blend of herbal tea. *What is Griffin up to?* It was hard not to be pleased with the gift, but so far, Griffin was running hot and cold on her, and she was afraid of whiplash, trying to decipher his next move. A card was tucked inside the box, and she pulled it out. **Helen Keller said, "Walking with a friend in the dark was better than walking alone in the light." I wanted to let you know how much I enjoyed our walk at the harbor the other night. Griffin**

She wondered if he would come over that evening, but the only sound she heard was his boots on the stairs and then his door closed. She wondered if she should knock on his door but decided to wait. If he was just making amends for his brusque behavior and rude comment, then she didn't want to read more into it.

Before she went to bed, she stood at the glass door to her balcony, her fingers gripping the handle, hesitating. She heard his door open and easily imagined him standing as he looked out over the yard. He had no chair out there to sit on, unlike her who reveled in her outdoor space regardless of its small size. It would be so easy to throw open the door and step out if for no other reason than to thank him for his gifts. God knows she was interested in him.

But then, if he'd wanted to see her, he could have come over. Frustration at her indecision speared through her, but before she had a chance to act, she heard his door open again and he'd gone back inside. Slowly, her fingers released the door handle, and she pulled the curtains closed.

She lay in bed, staring up at the rotating ceiling fan, her thoughts in turmoil. When sleep finally claimed her, it wasn't peaceful. Dreams of racing down the halls of her school with something dark and unknown coming after her filled her nightmares.

Racing out the door the next morning, she was surprised to see Griffin across the hall, stepping out of his apartment. His eyes held uncertainty, or maybe it was hopefulness. *Or maybe I'm a nutcase, and he simply hasn't had his caffeine yet!* Offering a soft smile, she greeted, "Good morning."

"Good morning, Caitlyn." He stepped closer, then stopped at the top of the stairs.

"I wanted to thank you for the flowers and the tea. They weren't necessary but were very appreciated."

His shoulders seemed to relax ever so slightly, and his lips curved. "I'm glad you like them."

"And, to be honest, the quotes were beautiful."

"I hoped they were appropriate." He stepped closer, looking down so that his gaze remained on her. "I really am sorry. I desperately need you to know that what you overheard has plagued me since yesterday. It's not how I talk. It's not who I am. I've always been... well, careful in relationships. In the few apartments I've lived in, I never went out with someone who lived there. It seemed easier to make sure my home was always kept free from an uncomfortable situation. And yet, my stupidity has made this place just so."

She nodded, forcing her hands to remain still so that she wouldn't reach up and brush the wayward lock of hair from his forehead. "I appreciate the apology, Griffin. I shouldn't have pushed. You're right, I'm sure. It would be best to remain friends." At her words, she expected relief to flood his expression, but instead, he winced, opening his mouth but snapping it shut before speaking. Shifting her purse higher up on her shoulder, she licked her lips, pondering whether or not she should bring up what was on her mind. With a slight shake of her head, she blurted, "Listen, Griffin, I'd like to ask you something, but it doesn't have to be now. I know you're going to work, and I am, too."

His eyes lit. "All you have to do is ask, Caitlyn."

"Well, I don't want you to agree unless it's something you really want to do. So, I'll go ahead and mention it, and then you can think about it. Believe me, you can say no."

He chuckled, and she wished the sound did not reverberate straight through her. Forcing her mind to the business at hand, she sucked in a fortifying breath. "I have no idea if you ever hire a very responsible teenager to help out after school or on weekends. Someone interested in learning all they can about working on houses. Because they're not eighteen, you might not be able to do it for safety reasons. Or you may just consider it to be a risk that you're not interested in. Or maybe you just don't want to. Or maybe—"

He chuckled again, and said, "I'm not sure there was a question in all that, Caitlyn."

Realizing she'd blabbed the same way Terri had the previous evening, she grinned. "You're right. I didn't actually ask a question. I guess I don't really want to ask a question because you don't need to give me an answer. I just want to let you know about a teenager who could use a break." Sighing, she amended, "Honestly, I know a lot of them that could use a break. But this is a student who mentioned that he wants to learn to work on houses. Right now, he has a part-time job bagging groceries. But I know that he would devote whatever time he could arrange to help out. He's not afraid of hard work. He's very smart. And while I don't know if it's anything you're interested in, if you'd even just let him come by sometimes to see what you do, it would be great. If you said no right now, I do understand. If you want to think about it, that's fine too—"

"Yes."

Blinking, she tilted her head to the side. "Yes?"

"Yes."

"At the risk of sounding foolish, Griffin, yes to what?"

His smile widened, hitting her in the gut. Trying to focus on his words and not the way his smile made her knees want to buckle, she cleared her throat, waiting.

"I don't need to think about it. I'd need to talk to him and get parental permission first. Then, if he really wants to learn and is willing to work, I could hire him for basic cleanup after school, and he'd get some field training on weekends." Shrugging, he added, "He and I could figure out what would work once we meet."

Swallowing deeply, she stared. "Really? Please, don't agree just because you feel like you should. But, honestly, it would mean so much to Russ."

He stepped closer, his smile softer now. "I'm not agreeing for any reason other than it sounds like a good plan. I'm not doing this to get back into your good graces although that's where I want to be."

"Okay," she breathed, fighting the desire to lift on her toes to kiss him. "I've got to get to work but I'll talk to him. Thank you. I know he'll be excited." Darting around him before she gave in to urges better left buried, she jogged down the stairs, a smile splitting her face.

16

"We have got to keep things moving."

"You don't think I know this?" One person slumped into the chair, swiping their hand over their face, looking at the two others in the room. "You think I don't know the risks?"

Another stood with hands on hips. "I don't know how we let ourselves be talked into dealing here. It was supposed to be so easy, but now there are too many people involved. Too many variables. Too many things that can go wrong."

They looked at the young person standing near them. "You've been sloppy in recruiting. If one of your protégé's can't keep their fucking mouths shut, we're all going to prison."

"Shit," they said, clutching their stomach.

"Contain whatever has gotten out. Plug the holes and pull in the dealers that we can trust. All others are out."

"I don't know how well that'll go over—"

"And I don't give a fuck! The dealers that can be trusted will make a whole lot more money moving the product. I've got someone cutting the H with fenty. The ones using will need more and will keep their damn mouths shut because if not, we'll cut off their supply. Also, get more of it off the school campus. Too many fucking eyes around."

The teen nodded, fear written on their face. "Sure. I'll take care of it."

The first one chuckled. "And that's why you're so good… fucking responsible. And you get the payments to prove it."

The teen left the room and the others looked at each other. "You got it safe?"

"Of course. No one will know. No one will suspect. It's all good."

"It'd better be. We do this a little bit longer, and we'll have enough to get the fuck away from Hope City and with money to live off of."

Closing their eyes, they sighed, nodding slowly.

17

Three days. For the past three days, Griffin had endured the polite, friendly, but not quite exuberant smile and greeting each morning and afternoon from Caitlyn. He'd made a point to be outside when she left for work each morning so that he would have the opportunity to greet her and hopefully have a chance to say something more than just 'Good morning,' or 'How are you?' or 'You look nice today.' But each morning, she'd smiled, nodded, answered in short, polite sentences, and then hurried out to her car.

And now it was Friday, and he was no closer to asking her out than he had been at the beginning of the week. Shoving his hands into his pockets, he sighed. *Maybe it's for the best.* As soon as that thought hit him, he immediately dismissed it. *It's only for the best if I want to keep being a scared chickenshit who'd rather be alone than take a chance with a wonderful woman.*

Going over his crew's instructions for the day, he climbed into his truck and headed to the Victorian house near the high school. He was splitting his time between this house and Margaretha's as well as looking at another one to begin. He already had two other crews working on townhouse flips that didn't require his special woodwork, and while thrilled that Jack supervised those, he knew he needed to stop by to check on their progress, as well.

Spending most of his day near the high school, he knew he was a glutton for punishment. Working on the back porch of the Victorian, all he had to do was glance across a deep, wide, fenced-in yard to the street that divided the neighborhood from the back of the high school property. From there, he could see the stadium and practice field locker rooms.

Feeling his phone vibrate in his pocket, he pulled it out and glanced at the caller ID. Not recognizing the number, he almost didn't answer. At the last second, he hit the answer button. "Capella Construction."

"Griffin?"

Instantly recognizing Caitlyn's voice, he sucked in a quick breath as his heart jolted. "Caitlyn, hey. How are you?"

Her laughter met his ear, and he closed his eyes. There was such a lightness about her that he felt it even through the phone. He was so grateful she was speaking to him, hopeful for more than friendship but willing to take whatever he could at this point.

"I'm fine. I talked to the student, Russ, and I talked to his mom. He'd love to meet with you and his mom says it's fine if I bring him to wherever you're working this afternoon. He doesn't have to be at the grocery store until later this evening."

The idea that he'd get to see her for more than just saying hello rushed over him and he grinned, staring down at his boots. "That'd be great. I'm at the house behind the high school. But I can—"

"Oh, that's perfect! The school day is almost over, and I can bring him there. Well, if that's okay."

"It's no problem." He rattled off the address just as he heard a bell ring. Watching students swarm out of the school building like ants, he smiled again.

"Wonderful! He's going to stop by my room, and we'll be there in about fifteen minutes."

Disconnecting, he felt lighter than he had in days. Shoving his phone back into his pocket, he ran his fingers through his hair, snagging them on his sunglasses, which he'd forgotten were perched on top of his head. They clattered onto the floor, and he emitted a rueful snort. *Smooth, real smooth.*

The fifteen minutes passed quickly, and he watched as Caitlyn's car parked out front and she alighted, looking just as fresh as she had when he saw her that morning leaving for work. He couldn't imagine how she managed that feat after working with teenagers all day. She looked up toward the house, her gaze landing on him, and smiled widely. And he wondered how he could have ever doubted having her in his life.

His gaze jerked to the young man climbing out of the passenger side of her vehicle. Tall, muscular, with long brown hair, half falling in his face. Jeans, a black T-shirt, and motorcycle boots completed his outfit.

Staring at the young man was like staring into a mirror into his past.

Giving a mental shake, he smiled as Caitlyn and the young man made their way to the front porch. Unable to keep his hands to himself, he reached out and clasped her hand, squeezing it. "Caitlyn, good to see you."

Her smile punched him in the gut as she stared up at him. "Hey, Griffin. This," she said, turning to the young man, "is Russ. Russ, this is Griffin Capella."

Russ stuck out his hand, but Griffin recognized the wary expression in the young man's eyes. Again, like looking at a fuckin' mirror into his past. He clasped Russ' hand firmly. "It's nice to meet you, Russ."

"Thank you, Mr. Capella, for taking the time to talk to me."

"First order of business is for you to call me Griff." The change was almost imperceptible, but Russ' shoulders seemed to relax ever so slightly. Looking toward Caitlyn, he said, "I'm going to show Russ around and talk to him about what my company does and get a feel for what he's interested in. You're more than welcome to look around or hang with us. Whatever makes you and Russ comfortable."

Her eyes widened as they darted toward Russ. "I wouldn't want to interfere, so I'll just wander around and look at the house if that's okay." She turned to Russ, still smiling. "Take your time. I love wandering through old houses, so I'll be great. When you're finished, I'll drop you off either at home or at the grocery store."

She beamed her smile back toward Griffin before turning and moving into the house. It took him a few seconds to drag his gaze from her and focus on Russ, who was staring at him.

He thought talking to Russ might only take a few minutes, but Caitlyn had been right about the teen's interests. Russ had lots of questions, listened intently, and it didn't take Griffin long to discover Russ had not only interest but aptitude and what appeared to be a strong work ethic. He'd been fascinated to watch Griffin work with a lathe after explaining the various spindle styles throughout the years in American architecture. To be honest, Russ reminded him of himself at that age—ready to learn and do something besides just school.

"That's amazing, Griff," Russ said, his gaze staring at the drawings and then the finished product. "I can't believe you've taken the time to show me this. I originally just thought that the construction work in these homes was what would interest me, but what you do to restore them... I never really understood what all went into this kind of work."

Griffin noticed Caitlyn leaning against a doorframe on the other side of the room. He had no idea how long she'd been standing there, but her soft smile was directed at him. He wanted nothing more than to go over to her, but her smile widened before she moved into the other room. Turning his attention back toward Russ, he said, "I have to admit, you've impressed me. Your questions were well-thought-out, your interest is obvious, and the recommendation from Ms. McBride is high praise."

"Thank you, Griff. I'd be honored if you'd allow me

to spend some time helping in any way I can, giving me a chance to learn."

"I'd like to do more than that, Russ. I'd like to offer you a job, but it'll be up to you. If you feel that you'd rather just give this a chance to see how things work, then as long as I have a waiver signed by your mom, you can come by after school or on weekends. On the other hand, if you'd like to get more formal training as well as help out, I'll hire you as a part-time site intern. You'd be responsible for helping to clean up at the end of the day or on weekends, plus we could show you more of the trade and you can learn as you go."

Russ' cool demeanor fell away as his eyes widened and his mouth dropped open. "You're offering me a job? A chance to get paid while learning?" His brow immediately lowered. "I… I know I wouldn't make much." He winced before rushing, "And that's fine. It's just that most of my money is used for the family." He shoved his hands into his pockets and looked down before lifting his gaze back up.

Griffin's chest squeezed at the young man's visible struggle. Remembering what it was like for him when he was young, he remained quiet, giving Russ a chance to pull his thoughts together.

Clearing his throat, Russ admitted, "My dad's not in the picture, but that's okay. His signing the divorce papers my mom served him was the best thing he ever did. I'm the second oldest, the oldest boy, so I help out as much as I can. I don't make a lot at the grocery store, but I've been there for two years, so I make a little more than minimum wage. But Griff, I really want this chance. I'd make it work even if you didn't pay me anything."

"What I'm offering you would be more than minimum wage," Griffin said, ignoring Russ' startle at his words. "If you want to keep your grocery store job, that's up to you. My guys don't work on Sundays. Now, I'm not going to convince you that you should just work for me, or not work for me and keep your grocery job, or try to do both, but I want you to think carefully. You're the man of the family, you've got to keep up with your school, and spreading yourself too thin isn't going to do anybody any good. So, you think about it and then you can let me know."

"I don't want you to think I'm not giving a great consideration, because I am. But I want to work for you. I'd have to talk to my mom, but she'll be thrilled. I figure the money I make with you will go just as far with my family, and I'll be learning a trade. That's not only helping me now but helping my future."

Impressed as hell with the young man, he grinned as he stuck his hand out. "Well, all right. Welcome to Capella Construction. I'll have my office manager email some forms to you that you're going to need to get signed and get your mom's signature. Once we get all that taken care of and you've turned in your notice to the grocery store, I'll put you on the schedule. And we may have to tweak your schedule as we go along. Schoolwork is most important. And I need you to stay out of trouble, stay clean and sober, and show me the work ethic that I believe you have. You do all that, I promise to teach you what I know."

Staring at Russ now that he knew a little more about his background was truly like looking into a mirror. He watched Russ swallow deeply, visibly holding himself in check. He remembered doing that a few times himself when he was young and someone gave him a chance.

"You guys all finished?"

Griffin turned and watched as Caitlyn moved into the room. Her blue eyes moved between them, her smile beaming. "Yes, we are. And as soon as he gets the paperwork done, you're looking at my newest employee."

He couldn't help but laugh as Caitlyn clapped her hands, giving a little hop in the middle of the room. "Oh, how exciting!"

Russ ducked his head, pink staining his cheeks but a smile curving his lips. Looking back up, he said, "Thank you, Ms. McBride. This wouldn't be possible without you."

She waved her hand, dismissing his words. "You would have found a way to make your dreams come true." She glanced at her watch and said, "I know you have a later shift at the grocery store, but we'd better go if I want to get you there on time."

Waving goodbye to Griffin, Russ thanked him again and then walked back out to the front porch. Mouthing her thanks, Caitlyn followed, and Griffin watched as they made their way back to her car and disappeared down the road. Sucking in a deep breath, he let it out slowly, tension easing from his body.

"Griff!"

Turning as one of his men called, he went through the house to the back porch, continuing to finish the work. Occasionally, his gaze would drift across the street as the athletes left the practice field and dissipated. He remembered his adolescent envy of the jocks, wishing he could play sports when instead he had to get to work or help with his siblings.

As the last of his crew left, he walked around, making sure the area was clean and the tools put away. It dawned on him that he hadn't had any new worksite thefts recently, now glad that he'd forced his crews to remember to secure the workspace at the end of the day.

Shadows were forming in the yard when a slight movement caught his eye. Leaning to the side, he watched as two boys left the fieldhouse. Even from a distance, he could see how they jerked their heads from side to side before running toward one of the back gates, scaling the fence, and disappearing down the sidewalk. While it didn't appear they had anything in their hands, their actions appeared suspicious. He wondered if they'd snuck back in because they forgot something after practice. *I'll mention it to Caitlyn, nonetheless.* After locking up, he climbed into his vehicle, grinning at the idea he had a reason for searching her out when he got home.

18

Griffin climbed the stairs to his apartment, startling when he saw Caitlyn's door wide open, hearing voices from inside. Just as he put his key into his door lock, she popped out.

"Griffin! I was hoping to hear you come in."

He smiled as he turned around, tilting his head to see what she needed.

"I was helping Terri and Bjorn pack up some items, then invited them to dinner. Margaretha came up, and we were hoping you'd join us. Sort of an impromptu apartment party."

He held her gaze, wondering if he was being invited out of politeness, but decided it didn't matter. If she was inviting, he was going to accept. Before he had a chance to speak, she stepped closer.

Her chin jutted out slightly as she held his gaze. "Please, Griffin. I'd love it if you join us."

"I'd like that, too." Her gaze drew him in, and he could have stood in the hall, mesmerized by her blue eyes all night. Laughter from inside her apartment caught their attention, and they both turned to look, seeing Terri twirling in the middle of Caitlyn's living room, wearing a skirt that appeared to have been sewn together from multicolored scarves with another one tied around her braids. "Is there anything I can bring?"

"Just yourself," she said, her smile sending shivers down his spine.

She turned and walked into her apartment, and he followed eagerly. Once inside, he was greeted with enthusiasm by the others. The tantalizing scents of roasted meat and vegetables wafted by, and his stomach growled.

"Here, here!" Bjorn pressed a glass of amber liquid into his hand. "It's my special homebrewed beer. I've been experimenting so you'll have to tell me what you think."

Taking a sip, his eyes widened as he fought to keep from choking. Coughing slightly, he looked to see Bjorn's eager, puppy dog expression. "It's... um... certainly different." Glancing beyond Bjorn, he caught Caitlyn staring at him, her eyes twinkling as her hand slapped over her mouth. She managed to quell her laughter but snorted instead.

"I never developed a taste for beer," Margaretha said, walking over to offer Griffin a saucer with several small food items—and he had no idea what they were. She winked as he set the beer down so that he could try one. "That is a saucijzenbroodjes."

He'd picked up one of the small pastries and had it

almost to his mouth. Stopping, eyes wide, he said, "It's a what?"

"Don't let her scare you," Caitlyn called from behind her kitchen counter, her eyes still twinkling. "It's a Dutch sausage roll."

With that information, he took a bite and groaned in delight as the delectable flavors and spices hit his tongue. Popping the rest of it into his mouth, he eagerly reached for the next treat. "And this?"

"Beef Bitterballen. It's often served in bars and cafés to be eaten with beer." Margaretha inclined her head toward the beer that he'd set to the side, she grinned. "But I think in this case, you can enjoy it by itself."

Quickly polishing off two, he reached for the last appetizer on his saucer. "This looks like fried cheese."

"You're right! It's fried camembert."

He finished and hoped no one minded that he licked his fingers. It appeared that Terri and Caitlyn were setting out several platters with a variety of delicious-looking appetizers along with a plate filled with veggies and dip.

Making his way toward Caitlyn, he asked, "Is this a special occasion?"

She smiled, and he felt his chest twinge, both loving the look on her face and that she appeared to have forgiven him.

"We do this occasionally. Although, the woman that used to live in your apartment was not very social. We'd always invite her, but she managed to be busy." She reached out and placed her hand on his arm. "I'm really glad you decided to join us."

"I'm really glad you invited me."

They shared a smile before everyone grabbed their small plates and loaded them with finger foods. It didn't escape his notice that Caitlyn managed to snag his beer and pour it down the drain, refilling his glass with a store-bought beer. He leaned closer and whispered, "I've had homemade beer before and liked it. I can't imagine what he's added to it."

Caitlyn glanced into the other room, seeing Bjorn talking to Margaretha, and she lifted on her toes to whisper in return. "Knowing him, I can't even imagine!"

They moved into Caitlyn's living room, everyone settling comfortably on the sofa and chairs. Margaretha claimed the comfy chair, and Bjorn sat cross-legged on the floor in front of the coffee table, his back near Terri's legs. This left the sofa for Griffin and Caitlyn. Conversation flowed, and Griffin relaxed.

By the time the platters were almost empty, Caitlyn stood and scooted past him, walking into the kitchen. She looked over her shoulder and smiled. "I've got several types of desserts. I'll bring them to the coffee table, and everyone can help themselves to whatever they'd like."

Bjorn turned around and looked up at Terri. "Babe, go get the brownies you made yesterday!"

Terri's eyes widened and she clapped her hands. "But, Bjorn, we ate them all!"

Caitlyn had walked over and set several platters on the coffee table. Griffin tried to keep his thoughts PG, but with her ass so close to him, it was hard not to fantasize. Considering she had set up residence in his brain, his fantasies were explicit.

Bjorn's face fell and he sighed heavily. "Oh. They were so good."

Terri smiled at the others and patted his shoulders. "We added some of our special ingredients, and they truly were fabulous."

Griffin's gaze snapped over to Caitlyn.

Margaretha lifted a brow and said, "I don't think those would be right for tonight. Those are probably best for you and Bjorn."

Caitlyn shot a glance toward Margaretha and then over to Griffin, making big eyes at him as she tried to stifle a giggle.

Finally, after all the food had been consumed, Margaretha stood and said, "Well, young people, this has been delightful, but I'm afraid it's time this old lady went to bed."

"Let me help Caitlyn clean up, and we'll walk out with you," Terri said as she and Bjorn stood as well.

"You go on, and I'll stay and help Caitlyn," Griffin said, thrilled at being able to spend extra time with Caitlyn when no one was around. Saying goodbye to the others, he closed her door and turned, seeing Caitlyn already in the kitchen rinsing off the dishes. "Let me help."

"You don't have to, you know."

"Hey, you fixed the food, so the least I can do is help clean. Plus, I was hoping to spend a little extra time with you anyway."

A smile played about her lips, but she remained quiet

as they worked side-by-side. It didn't take long till the kitchen was spotless. Not wanting to leave yet, he couldn't think of a reason to stay. Squeezing the back of his neck, he lingered near the counter.

"Would you like to stay for a little bit and have another beer?" she asked.

The air rushed from his lungs, and he chuckled. "I was hoping to stay longer but didn't want to overstay my welcome."

She handed him another beer before pouring a glass of wine for herself. "You won't overstay your welcome, Griffin. I was hoping to talk to you, anyway."

They walked over to her sofa, and he hesitated, waiting to see where he should sit. He wanted to be close to her but wasn't sure of her intentions. She sat on one end and immediately bent one leg underneath her as she twisted to face the other end of the sofa. Her gaze landed on him and she smiled, inclining her head toward the space next to her.

He sat closer to the middle, twisting his body to face her as well. Holding onto his beer bottle, he waited to see what she wanted to talk about.

"First of all, I want to thank you for talking to Russ. I never imagined that you'd offer him a job! And I realize he's limited in what he can do for you, but I know he'll be a hard worker."

"I have no doubt about that. And that's why I wanted to take the time to talk to him. If he was just looking for something to pass his time, I would have had him stop by occasionally to see what we were doing. But it was obvious he has a real interest and, I think, real aptitude for being able to learn construction as well as the specialty of restorative woodworking."

Her smile widened, and it was impossible to not notice the dimples that popped out in her cheeks. He had no idea why he'd never noticed dimples before. He couldn't even say if any of his family members had dimples, but Caitlyn's snagged and held his attention. It was hard not to reach out and touch her soft cheeks, so he focused on what she was saying instead.

"That's the other thing I wanted to say, Griffin. Your work is so beautiful. I had no idea! I'm embarrassed to say that even what you're doing here on this house had mostly caught my attention just as I came and went, but until I watched what you were discussing with Russ, I had no idea what went into what you do. The drawings. The understanding of historical architecture. The desire to recreate art."

Confident his work was quality, he nonetheless warmed under Caitlyn's praise, but she wasn't finished.

"And it struck me as you were talking to Russ how you combine art, geometry, algebra, and history. So many subjects that students struggle with because they think there's no practical application."

"Thank you." Uncomfortable with her effusive praise, he shrugged. "I'm a lucky man, being able to combine what I love with what I do."

"Yes, you are."

He took another swig of his beer, then said, "I really like being here. I've never had a caring landlady before, and the Sorensons are crazy." He wanted to add that meeting her had been the highlight, but she jumped on his comment about the others first.

She grinned. "Yes, they are! And who knows what they add to their brownies?"

"Does it worry you about the *special* ingredients that Bjorn puts in them?"

Her brows scrunched together, only making her cuter before she chuckled, making her dimple pop out again.

"Honestly, I've never been offered their brownies before, so I have no idea exactly what they put in them." Shrugging, she added, "Sort of don't-ask-don't-tell."

"Makes sense."

She held his attention as she leaned forward, and he met her actions, leaning in to focus on whatever she was about to say.

"Not only was my dad in the FBI, but I attended a Catholic elementary school. You might think that would only give me a strong sense of right and wrong, but actually, both my parents and teachers instilled in me a sense of nonjudgmental reality. It's not my place to judge other people, especially when I have no evidence. It's my place to make sure I make the choices that I believe in. That I help others." She tilted her head to the side, her nose scrunching a little once again. "Does that make sense?"

"Yeah, I think it does."

"That doesn't mean that if I saw a crime that I would turn a blind eye any more than I would ignore injustice. Terri and Bjorn are nice to Margaretha and me. They help whenever they can. And, in turn, I try to help them, as well. On weekends, I'll pack some of their wares so that they can keep their costs down by not having to pay another employee."

His fingers traced along her shoulders. "You're a good friend."

"I like them. They're funny and nice. I've never seen them use any drugs although I have to admit there's been a few times they were definitely more mellow than others. But I know many who abuse alcohol and I've seen what drinking does to many people who become angry, belligerent, or downright mean."

Nodding slowly, Griffin understood what she was saying. "Like my dad."

Caitlyn gasped, her eyes shooting open wide. "Oh, my gosh, Griffin, I didn't mean to indicate him—"

"Hey, don't apologize. You're exactly right."

They were silent for another minute before she said, "Now, when it comes to drugs and teenagers, that's a different thing. I know we've got a problem with drug sales in our school... hell, in every high school. It's so funny how people think that there are no drugs in a private or religious school. Sometimes those kids can afford the more expensive or designer drugs. But believe me, they're everywhere. I hate the effect, but so many kids are taken in by the lure of the money they can make running drugs."

"Do you see it a lot yourself?"

She shook her head. "No, not my classroom. I know there are drop-off points around the school but have no idea where they are. I know there are drug runners, but other than rumors I don't know them, either. And I can't act on a rumor. I know money is a problem for many of these kids and their families. That's why I'm so glad you can hire Russ. I promise, you're making such a difference in his life."

"Caitlyn, I think you've got that backward. You're the one who's making a difference in his life. By taking an interest. By caring about him. And I know you do that for so many students, not just Russ. I can't imagine how many pieces of yourself you give away every day."

Her mouth opened, then snapped closed, her face scrunching slightly.

Pressing forward, he added, "I don't see how you do it. I don't see how you keep giving pieces of yourself away and stay so positive." Her gaze slid to the side, she remained quiet for a moment, and he was uncertain of her thoughts behind her masked expression that gave nothing away.

Finally, looking back at him, her lips curved ever so slightly. "I've never thought of teaching that way, but you're right. I do give away bits of myself every day. Whether it's a smile, a listening ear, advice, or just a lesson, I always hope that my students walk out of class feeling better because they had me for a teacher."

He leaned forward, his arm resting along the back of the sofa cushions, his fingers barely grazing her shoulder. Holding her intense gaze, he asked, "How do you keep from ending up empty?"

"Because every day I receive pieces of them that fill me up."

Uncertain of her meaning, he waited, hoping she'd

give him more. And just like the Caitlyn he was getting to know and admire, she did.

"When they share their lives. When they share their problems. When a student who's struggled allows me to work with them and their grades go up and I see their pride. When they seek me out to share something good that's happened to them. When they come to me for advice. When I have a student, especially like Russ, that can sometimes be overlooked in a class filled with more verbal achievers, and then I realize the depths of their thoughts and am humbled that they allowed me to see how great they are. All of those things are pieces of students that they give to me every day. It breaks my heart that some teachers don't understand the give-and-take process. But for me, that's why I don't become depleted."

It was hard to drag air into his lungs as he listened to her. There was so much more to Caitlyn McBride than he'd ever imagined. More than he'd ever allowed himself to imagine. By now, they'd leaned closer together, their voices soft. He slid his hand from her shoulder to her face, his fingers threading through her dark, silky tresses and his palm cupping her cheek. Her eyes remained pinned on him as he closed the distance. Smart or not, all he wanted to do was taste her lips again. He hesitated a breath away, but she leaned closer, her mouth barely skimming over his.

That was all the encouragement he needed. Tilting her head slightly with his hand, he sealed his mouth over hers.

19

Caitlyn gave herself over to the kiss, unable to deny that she wanted it as much as ever while still uncertain where Griffin's head was concerning her. Refusing to overanalyze, she shifted closer until she was able to throw one leg over his thighs and straddle his lap.

The hand that had cupped her cheek slid to the back of her head and his other arm banded tightly around her back, pulling her flush against him.

His lips were strong. She'd read that description in a romance novel, and at the time thought it was ridiculous. *How can lips be strong?* And yet, his were. Firm, soft, taking charge, and leading. Lost in her descriptions of his lips, she was barely aware when he tilted her head with his fingers, gripping her hair gently, and his tongue slid into her mouth.

His talented tongue. *Christ, another romance novel description.* Perhaps it was more that he knew exactly what to do with his tongue that triggered the quick feeling in her belly as well as the singing between her nipples and core.

With another sweep of his tongue over hers, all thoughts, ridiculous and otherwise, fled from her mind. With a sigh, her body melted into his. Without losing a particle of space between them, he cupped her ass, shifted her hips, and twisted so they were lying flat on the sofa, she mostly underneath him. She wasn't crushed as he held his upper body weight off her with his forearms planted in the cushions next to her.

Her legs had slid apart, creating the perfect cradle for him with his hips aligned with hers. His tongue continued to explore, her body ready to fly apart. She welcomed his weight anchoring her in place. Her hands glided over his shoulders and down his back, tightening as she arched against him, her breasts pressing tight to his chest. He also arched, his erection pressing against the apex of her thighs.

He shifted ever so slightly, now balancing his weight on one forearm while his other hand glided over her shoulder, down her side, his thumb sweeping underneath her breasts. Her hands moved lower, gripping his ass and squeezing before slipping underneath his T-shirt. Feeling the hot, satin skin over the hard muscles of his back, she longed to know how it would feel when he finally plunged inside her body.

Just as the kiss was flaming hot, his mouth left hers, and he dragged in a ragged breath as she whimpered at the loss of his lips against hers. *Oh, God, please, don't let him have regrets again!*

"No, babe, no regrets."

Her eyes snapped open, realizing she'd spoken aloud. "Oh. Then why did you stop?" She heard the anguish in her voice and refused to care that it made her sound desperate.

"Because I want to do this right."

She blinked rapidly, not certain she understood his meaning. "This? What exactly is the *this* that you're referring to? And if you want whatever *this* is to be *right*, is there a *wrong* waiting in the wings?"

He pressed his forehead against hers, a chuckle rising from deep inside his chest, and she felt the rumble against hers. The feel of his laughter while laying on top of her had leaped into one of the top five most wonderful things she could ever remember feeling, obliterating all other experiences. If she discarded the excitement of Santa bringing an entire chest of dress-up clothes when she was five years old, her current delight moved up to a top-four. His kisses were up there as well, and she was sure that if they ever had sex, he would reign supreme at the top of her list.

Lifting his head so that his eyes could peer into hers, he said, "*This* is you and me. And there is definitely a *right* considering the last time we kissed I completely fucked up, and it didn't take long to figure out I'd been *wrong*."

"Griffin, I know you had a problem with us living in the same building. That hasn't changed." As much as she hated the idea of no more kisses, she hated even more the thought that she'd get used to those kisses and then he'd jerk them away with regrets.

"I know. In all honesty, Caitlyn, I'm not a player. I

don't date a lot because I've never had the time that it took to try to cultivate a relationship. The few that I have had weren't the best experiences. One, she didn't like that as I was building my business, I had to work a lot of hours. Another one thought that, as the owner of the business, I wasn't the one doing the work and my being a contractor didn't settle with her idea of dating a businessman. And the only other woman I tried to have a long-term relationship with wasn't happy with how important my family was to me."

"I want to tell you that they were all bitches, but then, if they'd been great, you wouldn't be laying on top of me right now, and I'm pretty happy with where you are." He chuckled again, but she wasn't finished. "I've got two brothers who work for the police force, another brother who's a paramedic for the city, a sister who is a social worker, another sister who's a nurse, and I'm a schoolteacher. Every single one of those jobs is important. Every single one of them is important to me. My family is hard-working, close, in each other's business, and loyal down to the bone."

His thumbs swept over her cheeks, and he bent to touch her forehead with his lips. She shivered at the light touch, not from a chill but from heat searing through her. Reaching up, she clutched his face also.

"And you gave me full disclosure with your past relationships, I'll do the same. In high school, I hardly had any dates because, with my three older brothers who weren't afraid to threaten anybody who came around, I mostly hung out with friends. I went a little wild in college but discovered early on that if I had more self-respect than what the guy was giving me, I wasn't interested. As an adult, it might seem like I've dated a lot because I've had a lot of first dates. I enjoy people, talking, and socializing, so I've never had trouble meeting a man. But there weren't a whole lot that got through to a second date, mainly because I have a low tolerance for bullshitters. I'm not impressed with a highfalutin job, or a big bank account, or fancy cars, or expensive suits. So, a man had to have some substance to make it to a second date. And even more substance to make it to a third date. I can count on one hand the number of relationships that I've had that have lasted longer than a month, and each time, we parted on friendly terms because, by the time we got to that point, I knew they were decent guys but just not right for me."

"So, there's still a chance for me even though I fucked up earlier?"

Grinning, she said, "I think we can already consider this our second date."

"As nice as that sounds, darlin', we've only had getting-to-know-you times. What I really want to do is take you out on a real date. And that's why I halted our kiss earlier. Not because I didn't want to keep going or had regrets but because I want to do this right."

She slid her arms down his back, her fingers now digging in as she clutched him tighter. Nuzzling his nose, she whispered against his lips, "And that, Griffin, is how you make it to a second date."

Caitlyn had stepped into the teachers' lounge to eat her lunch but was now regretting the decision. The topic of conversation revolved around the faculty meeting the previous day that had ignited opinions on all sides of the topic of drugs in the schools.

"The security officer knows who a lot of the players are. I don't see why he can't just handle it himself and arrest them. We're teachers, not policemen," one of the teachers said.

"Arrest them with no evidence? Based on hearsay?" Caitlyn looked over at the older man, whose face appeared to be set in a permanent frown, and she wondered what it would take to make him smile.

Barbara piped up. "We know it's going on, so I don't know why the principal acts like the school will lose all credentials if it's being addressed!"

"But it's everywhere… all schools, all over the place. I don't see that there's much we can do. It's like playing whack-a-mole," Renée added, sticking her plastic container back into her thermal lunch bag with the words *Chemistry Teachers Know How To Mix It Up* written on the side.

Jamie sighed. "Hate to admit it, but a lot of the coaches don't want their kids using, but they also don't want anyone kicked off their teams."

"Oh, that's perfect," another teacher said, rolling her eyes while pouring what was probably their fifth cup of coffee for the day. "Sports… just what the American education system runs on!"

Jon walked in and slid into the seat next to Renée. As soon as he did, Caitlyn watched as Renée's smile softened and all her attention went to him. She was glad for her friend but even happier that the twinge of envy that she used to feel wasn't present considering she had a date that weekend with Griffin.

"I heard the security officer thinks there might be a teacher involved."

Caitlyn had so focused on Jon and Renée that the words from Mack almost went past her. Silence filled the faculty lounge, and she jerked her head around to look at him. "Involved? What does he mean by that?"

Mack shrugged, his palms turned up as his forearms lay on the table. "Who knows? I just overheard him talking to one of the assistant principals, telling him that he felt certain a teacher was allowing students to stash drugs in various places."

Shocked, Caitlyn leaned forward. "He thinks a teacher is actively selling drugs to the students?"

"As I said, Caitlyn, I don't know what he meant. As soon as I turned the corner, they both shut up real quick. So, I don't know if he thinks the teacher is selling."

No one said anything, but furtive glances were darting all around. In a high school the size of North Central, there were almost one hundred thirty teachers, another thirty aides, and at least twenty support staff and administrators. The idea that any one of those people could be helping pass drugs along to teens made Caitlyn ill, but as she walked back to class, it wasn't hard to imagine a few of them who might.

Glad when the end of the day came, she ran into

Russ as she left the building. "Hey! Are you starting work for Griffin today?"

A smile crossed his face, but she could see nerves flashing through his eyes. "Yeah. I'm pretty stoked. Just hope I don't fuc—screw up."

Stepping closer, she said, "You're going to be great. Just listen and watch as you do in my class, and you'll be amazed at what all you learn." Glancing up toward the sky, she scrunched her nose. "It looks like rain. Why don't I give you a lift?"

"You sure, Ms. McBride?"

"It'll take two minutes to drive, and since you'd have to walk around the stadium, it would take ten minutes to walk. And if it starts raining, you'd start your first day drenched."

He nodded his agreement and threw his backpack into the back seat before sliding into the passenger seat. "I really appreciate this."

She smiled, and true to her word, it only took two minutes to pull up outside the house where Griffin was waiting on the front porch. She wanted nothing more than to jump from the car and race to him, planting a wet kiss on his delectable lips. Instead, she winked when Russ' back was turned and grinned. Griffin offered a smiling chin lift, and she laughed as she drove away.

She ran by the grocery store on the way home, and when she was putting the bags into her car, she realized Russ had left his backpack. She was so close to home, not to mention exhausted, she dreaded driving back to where he was working with Griffin. Pondering her options, she pulled out her phone and called. "Griffin?"

"Hey, is everything okay? Surely, you're not calling to check up on Russ. But if you were, there are no problems at all."

Laughing, she said, "Glad to hear it. But no, I'm not checking up on him. He left his backpack in the back of my car. It's no problem to bring it, but I've just been to the grocery and wanted to drop my cold and frozen items off first. I didn't know how long he was going to work today, so can you ask him if he needs it now?"

She could hear Griffin talking in the background before he got back on and said, "Russ says he doesn't need it tonight. You could just bring it to school tomorrow."

"He doesn't need it? He didn't have any homework?" She waited while she heard Griffin talking again.

"Ms. McBride? This is Russ. I'm sorry I left my backpack in your car, but no, I don't need it. I've got a couple of assignments that I'll be doing on the computer, but I don't need my backpack tonight so there's no reason for you to drive it all the way over here. If it's okay, I'll just stop by your classroom tomorrow morning."

"That'll be perfect. I'm glad everything's going okay, and I'll see you tomorrow." She waited until Griffin came back on.

"Griffin, I'm getting ready to get my groceries in and fix dinner. It's just going to be something simple, but you're more than welcome to come over when you get home if you're hungry."

"Thanks! It sounds perfect." Lowering his voice, he

added, "But this still doesn't count as a date. That'll come this weekend when I take you out."

"Well, don't forget I've got the fundraising fair on Saturday. I'll probably be dead on my feet, but I promise I'll put on something cute for our date."

"Can't wait for that, but until then, I'll see you as soon as I get home."

Disconnecting, she shoved her phone into her purse and smiled. Leaving Russ' backpack in her car, she grabbed her grocery bags and made her way inside, looking forward to having someone to share her dinner with. *Now, if we can just get a real date over with so he'll feel like we're doing things the right way, I'll have a lot more to share with him!*

20

"Are you sure you don't want to take my truck?"

Caitlyn closed the trunk lid to her car and looked over her shoulder toward Griffin as he walked over with another box in his hand. "That's okay. You've got the last box and it can go into the passenger seat since every other inch of my car is filled."

She'd volunteered the previous evening to help Terri and Bjorn package the items to sell in the school fundraiser, but they'd insisted they needed to do it themselves to make sure the packages were packed and labeled correctly. Terri had had the brilliant idea to post about the fundraiser on social media and even allowed customers to preorder the candles, potpourri, or tea that they wanted. Caitlyn had been surprised at how many people had done so.

Terri and Bjorn hustled out of the house, calling to Griffin. "Can I see the last box you carried out?" Bjorn said as Terri shuffled pieces of paper in her hand.

Griffin pulled out the box that he'd just set in the

passenger seat and held it for Terri to compare it to her list. Beaming up at him, Bjorn nodded. "Excellent, excellent!"

Walking over, Terri handed Caitlyn a check. Looking down at it, her mouth dropped open. "Terri, are you sure this is half of your preorders?"

"It's not only half of what was already preordered and prepaid, but this fundraising event saves us postage, so I'm including that as well." She smiled and squeezed Caitlyn's hand. "Bjorn and I want to help all we can. The items that already have a name on them, you can just hand them to the customer when they come and mark them off the list. Everything else has prices for you to sell. Just keep a running tally and give half to the fundraiser and then the other half to us."

"Are you sure you two don't want to come with me? You could greet your customers and talk about your products to anyone who comes along."

Terri and Bjorn shared a look before they both shook their heads. Leaning closer, Terri said, "Bjorn read his horoscope this morning and it says his stars are out of alignment. He really should stay home today."

Sucking in her lips to keep from grinning, she nodded as she hugged Terri before moving over to Bjorn, hugging him as well. "Okay, then it looks like I'm ready." Turning to Griffin, she said, "I'll see you later?"

He wrapped his arms around her, and with her back against her car, he pressed against her front and kissed her. "Absolutely. As soon as I finish up the house near the school, I'll come over." He glanced over her shoulder and down into her car, his brow furrowing. "Are you sure you have help getting set up? I don't want you to have to do everything by yourself."

"Don't worry, there will be lots of people to assist. Russ said he'd help and then head over to the house where you are." Seeming to have satisfied him, she lifted on her toes and kissed him lightly, cognizant of Margaretha, Terri, and Bjorn standing on the sidewalk. He had different ideas with his arms banded around her and he pulled her flush against his front, kissing her deeply. As he lifted his head, she hated that there were hours before she could drag him inside. Giggling from behind her had her glance toward the sidewalk. Terri was jumping up and down clapping, Bjorn was nodding his approval, and Margaretha had a peaceful expression on her face as she winked toward the couple.

Laughing, she climbed into her car and headed to the school. An hour later, she was already exhausted and grateful for Russ' assistance. He'd brought a handcart, and between the two of them, they managed to get all the boxes over to her assigned place. The parents' athletic group had tents for them to use, and she and Russ wrestled with the large tent until they finally got it completely opened. Next came the portable tables that were available, and she'd had the foresight to reserve two of them.

Once their tent was in place and the tables set up, they began placing the T&B items out for sale. By then, Russ needed to get over to the house where Griffin was, so she thanked him and sent him on his way.

Looking out over the football field, she loved seeing the colorful tents all along the track, adding to the fair atmosphere. Turning back to her tables, she looked at the boxes and sighed. With less than an hour until the public could arrive, she still had a lot of work to do.

Barbara and Renée wandered over, offering to help since they brought baked items for the large bake sale tent but didn't have a tent to run themselves.

"How do you want to organize the boxes that people just have to pick up?"

Taking the list that Terri had provided, she breathed a sigh of relief. "Thank God, they're listed alphabetically."

Scrunching her brow, Barbara asked, "How else would they be listed?"

"Knowing them, I was afraid they'd be listed by customer astronomical sign or something."

"I've bought things from them for a couple of years," Renée said, looking down into a box. "I had no idea you knew them." She pulled out a smaller bag. "I hate to run, but I promised Jon I'd help at his booth. Um, this was what I'd ordered. I'll just mark my name off and take it with me."

"Sure," Caitlyn mumbled, her attention on stacking the bags in some semblance of order. "See you later."

"I've got to go to the Fine Arts department booth to help," Barbara moaned, tossing a wave as she walked away as well.

Hustling to meet the opening time, Caitlyn finally stood with a smile on her face as the first customers came along.

There were lots of customers who wandered past her booth, but the intriguing scents from the T&B

products drew them back to sniff the candles and potpourri or have a tiny tasting cup of brewed tea samples. Then their wallets came out.

Grinning, she worked continuously, barely having time to greet her family members that came along to support the school's fundraiser. Looking up, she spied her sisters-in-law Harper, Sandy, and Kimberly as they sniffed candles, each choosing one. Hugging them quickly, she waved to Sean, Kyle, and Rory standing behind them. Sean's keen gaze was moving over the crowd, Rory was smiling at something Sandy said, and Kyle moved next to Kimberly, his face hard as he looked over the potpourri.

Sniffing, he growled, "Smells funny. Smells like that crappy incense college kids use to cover up their weed smoking."

Blinking, she plopped her hands onto her hips. "You are ridiculous. Just because there are herbs, spices, and dried flowers in something, you think it's for some kind of illegal use."

"Sweetie," Kimberly said, placing one hand on Kyle's arm, holding up a small bag in the other. "This one smells like Christmas."

His face softened. "You're right, that one's good. Get it, babe."

Caitlyn smiled at the sight of her tough brother giving in to the woman he loved, his *someone,* and the familiar pang went through her, only lessened this time. Thinking of Griffin, she smiled wider, wondering if he might be her someone.

Selling several items to her family, she waved them

off as more preorder customers came by to pick up their purchases.

"Hey, girl." Renée walked back over. "I've got some time, so how about I run your booth for a few minutes while you take a break?"

"Are you sure?"

Nodding, Renée said, "You've sold so much, there are just a few more pickups, anyway."

Glad for the reprieve, she hurried to the stadium bathrooms for a quick trip to the ladies' room and then off to wander amongst the food tents. Finally making her decision, she bought a hot dog, chips, water, and then a funnel cake because nothing says *'fair'* like fried dough covered in powdered sugar.

Making her way back to her tent, she saw students around, sniffing the items while talking to Renée. "Hi, Ms. McBride," called several while a few others looked up and simply nodded before going back to their perusal. She was surprised at the diversity, having to admit that a few of the students hadn't struck her as "fair-goers", but as they purchased several items, she realized that T&B's products held a wide appeal.

Waving goodbye to Renée after thanking her profusely, she stuffed her face while chatting with the students. It took another hour, but the last of the preorders were picked up and she marked the final name off Terri's list.

"Hey, babe," Griffin's rough voice sounded in her ear as his arms banded around her from behind.

Twisting around, she grinned up at him. "Hey, to

you, too." She glanced around. "Did Russ come back with you?"

"Yeah, he ran to grab something to eat, and said he'd be back to help load things up." He tucked a wayward strand of hair behind her ear. "He's a good kid, Caitlyn. I think he's gonna work out fine."

She wrapped her arms around his waist and held him tight with her head leaned back, holding his gaze. "And I think he's lucky to have you. For that matter, so am I." The noise of the tent next to her being taken down interrupted her moment of enjoyment at just being in Griffin's embrace.

"I guess we'd better start breaking things down, also."

As she was struggling with one side of the tent, Russ jogged over. "I'll get this, Ms. McBride."

Stepping out of their way, she watched as Griffin and Russ made quick work of getting the tent and tables folded up. Using the handcart provided, Russ rolled them back to where the administrators were collecting the items. While Griffin carried the empty boxes back to her car, she counted out the day's sales, and pocketing half to give to Terri and Bjorn, she shoved the other half into an envelope and walked it over to the school's bookkeeper. After it was counted and she was given a receipt, she hurried into the parking lot to find Griffin standing at her car.

"I'm gonna take Russ to his house, and then I'll come home," he said, bending to offer a light kiss. His nose glided along her cheek as he whispered, "Remember, tonight's date night."

A shiver ran over her and she grinned. "I can't wait." Waving goodbye to Russ and him as well as a few of her friends, she climbed into her car and drove home.

Terri and Bjorn came out to get the empty boxes, thrilled that everything they'd sent had sold, especially when she handed them their money.

"Oh, wow!" Terri threw her hands upward and shook her hips, her broomstick skirt swishing about her ankles.

Bjorn rubbed his hands together. "We've got to get busy and make more T & B brilliance!" The two of them hustled back into their apartment, leaving Caitlyn climbing the stairs, excited to get ready for her evening.

21

Griffin stood in his bathroom, a towel wrapped around his hips and another one in his hand as he swiped the condensation off the mirror. He'd showered and shaved and now ran a comb through his wet hair. Staring at his reflection, he tried to ignore the nerves fluttering. *Shit, when was the last time I was nervous before going out on a date?*

As he continued to stare, he snorted. *When was the last time I was excited about going on a date?* When he couldn't remember the answer to that question, he turned from the mirror and jerked off the towel before stalking into his bedroom. Once dressed, he shoved his wallet and keys into his pockets, swiped his fingers through his almost-dry hair, and headed into his living room.

His phone vibrated on the coffee table, and he glanced down, grinning to see his mom on caller ID. "Hey, Mom. What's up?"

"I hear you have a date tonight," she said.

Chuckling, he shook his head. "I ran into Marcie at the grocery store and she invited me to dinner. I kept trying to give her excuses, but she weaseled it out of me. Damn, she's good."

"I think that comes with being a mom. We have a way of knowing when something's going on, both good and bad." She laughed and added, "In this case, it's something good, right?"

"Right, Mom. I pulled my head out of the sand and realized that not pursuing Caitlyn just because she lived in the same building didn't make any sense. As you said, I was passing up something amazing. And I don't want to live my life constantly worried about the what-ifs."

"Hallelujah! I'm glad to hear you say that, Griffin. So, when will I be able to meet her?"

"Tell you what, Mom, let me and Caitlyn have a chance to see how this is going first."

"That's probably a good idea. I'll let you go and have fun."

He disconnected and glanced at the time. Shoving his phone into his pocket, he headed across the hall. His knuckles had barely met the wood of Caitlyn's door when it swung open. All thoughts of a suave greeting fled as his gaze landed on the beauty standing in front of him.

Her black hair fell in waves about her face and over her shoulders. Her makeup was a little heavier than what she usually wore, making her blue eyes appear even more brilliant and her pink lips begging to be kissed. Her curves were wrapped in a deep blue dress, fitted at the top with a hint of cleavage showing, then swirling out over her hips and thighs, ending just above her knees. And as his gaze continued downward, he feasted on her long legs, ending at her black heels, a little cut-out where her pink toenails could be seen.

Each part of her was gorgeous, but the entire package altogether was breathtaking. Dragging his gaze back up to her face, he was surprised to see the uncertainty in her eyes. "Babe..." He knew there was more he needed to say, but her beauty had his tongue tied.

She looked down and swiped at her skirt as though to brush away an imaginary wrinkle before lifting her chin. "Is it okay?"

Stepping forward, he tried not to rush as he enveloped her in his embrace. "Oh, hell, babe, I'm speechless. I know there are all sorts of things I should be telling you, like how gorgeous you are, how beautiful your dress is, how perfect you look, but I swear I can't think of anything that would begin to express how bowled over I am right now."

Laughing, she wrapped her arms around his waist and squeezed. "That was a pretty damn good speech for someone who's speechless. In fact, I've never received a better compliment in my life."

He held her close, cupped her face, and bent to gently kiss her lips, careful to not smudge her lip gloss even when the bubblegum taste hit his tongue. Stepping back, he sucked in a deep breath through his nose and let it out slowly, willing the blood to stop rushing from his head to his dick. Clearing his throat, he smiled down at her. "We need to leave so that we can start this formal date. If we keep standing here much longer, the only place we're going is your bedroom, and that is not the kind of date you deserve."

She laughed and turned to the small table next to the door. She picked up a small purse, locked her door, dropped the keys into her purse, and slid the thin strap over her shoulder. "Then let's go, because I'm excited to go on a real date with you!"

They headed toward the Inner Harbor, parking along one of the side streets. Jogging around the front of his truck, he opened her door and assisted her down. "I made a reservation at the Pier Restaurant."

They'd already begun walking toward the harbor, hands linked, when she jerked to a stop and looked up. "Griffin! I haven't been there in ages. They had the best seafood."

"To be honest, I tried to make a reservation at the Harbor Emporium, but they were already filled."

"No, no," she said, shaking her head emphatically. "The Harbor Emporium is super fancy but also super-expensive. And, to be honest, you pay a lot of money for a meager portion. Granted, I've only been there once, but I'd so much rather go to the Pier Restaurant. There, I can order what I want, eat to excess, and enjoy your company without worrying if I'm spilling something on my dress."

Her words hit him, and he breathed a sigh of relief. When he wasn't able to get reservations at the fancier restaurant, he debated where to take her. He wanted their date to be memorable, but looking down at her wide smile as they continued walking along the harbor, he realized that any date with her would be memorable.

When they got to the restaurant, there was a line out the door with a hostess standing near a small podium. Bypassing the line, they were able to go straight in since he'd made a reservation. As they followed the next hostess to their table, Caitlyn leaned in, pressing close. "Good job on making a reservation. I had no idea they'd be so crowded!"

They were led to a table in the corner of the restaurant that jutted out over the water. Glancing around, he knew it had to be one of the best views in the restaurant.

They looked over the menus after giving their drink order to the server. He glanced up to see Caitlyn studying the menu closely, her nose scrunched. *Christ, she's cute.* When she finally looked up and saw him grinning, she scrunched her nose even more.

"What are you smiling at?"

"You. You're studying that menu like you're going to be quizzed on it later. And yet, you've got the most adorable look on your face."

"It's because everything sounds so amazing. Sometimes, it's easier in a restaurant when they only have one or two things that I like. Of course, that rarely happens because I like to eat almost anything! But a place like this? Holy moly, this is going to be a hard choice."

"Well, they've got some great platters that include a lot of different things."

Her eyes twinkled in the candlelight as her smile widened. "I know!" She sighed and rolled her eyes. "You know, we really can't call this a first date because that will totally ruin what I order and eat."

His chin jerked back as his head tilted. "What? Why?"

"Because if this was a first date, I'd order something small. Not a salad... I'm not one of *those* women who want to make you think that's all I eat. But I definitely wouldn't go big. But, if you agree that this is at least our third date, then I think I'll get the broiled seafood platter and a baked potato."

Laughing, he nodded. "Fine, fine. This is our third date."

She clapped her hands right as the server came back and asked if they were ready to order. Looking up, she nodded. "Absolutely!"

He settled back in his seat after they ordered and relaxed. She was right. This was not a first date with the typical first date nerves and wondering if he was going to click with the person or end up wishing he'd stayed home watching TV alone instead. Glancing around the restaurant, he noticed several men's gazes on her, but she was blissfully unaware as she stared out the window over the harbor with a delighted expression on her face.

"Oh, look! It's the pirates!" she exclaimed, drawing his attention to where she was pointing. A tourist boat was in the water and another smaller boat with costumed pirates was racing around, calling out for the tourists to walk the plank.

Chuckling, he leaned forward and admitted, "I never got to ride one of those boats, but when we were kids, Mom would let us take the water taxis and go from one side of the harbor to the other. It was no-frills but cheaper." For a second, he wondered if admitting to his more impoverished childhood was the right thing to do.

Eyes bright, Caitlyn laughed and nodded. "We did the same! Those tourist boats were always so expensive, and with six kids, you can imagine that Mom and Dad wanted to cut corners where possible. So, we'd come to the harbor, walk around, and then use the water taxis to get from one side to the other." Still smiling, she added, "I think it makes you a Hope City original to have spent part of your childhood riding the water taxis!"

Their dinner came and both made big eyes at the huge platters filled with food after the servers had walked away. Caitlyn lifted her brows then picked up her silverware and pronounced, "Okay, thank God I'm in a stretchy dress!"

They continued to talk over dinner, both making a decent dent in their meal but neither able to finish. Skipping dessert, they wandered out of the restaurant, their pace leisurely. His hand had rested lightly on her back but now he linked fingers with her as they watched the street lamps illuminate and the shadows lengthen over the water.

They were quiet, but it was a comfortable silence as they walked. They stopped at one point to watch one of the water taxis as it approached. Looking at each other, they grinned at the same time. Her eyes lit, and she nodded just before he led her over to the pay booth. Soon, they were ensconced at the front of the boat, laughing as the breeze blew as they moved across the water.

Sitting side-by-side, he wrapped his arm around her shoulders, pulling her in close. Arriving at the other side near where he'd parked, he held her close as they left the boat, making sure she didn't stumble in her heels. As soon as they were back on the brick walk, she whirled around and plastered herself to his front, her arms tight about his waist and her face turned up toward him.

"Oh, Griffin, first date, third date… it doesn't matter. This has been the best date ever!"

Throwing finesse to the wind, he bent and took her lips in a searing kiss, his tongue plunging, immediately tangling with hers, both pushing for dominance. Their noses bumped as they twisted back and forth. He'd love to be able to say that he gave as much as he took, but all he could think about was the soft feel of her lips, her breasts crushed against his chest, and her curves fitting neatly in his arms. That, and the fact that his cock was now painfully pressed against his zipper.

She broke the kiss first, her fingers still clutching his shoulders and her eyes staring up into his. Licking her swollen lips, she said, "When we get home, Griffin, I don't want to kiss you good night."

He blinked, jolting slightly as he wondered how bad his kissing had been. Heat filled his face and his arms loosened. "You… you don't want to…"

Shaking her head, she whispered, "No. I don't want to kiss you *good night* because I'd rather kiss you *good morning* tomorrow when you wake up in my bed."

It took his brain a second to catch up with her meaning, then his arms jerked her tightly against him again. "Fuck, babe, you just gave me everything I wanted, making this absolutely the best date ever!" Fighting the urge to throw her over his shoulder, he slid his hand down to link fingers with hers, and they hustled away from the harbor and across the street to his car. Throwing open the door, he scooped her up and set her gently inside. "Buckle up."

They barely spoke as he drove back to their house, but they stayed connected through their linked fingers between their seats. He tried to drive responsibly but could barely keep his foot off the accelerator, feeling the need to race. Praying they wouldn't see any of their neighbors when he parked, he jogged around the front of the truck and helped her down. He locked his car, eschewing the key fob, not wanting to make any extra noise. Linking fingers again, they walk-trotted up to the porch and through the front door. He scooped her into his arms again and took the stairs two at a time, not stopping until they stood outside her door.

Setting her feet gently onto the floor, he cupped her cheeks and stared into her eyes. "Are you sure, Caitlyn? I want you to be sure. I *need* you to be sure."

She lifted on her toes and placed a soft kiss on the underside of his jaw. "I've never been more sure about anything."

With that, he slid her purse from her shoulder, snagged her keys from inside, and unlocked the door. Scooping her up into his arms again, he was determined to not act like a caveman, but once inside her apartment and the door kicked shut, it was all he could do to not press her against the wall. He had no doubt they'd try wall sex at some time, that wasn't how he wanted their first time to go. Tremors ran through his body, every cell vibrating.

As though she knew the battle going on inside him, she kissed him lightly again and said, "Take me to bed."

He didn't need to be told twice.

With her still in his arms, he stalked past the kitchen counter and down the hall. Her apartment wasn't a mirror image of his, but he had no doubt he was heading toward her bedroom. Turning to the right, he guessed correctly and entered a large room, the wooden floors and tall windows like his, but that was where the similarity ended. Whereas his was furnished minimally, hers was decorated in a style that matched her personality.

Colors melded and meshed throughout the room without overpowering the space. Pastels in blue, green, and yellow covered her queen-sized bed, both in the spread and the pillows scattered on top. Her curtains were white, perfect against the pale blue walls. A large blue and green rug was centered in the room, and in the corner was a reading nook, complete with a window seat covered in a deep green cushion and blue and yellow pillows.

He took all this in almost instantly, needing something to focus on to slow down his ardor, not wanting to overpower her with his need to strip her naked and plunge into her body.

Walking to the bed, he set her down gently, then bent to slide her shoes off. He knew some men talked about sex with a woman wearing sky-high heels, but his fantasy was just her. Pure, unadorned Caitlyn.

She wiggled her toes, moaning slightly, giving evidence that he was making the right decision to rid her of her shoes. Squatting in front of her, his hands glided up her calves, slipping underneath the hem of her dress. Her gaze was pinned on him, and another little moan left her lips as her head fell back, this time in response to his ministrations.

The material of her skirt shifted upward as his hands continued to skim over her thighs, her soft skin making it almost impossible to go slowly, but the desire to commit each sensation to memory kept his movements deliberate. Her pale blue, silky panties came into view as her skirt was now pushed up to her hips. The scent of her arousal wafted past, and he breathed deeply as his fingers gripped her thighs before he smoothed them over her flesh.

She dropped her chin, her gaze holding his, and while her chest heaved, her smile widened. Swallowing deeply, she nodded, answering his unasked question. She lay back on the bed and unfastened her side tie, loosening her dress. The material fell open, and he marveled at the simplicity, wondering if he could request that all her dresses be made in the same fashion. Her blue panties were now in full view as was her matching bra, the silky material barely covering her breasts.

Nuzzling her panties, he hooked his fingers into the elastic, dragging them down her legs and tossing them to the side. She lifted her legs to rest over his shoulders, and he dove in as a man starved, and in truth, for her, he was.

He licked, nipped, sucked, and plunged, drunk on her essence, determined to make her feel everything he was feeling. She gasped, chest heaving as her fingers gripped the bedspread.

"Griffin, please..."

Mumbling against her sex, he asked, "What, baby? What do you need?"

Her voice rasped, "You. Just more you."

Grinning, he slid one finger inside, tweaking until she cried out her release, and he slowly licked her essence before kissing over her mound and stomach. Seeing her front snap bra, he once again decided that was the clothing of choice just for its convenience. Her fingers had already found the snap and her breasts spilled free. "Gorgeous... fuckin' gorgeous, baby."

He stood, his fingers now fumbling as he quickly undid the buttons on his shirt before tossing it to the floor. As he unbuckled his belt, she leaned up and wiggled out of her bra and dress before laying back, now completely exposed. Her eyes lit as her gaze moved over his body while he kicked off his shoes, slid off his pants and boxers, and ditched his socks. Fisting his cock, he grinned, loving the unfettered access to her body as well as the appreciative gleam in her eyes.

Her arms lifted, fingers wiggling, beckoning him in, a siren's call he intended to answer just as quickly as he could reach down to snag a condom from his wallet. Rolling it on, he looked up, seeing her gaze on his cock, her tongue darting out to moisten her lips. *Christ, now I want her mouth on me.* Giving a mental shake, he pushed that desire down, wanting to fill her instead. Climbing over her, he kissed each breast before sucking a nipple deeply, eliciting another moan as she writhed underneath him. Settling his thighs between hers, he aligned his cock to her entrance. Resting his weight on his hand, he leaned over, dragging his other hand between her breasts to her chest, feeling her heart pounding underneath his fingers.

He lifted his brows, waiting. She smiled and nodded. "I want you, Griffin. Only you."

Easing in, she lifted her legs and wrapped her calves around his back. Plunging, he was sheathed in her tight warmth, and she gasped just before her hands clutched his arms. Over and over he thrust, and she lifted her hips to meet his movements. It had been a while since he'd been with anyone other than his hand. Afraid he'd unman himself, he forced his mind off his cock and focused on the woman underneath him. Her dark hair spread over the pale colors of the bedspread. Her upper chest was flushed pink, the same color rising up her neck and to her cheeks. Her blue eyes stayed pinned on him, seeming to take him in as much as he was admiring her.

He dropped down from his hands to rest his weight off her chest with his forearms, his hands palming her cheeks. Her breathing increased, her breasts pressing against his chest with each inhalation.

"Griffin…"

"Come on, babe."

"Griffin…" Each time she called his name, her voice became more desperate. "I need… I need…"

"Tell me what you need, sweetheart."

"I… oh, Griff..." Her fingers dug into his arm, her fingernails leaving little crescents as she cried out her release.

He felt her core tighten, and he fell over the precipice after her. Pumping until every drop had left his cock, he rolled to her side as he dropped, wrapping her into his arms. His body shook with his orgasm as well as the emotions crashing into him. He held her tight until their heartbeats returned to normal and his cock slid from her body. They lay facing each other, gazes never wavering. Brushing her damp hair from her face, he swept his thumb over her cheek. Kissing her softly, he whispered, "Christ, babe, you are so fuckin' beautiful."

22

Caitlyn stirred, her eyes blinking open. She normally woke fully alert, and this morning was no different... except she was instantly aware there were a lot of things not the same. A delicious twinge in her core. The extra heat in her bed. The heavy weight that lay across her legs. The arm that was slung over her waist. Shifting gently, she stared at the face of the man who'd given her all the feels last night. From dinner, to laughter, to a water taxi ride, to sex that was so far better than any she'd ever experienced. And now, to waking up to him wrapped around her.

His long hair was swept back from his face except for the curl that lay across his forehead. The sun-lines that emanated from his eyes were softened in sleep. His jaw was covered in a shadow of a dark beard.

The sheet had slipped to his waist—his trim, muscular waist, giving evidence to the fact that he worked for a living. Real, physical work. His muscles were honed, and she knew from her intimate perusal last night that his body fat was almost nil. A flash of Jamie bragging about his body on their one date ran through her mind, and she battled back a grin. Griffin didn't need to brag. He simply was the real deal.

She wanted to kiss him, taste the underside of his jaw. Slide down and take him in her mouth. Run her fingers over his body, exploring the dips and hollows. But… she desperately needed to visit the bathroom. Her bladder was calling, and her morning breath made her afraid his cock would wither if she didn't take care of that first. *Why do romance novels always talk about morning sex without taking care of certain bodily functions first?*

Hating to leave the warm bed, she gently eased away from him and tiptoe-ran into the bathroom. Taking care of business, she then looked in the mirror. Always careful to remove her makeup before bed, she was agog at the raccoon-eyed sight before her. Quickly washing her face, she moisturized then brushed her teeth. Peeking into the bedroom, she was thrilled to see that he was still asleep.

Now, ready to pounce, she slid back underneath the covers and settled near his hips, her fingers surprised to see that his cock was hard. She licked her lips then slid them over him. He stirred, and she took the rest of him, or as much as she could, into her mouth. Unable to completely sheathe him, her hand wrapped around the base, pumping as her mouth bobbed over his length.

She felt the instant he woke, his whole body jerking, his hips lifting, his cock surging into her mouth.

"Christ Almighty, Caitlyn," he groaned.

She peeked up at him, continuing to lick and suck, loving the look on his face as he lifted his head to peer down at her. Her movements halted as she grinned, then began again as she dropped her gaze, torn between the desire to see his face and continuing her ministrations.

He flopped back onto the pillow, groaning, "Fuckin' hell," as his fingers found their way into her hair, tangling and gripping. It didn't hurt but spurned her on faster.

"Condom," he growled, twisting slightly to the side.

"Uh-uh... wanna fini..." she garbled, not stopping.

"Babe, I'm gonna—"

"Goo..." she continued.

With a few more sucks, she felt his hot release and swallowed it all, licking him when it was over.

His body, now relaxed with a sheen of sweat coating it, was the perfect canvas for her to explore as she kissed her way up to his mouth.

"Damn, woman, you may have just killed me." Opening his eyes, he held her captive with his blue-eyed gaze.

"Death by morning blowjob," she giggled.

"Come here." His hand left her hair and reached underneath her arms to haul her up against his body to where she lay on top.

He kissed her, and she melted, her body liquid as soon as his mouth sealed her. Their tongues tangled for just a moment before he pulled back. Looking down, she was about to ask why he stopped when he mumbled.

"Huh?"

"You smell like mint, which means you brushed your teeth, which means I'm the only one with morning breath. And that means you snuck out of bed."

She giggled again and stuck her tongue out, licking the pout on his face. "You taste amazing. I, on the other hand, had to pee, then looked at myself in the mirror. It was rather frightening, totally non-sexy, and I smelled icky."

"Icky?"

"Yeah, icky. What's wrong with saying icky?" she asked, propping her forearms on his chest, trying to ignore the feel of his cock firming against her tummy.

"Nothing's wrong with icky if you're five years old."

Elbowing him in the ribs, eliciting a grunt, she asked, "Did it feel like a five-year-old had her mouth —umph—"

He flipped her so she was now underneath him and sealed his mouth over hers, the kiss flaming as his hips pressed and his cock was nestled against her heat. All thoughts fled her mind other than this man in her bed on a Sunday morning, nowhere to go, nothing to do but just hang on for the ride. And she hung on…

Caitlyn pushed her plate back after having sopped up the last dibble of syrup with her final bite of pancake. Leaning back in her chair with her sweetened and creamed coffee in her hand, she looked over as Griffin polished off the last of his breakfast as well. Everything about their date played on a loop in her mind, from the moment she saw him until they woke up together this morning. Part of her was searching for any sign that he was not as wonderful as he seemed. But she came up empty.

She couldn't remember the last time she'd felt so comfortable with a man whose last name wasn't McBride or King. She tried to rein in her stampede of emotions, not wanting to overwhelm him by being too needy, too clingy, too demanding. But, if she was honest, she hoped they had more time to enjoy each other. Adopting a casual tone, she asked, "So, what have you got going on today?"

He also pushed his plate back, took a long sip of his coffee, and smiled. "I've got nothing special other than spending time with you, I hope."

His words so mirrored her own thoughts, she forced down the squeal that threatened to erupt. His eyes jerked open wider, giving evidence that she hadn't completely swallowed her excitement.

"I take it that's okay with you?" he asked, chuckling.

"Well, my attempt at being coy has obviously failed miserably. So, yes, spending as much time as possible with you today is exactly what I'd love to do."

"Good." He set his mug back on the table and leaned forward, taking her hand in his own. With his thumb driving her to distraction as he rubbed it over her knuckles, he said, "I just need to run by a couple of my other worksites to simply make sure everything is secure."

"Wouldn't that have been done when your crews left at the end of yesterday?"

He nodded, then sighed. "I'm having a little trouble with some worksite thefts. I don't want to think that it's anyone on my crew, but I have to admit that I'd be foolish to not consider it might be someone that works for me."

Rearing back, she gasped. "You're kidding? I can't imagine who would steal from their own team."

Lifting a brow, he reminded, "And didn't you mention that there's always the possibility someone in the school system is helping the kids pass on drugs?"

She nodded slowly, her shoulders slumping. "You're right. I suppose no one's above suspicion, are they?"

"Do you remember the night at the ER?" She rolled her eyes and he quickly continued, "Yeah, I guess you do. Anyway, one of my newer hires, Roscoe, had gotten hurt and has been out since then. Right after he was injured and stopped coming to work, the thefts stopped. One of my other men suggested that it might have been Roscoe who wasn't leaving the work area secure. But he's not scheduled to come back for another week, and I had a few things missing the other day. I've been after everybody to take equipment with them or lock it up, but somehow, I'm still losing shit."

It struck her how much he carried on his shoulders. He wasn't just a woodworker who created historical art but ran his own business. The responsibilities for his clients as well as his employees must weigh heavily on his shoulders. She stood and walked to his chair, straddling his lap, placing her hands on his shoulders.

"I'm so in awe of you, Griffin." He cocked his head to the side, a crease settling between his brows. "I am in awe of you because of everything you do. All that you're responsible for. And if you'd like some company, I'd be honored to visit your other worksites with you."

He laughed, his hands sliding down her back to squeeze her ass. "You might be in awe of me, but sweetheart, I can't imagine spending my day with a bunch of hormonal, attitude-riddled teenagers. Give me my historical houses and my crew any day."

She leaned forward and kissed him lightly, and just as he was about to take the kiss deeper, she pulled back. "As much as I'd love to do nothing more than kiss you, that's gonna lead us to being right back in bed. I really want to see your houses."

It didn't take long for them to get dressed and back into Griffin's truck. He drove them to several houses, all with residents living inside, but they walked around the outside, checking to make sure there was no equipment or materials left unsecured. Driving toward the high school, he said, "I know you got to look at this one when you brought Russ over, but I can show you some more details."

Excited, she hopped down from the truck and eagerly linked fingers with him as they walked toward the home. "Where are the owners?"

"They bought the house about six months ago, and it was in good shape. But, unfortunately, there had been some renovations that, while decent, had completely taken away the historical accuracy of a house like this.

So, when they hired me, they're staying in their Florida vacation condo until the inside work is complete."

"I see those shows on TV and they're always tearing down walls and ripping out cabinets to do renovations. How do you take an old house and renovate it without demolishing so much of what's inside?"

"A lot depends on what the owner wants to accomplish. If they just want a modern renovation, then I usually refer them to another contractor. Not that we can't do that, but I prefer to maintain some of the historical integrity of the original home or even bring back features that were obliterated in a previous reno."

Stunned, they walked hand-in-hand into the house. She'd seen it when she came with Russ, had wandered into a few rooms, but was mostly so anxious that Russ presented himself well and for Griffin to appreciate all the young man had to offer that the house was secondary to anything else. But now, she entered, her mind fully on what Griffin was describing, seeing the history through his eyes.

"So, your specialty is Victorian?"

"I can work on others, but Victorian homes are my first love. It's the details. The stair and porch spindles that weren't just a rectangle of wood but were turned and carved, creating works of art. Wood cutouts and reliefs." He rested his hand on a beautifully carved mantle over the fireplace and turned his attention to her. "But, you'd know all about this period in literature."

She smiled. "It was during the Victorian era in British literature that the novel became the literary genre. The novels reflected the change in the times from scientific and economic to struggles of class structure and the role of religion. Dickens, Eliot, the Brontë sisters. In America during that time, it was when American novelists became more popular, as well. They no longer just focused on adventure and imagination but on daily lives and struggles." She turned around in the room and shook her head. "It's almost like as the literature became more stark, the architecture became more beautiful."

"I never thought of it that way," he admitted. Taking her hand again, he said, "Come on. Let's keep exploring."

For the next hour, they wandered through the house, and she listened intently as Griffin showed her all the work he and his crew had accomplished as well as the special designs he'd crafted. As they moved out onto the balcony leading from the owner's upstairs bedroom, she looked across the backyard and street.

"Oh, you can see the high school from here!"

"Yeah, I noticed that the day I was waiting for you and Russ to arrive. When school let out, it was like an army of ants."

Laughing, she nodded. "I can understand that analogy." Seeing the faraway expression on his face, she moved in front of him. "What are you thinking about?"

"I remembered something about that day. There were a couple of guys that came out of the stadium locker room when everyone else was gone. No practices were going on down on the field and it made me wonder what they were doing there."

Caitlyn nibbled on her bottom lip. "I worry about

kids using certain areas at school as a drop-off point for drugs. Like lockers, for instance."

"That seems really risky. They could easily get caught."

She shrugged. "Halls are crowded. Kids are in such a rush to get to their next class or catch the bus at the end of the day that it wouldn't be hard to have a designated drop-off place."

"I remember in high school knowing whose locker was around mine because I saw them all the time. Wouldn't it be obvious to others if there was a locker that different people were going to?"

"We tell kids they shouldn't share lockers for the very reason that anything in that locker is the responsibility of the person who was assigned that combination. But, so often, kids share lockers anyway. Their friend might have a locker that's a lot closer to most of their classes. Boyfriends and girlfriends share lockers." She sucked in her lips, then added, "Even gym lockers. Or the ones down at the fieldhouse."

They were quiet for a moment, standing side-by-side looking out toward the high school, lost in thought. Finally, she looked over and asked, "How is Russ doing for you?"

He dropped his gaze back to her, studying her carefully. "Fine. Why?"

"I just wanted to make sure. I was the one who recommended him to you, and I still stand by that recommendation, but I have to admit I pray he doesn't do anything to make you regret hiring him."

He wrapped his arm around her, pulled her toward

his front. He kissed her forehead, then held her gaze. "You took a chance on a kid that had a lot of potential. So did I. But the choices that Russ makes are his own. He either builds something for his future, or he chooses a path that isn't good. But if he does, that's on him."

Her arms snaked around him, her fingers gliding up his back. "You're pretty awesome, you know?"

"I don't know how awesome I am, but I have to admit that when I'm with you, we feel awesome together."

23

"Ms. McBride, can you come with me, please?"

Her last class had just left as the assistant principal, Robert, stood at her door. "Sure, what's up?"

"I'm afraid I can't say right now. But I need you to come down to the office with me."

Nervous squiggles hit her stomach as she smiled politely, opened her desk drawer and pulled out her purse, then stood and walked to the door. Her mind raced as to why she was being summoned. *Student grades are all in. Student test scores are above average. All duties completed, as well as lesson plans.* Just like with students who get summoned to the principal's office, the sick anxiety that hits the stomach happens to adults, as well.

She'd heard the kids grumbling earlier about the drug-sniffing dogs in the parking lot but gave it little thought since on this trip they didn't enter the school building. Not having to put a class in lockdown, her day had progressed as normal. Barbara had mentioned earlier that several students had been summoned by the administration due to the dogs' reactions at their vehicles. She'd also heard a few rumors flying around about a couple of teachers. One of them had boots in his trunk that were covered in grass where he'd mowed his lawn, and it appeared the dogs reacted but nothing untoward or illegal was found.

Once they'd entered the main office, she followed Robert into one of the conference rooms, shocked to see her brother, Kyle, and brother-in-law, Carter. Gasping, she rushed forward, "What's wrong?" The idea that they'd been sent to give her bad news about someone in the family almost had her drop to her knees.

"The family's fine," Kyle said, his lips tight.

Unable to read the expression on his face, she stood with her fingers gripping the back of the nearest chair. "Then… what's going on?"

"We need you to sit, Caitlyn," Carter said, his voice softer than Kyle's.

Her gaze bounced between the two of them, still unable to discern the situation but following his direction. She walked on stiff legs around the chair and sat, perching on the edge, her hands clasped in her lap. Refusing to speak until they told her what was going on, she clamped her lips shut and stared.

"The dogs reacted to your car."

Kyle's voice clipped out each word, hard and unyielding. She blinked, not understanding. "The dogs reacted to my car?" she repeated.

Carter shot Kyle a glare and then turned back to her. "The drug dogs were brought in today but only for the parking lot. They were taken around and allowed to sniff all of the vehicles. The students' cars in the student parking lot were done first, and some had to be searched. Occasionally, nothing was found, but in others, drugs or drug paraphernalia were discovered."

Still not understanding what this had to do with her, she forced her body to remain still, waiting to see what they had to say.

"Near the end of the day, the dogs were taken around the building and also moved through the teachers' parking lot. Where the dogs reacted, we asked teachers to allow us into their vehicles. The dogs reacted to your car, and we need to be able to do a search."

"Okay." She reached her hand into her purse and pulled out her keys, holding them out toward Carter.

"Thank you," he said. Glancing down at Kyle, he then turned to another man in the room and handed them to him before turning his attention back to Caitlyn. "Because we're related, we can't be in on the search."

Trying to keep her voice from shaking, she forced her breathing to steady. "I can't imagine what the dogs reacted to, but I have nothing to hide." Looking over to the other side of the table, she held Kyle's gaze, the McBride blue eyes staring back at her. "Kyle, talk to me. You can't possibly think I have anything in my car."

Of all her siblings, Kyle was the most intense, sometimes hard to read. He sighed heavily, scrubbing his hand over his face before leaning forward, placing his forearms on top of the table, his hands also clasped together. "I know you, sis. No, I don't think you have anything in your car. I'm just pissed that of all the people I know in the school that have shit and deal shit, you have to be faced with this because the dogs reacted."

Her brow furrowed as she tried to imagine the scene in the parking lot. "They're trained to just sit when they smell something, right?"

Nodding, he said, "Yes. Generally, it's with drugs but there can be other things that might confuse the dog, so that's why we check it out."

It only took a few minutes for the other officer to come back into the room, but each moment felt like an eternity. The battle between throwing up and passing out was real. He laid Caitlyn's keys on the table while shaking his head. "Nothing was found."

Even though she knew that there were no drugs in her car, she could not hold back the air rushing from her lungs.

"The dog reacted to a scent in the back seat, not the trunk. But, upon close inspection, there was nothing to be found."

While his words were exonerating her, she could not help but feel that his tone was implying guilt.

"Have you carried anything in your car that you think might have caused a reaction?" Carter asked. "Anything from someone else?"

Jerking slightly, her eyes widened as she looked at them. "I just had my car filled with potpourri, scented candles, and herbal tea for the Fundraising Fair. Good grief, all of that essential oils, dried herbs, various flavors, and scents has made my entire car smell strange but also very citrusy and grassy!"

Kyle jolted, his eyes wide. "All that crazy smelling stuff you were selling? Hell, no wonder they reacted."

"Yes," she groused.

He, Carter, Robert, and the other officer all nodded, their stances relaxing, as well. Seeing Kyle's face after she'd given her explanation made her love her brother even more. He trusted her, hated that she'd been put through this, but was relieved as fuck that there was a good reason. Carter grinned widely, his expression going a long way to helping quell the nerves still jumping around in her stomach.

The other officer who was writing looked up. "I'm taking all this down, and we'll just need you to sign it."

Carter stood, and as he walked out of the room reached over to squeeze her shoulder. "I know that was nerve-wracking. Sorry to put you through that. I'll see you at the next family dinner, okay?"

She twisted her head and looked up at him, plastering a wide smile on her face. It's not that it was fake, she truly loved her brother-in-law. But right now, her skin felt prickly as anxious nerves continued to slither over her. "It's okay, no worries. And yeah, I'll see you at the next family get-together." She watched as he and the other officers walked out of the room, probably to go question someone else.

Blowing out a breath, she signed the form the officer held out to her after reading it over. Looking up, she noticed Kyle remained in the room although he shifted to a chair closer to her. It was on the tip of her tongue to ask if he didn't have someone else to go question and terrorize but she knew that was petty. He had a job, and truth be known, she wanted him to help rid the drugs from her school. But, still raw, she sat waiting to see what else he was going to say, her gaze roving over him. Her three brothers were so similar in appearance, it was easy to tell they were siblings. But where Rory often had a smile on his face, and Sean had a benevolent maturity, Kyle had always been more of a loose cannon, and yet, one of the first to jump to her defense and make sure he was taking care of his baby sister.

"You okay?" he asked.

"Kyle, my car was so crammed with scented everything this past weekend that I'm not surprised the dogs trained for sniffing drugs reacted. But you've got to cut me some slack. Getting called down to the office at the end of the day, being questioned by the police, and knowing that the police are searching my vehicle was all a bit nerve-wracking."

He reached over and held her hand. "I'm sorry, sis." He stood and bent, kissing the top of her head before she stood and they wrapped her arms around each other.

"Don't be, Kyle. You've got a job to do and I'm glad you're here doing it. I know kids are using and dealing. And I'd like that shit out of my school, so if I have to be a little uncomfortable during the process, that's okay."

They walked out together, then said goodbye. She had no desire to go back up to her room, so she headed out to the teachers' parking lot. Approaching her car, she had the strange feeling of violation. Ridiculous, since the only thing they did was take a look inside her car and let the dog sniff. And yet, her insides still twisted and turned.

"Caitlyn!"

She turned at the sound of her name and saw Renée and Barbara hurrying toward her. A smile met her lips, the first real one she'd had in almost an hour. "Hey," she greeted, her voice weary.

"Are you okay? We heard they were searching a lot of vehicles," Barbara said.

Renée glanced toward her car before shifting her gaze back to Caitlyn. "What do you think it was?"

"I heard there were at least four cars where there was nothing but lawn grass or insecticides," Barbara continued. "Although, there were about six kids who had drugs or drug paraphernalia in theirs."

"It must have been all the stuff I brought to the fair," she replied.

Renée snorted, then winced. "Oh, my God. I'm sorry, but I just thought of how all that incense must have driven those dogs' noses crazy!"

"You're right. I had candles, potpourri, herbal tea. All those scents mixed together in my car must have set the dogs off."

The other two women nodded before Caitlyn hugged them goodbye. Climbing into her car, she heaved a sigh before pulling out onto the road. She tried to maintain the air of nonchalance but to no avail.

Arriving at home, she parked and looked toward the house, her gaze landing on Griffin and his crew working on the porch at the side of the house, Russ with them. Suddenly, hit with a thought, she jolted. *Russ' backpack! His backpack had been in my car also!*

Having no idea what to do, she climbed from her car, offering a weak smile when Griffin waved. Her smile faltered when Russ turned and looked at her, a slight grimace on his face. She forced the corners of her lips to lift again before heading to the front door.

She'd barely made it through the front door when Margaretha's door opened and her name was called. "Caitlyn, my dear, come and have tea with me."

She hesitated for a few seconds, battling between the desire to go home, break out the wine, and hide from everyone, or sit with her sweet landlady and let Margaretha's tea and cookies make life seem a little better. Her shoulders slumped, tea and cookies winning out. *After all, I can have wine later.*

Stepping inside, she felt the stress of the day ebb as she was ushered to the sofa, the tea set already on the coffee table along with the plate of cookies. Sinking into the soft cushions, she breathed in the scent of Margaretha's soft perfume blending delightfully with the apple-spiced tea. "I love the smell of your place." As soon as the words left her mouth, she scrunched her nose and said, "I suppose that sounded really weird, didn't it?"

Margaretha chuckled. "Not at all. I love the scent of fresh-baked cookies and tea, also." Leaning closer, she added, "Occasionally, the various scent experiments from across the hall are a little hard to take."

Laughing, she nodded. "Remember last year when Bjorn tried a new holiday potpourri and mixed juniper, apple, pumpkin, and sage? He tried to say it was for Thanksgiving, but it was horrible!"

"Oh, yes, I remember! I had some women from the church over and three of them left in a fit of sneezing!" Shrugging, she added, "But then, they get it right, and it smells wonderful!"

They sat in silence for a moment, sipping their tea before Margaretha finally said, "You look like you have something on your mind, sweetie."

She leaned forward and placed her teacup back onto the table. "I had a difficult afternoon, and now have some... concerns... uh... about something... about a student." She swept her hand through her hair, her fingers dragging through the tresses. "I honestly don't know what to do. To do something and be wrong could be devastating to them. To do nothing could be turning a blind eye to a larger problem."

"You work with youth all the time. What do you tell them when they come to you for advice?"

Snorting, she grinned as she looked up at Margaretha's twinkling eyes. "I tell them that no one can make up their minds for them. That they need to weigh the pros and cons and learn to make decisions for themselves."

"Then that is what you must do, my dear." They sat quietly for a moment, both still sipping their tea. "I have no photographs of my parents."

At the unexpected words, Caitlyn blinked, her attention snapping to Margaretha. A strange foreboding moved over her, wondering what was coming next while knowing something profound was moving through the room.

"The German army came through my town when I was only eight years old. We were not Jewish, but my parents had many Jewish friends. They did what they could to protect them even though it was declared against the law. But to no avail. My father was taken along with others. I never saw him again."

Caitlyn's breath halted, ignoring the burning in her lungs as her chest squeezed. "Oh, I'm so sorry."

Margaretha waved her hand, her gaze gentle as she looked at Caitlyn. "Oh, my dear… I don't tell you this for sympathy but to impress upon you that sometimes doing the right thing isn't always the right thing to do."

She stood, and Caitlyn took to her feet quickly. They remained silent as they gathered their cups and plates, taking them into the kitchen where they worked side-by-side at the sink. Caitlyn's mind whirled as they walked to the front door. Bending to wrap her arms around Margaretha, she whispered, "Thank you."

Margaretha smiled and patted her back. "No, my child. Thank you."

Just as she started up the stairs to her apartment, Terri and Bjorn came in through the front door. Greeting them, she felt her chest ease at their smiles.

"Oh, girl, we have to thank you for the fundraising money!" Bjorn said, his hands waving all around. "You sold everything, and even splitting the profits with the fundraiser, we came out ahead!"

"I'm glad," she said, her spirits lifting more. "I have to confess, though, that the drug-sniffing dogs came through the parking lot today and must have caught the scent of all the potpourri—"

"Oh, phooey!" Terri cried, her eyes wide. "That always causes such problems!"

"It does? What problems?"

Bjorn's shoulders slumped. "I was stopped at airport security. I called it profiling just because I had on a tie-dyed shirt!"

Terri nodded emphatically. "Yes! They searched everything, but all we had were candles wrapped that we were taking to his parents."

Bjorn leaned forward as though whispering state secrets. "They also had pulled over that woman with the bread."

Having trouble following their bouncing conversation, she tilted her head. "Bread?"

Not to be outdone, Terri jumped in. "Yes. The dogs sniffed a woman's suitcase, and the security came rushing over. Turns out, she had baked bread... you know, like naan—"

"Oh, it was so fresh and smelled divine!" Bjorn interjected.

"What happened?"

Terri shrugged. "The security walked off with her and the bread. Who knows?" Looking down at the bag in her hand, she said, "Oh, we've got to go. My frozen tofu is starting to melt."

Finally, ascending the stairs and into her apartment, Caitlyn crossed the living room to the large window overlooking the front. Griffin's crew was packing up, placing their tools in their trucks, and calling out goodbyes to each other. Griffin stood to the side with Russ, both smiling. *Looks like Griffin is taking him home.*

Moving away from the window, she walked into the kitchen and stared into the refrigerator until inspiration struck. Mindlessly pulling out ingredients, she thought of how Terri and Bjorn's scented products had caused the drug dogs to react at the airport, accepting it was just dumb luck that she'd had some of their products in her car.

But Russ' backpack had also been in her car. Could there have been anything in there to tip off the dogs? Giving the police Russ' name was the right thing, but staring out her window at the young man she knew was struggling to find his place in the world, she had to decide if it was the right thing to do.

24

Griffin stood in the front yard, his crew having secured their equipment. Russ stood near, waiting for a ride to his home. "You ready to go, Russ?"

Once inside the truck, Russ fiddled for a moment then drew a deep breath. Clearing his throat, he said, "I just wanted to thank you. I looked at the paycheck you gave out today. It's... well," he squeezed the back of his neck in a movement familiar to Griffin. "It's more than I thought. It's way more than I was making at the grocery store. My mom's gonna freak."

Griffin grinned. "It's well-deserved. You're starting out doing everything I ask. We'll move you to more construction soon, and if you want, I'll teach you more about the work I do."

"I'd like that. Thanks."

It only took fifteen minutes to pull up outside a small but neat house. He'd dropped Russ off several times, but instead of jumping down from the truck, Russ hesitated, looking out the window. A small woman appeared in the doorway, her hands clasped in front of her.

"Um, would you like to meet my mom? I know you talked to her on the phone, but she was off today so she's here now."

"Yeah, that'd be great." He climbed from the truck and met Russ on the sidewalk. Looking toward the house, he saw Russ' mom smile widely as they approached.

"Mom, I'd like you to meet my boss, Griffin Capella."

Griffin thrust his hand out, smiling as she took it gently. "It's a pleasure to meet you, Mr. Capella. I'm Karen."

"Karen, it's nice to meet you, as well. And please, call me Griff."

Russ reached into his pocket and pulled out the check, thrusting it toward her. "Mom, I got paid today."

She hesitated, pink dusting her cheeks, but looked at Russ before glancing back at Griff. Taking the check, she glanced down, and her eyes widened before darting up again. "This... this is very generous."

"He works two to three hours every day after school and five to six hours on Saturday. Believe me, Karen, it's well-deserved."

"Mom, that's a lot more than I was getting at the grocery store."

Griffin hid his smile, hearing the excitement in Russ' voice but knowing the young man was trying to maintain his cool demeanor.

She lifted her brow as she smiled. "You know what you have to do with that, right?"

"I know, I know. It goes in the bank." Russ looked over at Griffin. "Mom made sure I set up my own bank account. That way, I learned to save, it gets a little interest, and keeps us safe."

"Your mother's a smart woman."

Karen smiled up at him. "Griffin, would you like to stay for dinner? It's the least we can do for taking a chance to help Russ."

"Thank you, but some other time. I know my girlfriend has already got dinner started."

"He's dating Ms. McBride, my English teacher. She's the one that talked to Griffin about hiring me."

"And we'd love to have both of you to dinner. I'll have Russ check with your schedules, and he knows my work schedule. I do hope you'll make plans to come."

"Karen, it would be an honor. I'll talk to Caitlyn and we'll come up with a date."

She smiled, then turned to see the two younger children standing at the door. "Lovely. Thank you again." She turned and walked back inside, shooing the curious children back into the house.

Russ ducked his head. "I don't want you to think that I just blow my paycheck. Mom hates taking any, but I always give her a bit to help out—"

Throwing his hand up, Griffin said, "You don't have to tell me what you do with your pay."

"I know, but I just wanted you to know how much we appreciate the chance. Mom makes me save what I can in case I ever wanted to go to college, but I don't. I planned on a trade, but if I can learn from you and don't have to spend money for a trade school, then that's just more for my future and to help my mom." He drew in a deep breath and stuck out his hand, nervousness moving across his face.

Grinning, Griffin took his hand, accepting the shake. "Keep up the good work, Russ, and I'll see you tomorrow."

Driving home, a smile remained on his face. He liked Russ. Liked helping him. And liked thinking that Russ might find his way in life, following the same pursuits he enjoyed. Parking, he felt his phone vibrate. A text from Caitlyn had come in. **Come on over after shower. Soup's on.**

It was early days in their relationship, but they shared meals and nights in her apartment mainly because it was comfortable, and she seemed so at home in her place. The idea that he was encroaching niggled at him, but she always assured him she wanted him there.

After his shower, he walked across the hall, finding her door unlocked. "Hey, babe." He moved behind her as she stood in the kitchen, stirring a pot on the stove that smelled amazing. Nuzzling her neck, he loved the sound of her giggle, knowing he was creating goosebumps over her arms.

She let go of the spoon and turned, her gaze meeting his. "Hey, yourself. Good day?"

"Yeah, not bad. You?" She crinkled her nose, and he suspected a story was behind that expression. "What's up?"

"Dinner is almost finished. Then we can talk, and I'll tell you all about it."

"Sounds good. I wanted to talk to you about something also."

Soon, they sat down to bowls of clam chowder and fresh bread from the corner grocer. "So, you first," she said, breaking off little pieces of bread to drop into her soup.

"I met Russ' mom when I took him home."

Caitlyn sat back in her chair at his words, waiting.

"He'd expressed surprise and gratitude when he got his first paycheck. The pay period rolled around after he'd only been with me for a week, but it was more than he expected. He immediately showed it to his mom, and I can tell it meant a lot to her, as well. She asked us to dinner and wants Russ to coordinate our schedules and her work schedule. I told her we'd do that. I hope that was okay."

"Oh... of course. Yeah, that'd be fine."

"I think he just reminds me so much of myself. Dad's out of the picture. Mom's doing the best she can. And Russ has a lot of responsibility to help."

Caitlyn's face softened and she leaned forward, placing her hand on his arm, her fingertips sliding over his skin. "I'm glad he's working out for you."

"You're the one who has to take the kudos for sending him my way, Caitlyn. You're the one that saw his potential." She seemed to hesitate again, so he prodded, "Now, you were going to tell me about your day."

After a moment's prevarication, she finally opened up to tell him about the drug dogs indicating something at her car, her brother and brother-in-law being there as she felt interrogated even if it wasn't a true interrogation, and then ending with nothing being found.

Brow creased, he licked his lips before asking, "And they think it was the scent of all the boxes from T&B?"

She shrugged, her eyes staying pinned on her now-empty bowl.

"Hey, sweetheart. You okay?"

Her gaze lifted and a half-hearted smile curved her lips. "Yeah. I mean what else could it be, right? Even Terri and Bjorn told me that they've gotten stopped at airports when they pack some of their products. They even remember seeing a woman stopped by the drug dogs when all she had was some homemade naan bread in her suitcase."

"I'm sure it was upsetting, though. You probably felt as though everyone was wondering what you did, and then to have your brother right there, you really felt under the microscope."

"I knew I hadn't done anything wrong, but it was embarrassing, nonetheless."

He took her hand and drew her to her feet, guiding her to his lap. She settled on his thighs, her arms wrapped around his neck, and lay her head on his shoulder.

"So, is that it, or are there any lingering issues?"

She sighed. "That's it. I told them about T&B's products in my car and they searched and found nothing. So, it's a done deal. No harm, no foul as my brothers would say."

So many emotions crossed Caitlyn's face, and his heart ached for her. He wanted to be her champion in all things. Take away the pain. Keep the world at bay. But all he could offer was a shoulder to cry on. "And yet, it feels like a foul, doesn't it?"

She sniffed and nodded, her shoulders slumping as though the weight of the world rested on them.

"Was there anything else, babe?"

She stared at him for a long moment, but he had no idea what she was thinking. Finally, heaving another sigh, she shook her head. "No."

He wasn't entirely sure he believed her, but if she needed to work something out on her own, he wanted her to feel free to do so. He just hoped when she was ready, she'd come to him. "You need time to yourself tonight?"

She startled and leaned back, hitting him. "Time?"

"Yeah, babe. I know I've been over every night recently, but it hit me that I haven't asked. I don't want you to feel that you don't have a choice."

Her body relaxed, a soft smile curving her lips. "No, Griffin, I don't want to be alone tonight. I like having you here with me." Sucking in her lips, she inhaled deeply, her gaze dropping to his chest.

"Talk to me," he prodded. "Please."

"My parents want to meet you." Her words came out in a rush. "I know it may seem early in our relationship and I can tell them no. I don't want you to feel like—"

"My mom wants to meet you, too."

Her mouth snapped closed as her eyes widened. "Your mom? I didn't know you told her about us."

"Why wouldn't I?"

"Um... I don't know." A nervous laugh slipped out. "I

guess since we hadn't defined what we are, then I didn't know if you'd told anyone."

Lifting a hand, he brushed her hair back from her face. "Yeah, babe. My crew knows. My mom knows. My family knows. Even Russ and his mom."

"So, now, we have an invitation to my parents' for dinner, your mom's for dinner, and Russ' family for dinner?"

Chuckling, he slid his arms around her waist and pulled her tight. "Looks like we've got some people willing to feed us for a while."

With her arms now around his neck, she leaned in and placed her lips on his. "I guess we're going to need to work up an appetite."

Her words shot straight to his cock. "Can't think of a better time to start than now."

"I was hoping you were going to say that," she mumbled against his lips.

Not about to ignore that invitation, he sealed his lips over hers, stood with her in his arms, and stalked toward the bedroom. Letting her body slide down his, he slowly laid her on the bed and grinned. "This is the best way I know to make a crappy day better, babe. So, hang on and let me do the work. I promise, I'll take care of you." With her easy acquiescence, he settled in to do just that.

25

"I can't believe none of our carriers were picked up by the dogs that went to the school."

The leader looked over, nodding. "Even if the dogs reacted, our carriers know to not keep anything in their vehicle. It helps to keep the deals off school properties. It reduces the risks to all of us."

"Did you hear the police got some?"

"Yeah, but not any of ours. Dumb fucks."

"I can't believe they took the dogs to the teacher parking lot."

"No one had anything, though, so that just leads credence to try to keep the dogs off the school property. Someone will complain and maybe there will be pressure to stop the practice."

Two teens walked into the darkened room, their eyes darting all around. One took a deep breath and said, "Ms. McBride had to have her car searched."

"No shit," the other teen said as their eyes widened.

The leader flicked their hand out in a dismissing

motion. "It's all good. Nothing found. But again, just goes to show that the dogs can react to things besides what they're trained for."

The others continued talking, but the one teen remained quiet, their lips tight and heart pounding. *How did I get myself into this? And how am I going to get out?*

26

"Okay, Theodore Dreiser's *Sister Carrie* discussion today," Caitlyn announced, looking out over her advanced juniors, ignoring their groans. Teens always groaned when approaching literature, but she knew as soon as the discussion began, they'd jump in with insightful if not sometimes delightful comments.

Several weeks had passed in glorious reprieve of any drama in her personal life and with little out of the ordinary. After Griffin had talked about Russ' family reminding him so much of his own, she'd concluded that the last thing she wanted to do was make anything more difficult for the young man. To bring his name up to the police with no proof could have been catastrophic.

She and Griffin had made the rounds to their dinner invites, first tackling her family. She'd warned him that an invite from her parents would never involve just her parents. She never knew how many siblings and their significant others would come, but she should've known everyone wanted to spec out their baby sister's boyfriend. She'd threatened all of them to be on their best behavior but should have known that Griffin could handle himself with a large family. In fact, she thought her family was impressed with how well he fit in. Sean recognized another oldest sibling. Her sisters and sisters-in-law loved looking at pictures of some of the old houses he'd worked on. Kyle and Rory enjoyed listening to his stories of his own siblings' adventures and misadventures. And her parents loved the way he often reached over to touch or hug her.

Her next dinner invite had been with his family, and it was much like her own family. His siblings were sweet, his nieces and nephews were adorable, and his mother was delightful. It was obvious how proud she was of all her children and equally how much they all loved her. It was easy to see herself considering them her family, too. But she kept that thought private, too afraid to voice how much she could see a future with Griffin.

And then they'd gone to have dinner at Russ' house. She'd had reservations about having dinner with a student's family but pushed them down. Griffin was right about the parallels between his family and upbringing and Russ'. The house may have been much smaller than the one she'd been raised in, and no father was sitting at the head of the table, but pride was evident, all the children pitched in to help, and it was easy to see that love filled the home.

Russ appeared to be flourishing under Griffin's tutelage, and their crew had finished refurbishing and replacing much of the porch that encircled Margaretha's house, now moving to the inside. It wasn't the only house Griffin was working on, and since discovering that Nate didn't live too far from Russ, he had begun to take him home, freeing up more time Griffin had to spend at the different houses where his crews were working.

Now that school was firmly settled into the semester and her life was settled into the routine of dinner with Griffin at night and he in her bed each morning, she smiled out over her students.

"You've now read the entire book and have had a chance to start on your essays. Who can give me a sentence summary… just a sentence?" Looking around, she nodded. "Cora?"

The girl with multiple piercings that Caitlyn could see—and probably more that she couldn't—replied, "For all the critics go on and on about this book, it's really about a poor girl who rises in society and a man who started out high who falls down."

"It's more than that!" another student grumbled.

"Yeah," Cora said, "but Ms. McBride said to put it in one sentence!"

Nodding, she said, "What happens when you have to reduce a novel to a sentence is that you strip away everything except the one concept that stands out for you." Casting her gaze around she asked, "Who else?"

"I couldn't understand at first why this was such a controversial book," Marty added. "I mean, what's the big deal about a woman making money? But, when you talked about what society was like at the time, it's a big deal."

"Yeah, and how she made it. She became an actress... not exactly an honorable profession then," Joanne said, rolling her eyes.

"And she slept with men," another student called out, much to the rolling eyes and amusement of the others.

"Your American History teachers are at the same point we are," Caitlyn reminded. "What tie-in can you find?"

Another student piped up. "Capitalism! Anyone can earn money, make a living, societal norms are blown out of the water!"

"Some people only look after themselves, not caring about others or society."

At the last softly spoken words, Caitlyn jerked her head around to see Russ, his face tight. "Okay, Russ," she prodded gently, "can you explain a little more?"

He looked down at his opened, dog-eared book. "They have no feeling that any result which might flow from their action should concern them... They think only of themselves because they have not yet been taught to think of society." He looked up and continued, "It goes on to basically say that when they get caught and punished, they don't make the connection that it's due to their own misbehavior."

Nodding slowly, she licked her lips in hesitation of asking him for more considering his face held a multitude of emotions. Deciding to put the question to the class, she asked, "What do the rest of you think of this?"

"It's saying that some people don't care what they do as long as they don't get caught."

"Hell, that's like a lot of people I know, my stepfather included!"

The discussion continued until she gave out the next assignment just before the bell rang. As the students filed out of her classroom, she wanted to ask Russ to stay back but didn't need to. He was already waiting for her after the last student left.

"Ms. McBride, can I talk to you?"

Seeing his face twisted and his eyes flashing, her heart squeezed. "Of course. Let's sit down." She led him to the closest desk and settled into the one next to it. "What's going on?"

His forearms lay on the desktop, fingers gripping together tightly. He opened and closed his mouth several times, the struggle to form words evident.

The desire to take away his pain or at least give him the ability to speak of what halted his words was so strong that she gave up on trying to let him verbalize his thoughts on his own. "Please, Russ, just talk to me. Whatever it is, I'll help."

His gaze searched hers, peering deeply, and she remained still, hoping whatever he was looking for, he found.

Finally, he nodded. "I need to talk to someone, but whatever I do, it needs to come from me. So, if I talk to you, will you not go to Griffin?"

She blinked, trying to hide her surprise. She'd never been involved with someone that also knew her student, and the implications of that difficulty were now evident. But, whatever he needed, she'd give. "Okay. I won't tell Griffin what you tell me, but you have to know that I'll do whatever I can to help you with whatever you're struggling with."

He blew out a long breath, still looking down at his hands. "It's hard. Money being tight... it's hard. I used to peek out of my room at night and see Mom at the kitchen table, bills lined up neatly, her checkbook out, and a calculator in front of her. I'd hear her sniffling. I came out once and asked her what was wrong. She looked me in the eye, and I could see the internal debate going on inside of her and it killed me."

His voice broke a little and he cleared his throat while Caitlyn swallowed deeply to keep her own tears at bay.

"She told me that she would pay a little bit on each bill so that the creditors didn't shut off our electricity or water, but that she couldn't pay them all off each month." He looked up at Caitlyn and said, "I went to bed that night and swore that from then on, I'd do whatever I could to help. I told Mr. Jackson at the grocery store that I was fifteen. If he would hire me, then I'd work for whatever I could. Since he couldn't hire me officially, then I worked *unofficially*."

"What does that mean?"

"Until I turned fifteen, I worked at the grocery store after school and on weekends off the books. He paid me in cash and neither of us reported the arrangement."

"And your mom?"

His shoulders hefted. "She was upset at first, but Mr. Jackson was nice. I kept up with my schoolwork and still helped with the other kids. And when I handed over my first pay, she cried." His gaze jumped to hers. "You gotta understand that Mom didn't want to take my money, but I insisted. So, we agreed. She got part to help with bills, and I saved part for my future. My sister helps, too. As soon as I turned fifteen, he hired me officially, but Mom and I kept the same agreement. Now that my sister works also, she does the same thing. And, of course, now that I work for Griffin, the money is more. Plus, Mom has a raise, so the family needs less, and I put more into the bank."

"Okay... I'm glad you shared, but so far, I'm not hearing anything concerning." As the words left her mouth, she wondered if he was going to confess to illegal activity to bring in more money, and her stomach clenched at the thought.

"People think when you need money, you're willing to do anything. But to me, they're just like in *Sister Carrie*. They're willing to only think of themselves, not what's right or wrong. That's not how I was brought up."

Heart threatening to pound out of her chest, she nodded slowly, hoping to encourage him to keep talking, all the while terrified of what he was going to say.

"I'd been approached by another kid who just said that he was supposed to find someone good to join forces with. I turned him down, but one afternoon, I saw him going into the locker rooms after school. I followed him, and sure enough, he was searching through lockers, looking for stuff. He was confused, nervous, sweating, couldn't remember where it was supposed to be stowed. I found it but told him I was getting rid of it. He could tell whoever that he never found it. I stuffed it into my backpack. Coming out of there, we saw you. I felt like you could see right through me and right into my backpack. I was fucking scared. If you turned us in and they searched my bag, I was a goner."

"Oh, my..." she breathed, her voice as shaky as her hands. "What did you do?"

"I got to the nearest men's room down the hall and pulled out the bag. There was a smaller bag of pills and four bags of white powder. I emptied all the bags into the toilet and flushed them away."

The implications of what he'd done slammed into her, and she fought to keep from slumping into the floor. With her family's law enforcement background, it was impossible to keep work discussions out of their conversations. With her brothers, especially Kyle working for the HCPD Drug Task Force, she'd heard tales of informants going missing or turning up dead, gang-related executions, retaliations, and a host of other equally horrific punishments meted out for interfering with the drug-running trade. Questions rushed at her, but before she had a chance to verbalize her tumultuous thoughts, he continued.

"I know I was lucky as fuck to get away with it. Probably only because the other guy kept his mouth shut. I gotta tell you, I walked around fearing for my life for a while, definitely keeping an eye on my back. The only good thing is that since I had no idea who put the stuff there, I had nothing to tell anybody. So, I kept my mouth shut, my head down, and went about my business." He lifted his head and pinned her with another hard stare. "I'm no hero, Ms. McBride. I didn't want that shit to affect me or my family."

Leaning forward, she placed her shaking fingers on his arm, feeling the tension in his muscles. "You know, Russ, heroes aren't always found in uniforms on the battlefield or escaping burning buildings with a child in their arms. They don't always show up on a white horse. Heroes are everyday people, going about their everyday business, who step in and do something extraordinary for someone else. And most of the time, we never even know who they are or what they've done. You saved that other student, but more importantly, you saved countless others whose lives would've been affected if those drugs had gotten out into the pipeline of dealers and users."

"Ms. McBride, my backpack had been in your car, and the dogs smelled something. Everybody knows you got called down and they didn't find anything. But I could've said something. I should've said something. I just froze. Griffin had given me a job that's going to teach me a trade and make my life better. My mom was happy with the money. And I felt like I turned the corner. And then I thought about you being questioned by the police, and I should've fuckin' said something."

"No... no. It's okay."

Anguish distorted his features. "Why didn't you say something, Ms. McBride?"

Sighing heavily, she shook her head. "I thought about it. Honestly, Russ, I almost did after agonizing.

But there was nothing to tell. There was nothing to find in my car. To have said something could have set in motion things that couldn't be undone for no reason."

The two sat, staring at each other, their gazes not wavering as the room filled with heavy emotion. Finally, sucking in a deep breath, she whispered, "Why now, Russ? What's going on now?"

He swallowed deeply, waiting a moment before speaking, his voice stronger. "I was reading *Sister Carrie* and at first just saw it as a novel of social commentary on the times it was written. But I came to the passage about only thinking of self until caught… about thinking of the greater good." Blowing out another breath, he nodded. "Griffin's had some things taken at his work sites. I know it slowed down for a while, but it's started up again."

Griffin had talked to her about what was happening on some of his sites, now having to plan on renting a storage unit where they all took their equipment and tools that didn't go home with them. It was an added expense, but mostly, it was a pain for his crews.

Nodding slowly, she said, "Yes, he's told me."

"I… I don't know anything… not for sure."

She wanted to jump up and shout *'you have to tell him'*, but that would be hypocritical considering she'd kept suspicions to herself. "Okay." Her words were breathy, but the entire conversation had pulled at her emotions over and over.

"One of the… someone… well, someone came to me, probably thinking that since money is tight, I'd be willing to help them…" His face contorted again. "I owe

Griffin so much, but I've got no proof. And they said for me to keep quiet, or they'd make it so Griffin had to fire me—"

"Oh, hell, no!" Caitlyn jumped up from her seat, her blood firing through her veins as she marched back and forth in front of the desk where he was sitting. "Oh, no, Russ. You aren't going to be anyone's fall guy! This isn't right. You've done everything you could to do the right thing, even at personal risk." Dropping down to squat in front of him, she lay her forearms on the desktop near his. "We have to talk to Griffin." As indecision crossed his face, she reached out to take his hand. She couldn't imagine what all he had gone through but knew he was desperate to do the right thing. "Please... Russ, you came to me. You wanted advice on all of this. Let me help."

27

Griffin sat in the dark in the empty living room of the grand old Victorian house that he'd just taken on from clients who were out of the country, and they wanted the entire house to be refurbished to its original glory before they moved in. He loved a blank canvas, one where he could restore the special woodwork in the stairs, porches, detail work while his crew refinished floors, tile, and cabinets.

Taking on a new client at this time was stretching his crews thin, but the payoff would be worth it. The clients were willing to pay top dollar for his services. Both flattered and humbled that Capella Construction was finally taking off, he would be able to hire more workers. Bob and Jack were ready to become on-site supervisors, allowing him to turn over more responsibilities.

For some strange reason, perhaps the quiet of the night, his father ran through his mind. He had no idea where Gerald Capella currently resided. He also had no idea if his father ever thought about his wife and kids he left behind. What Griffin had become he owed to his mom and the people that had mentored him. But he couldn't help but spare his father a tiny thought, wishing the man knew that his son had become successful despite his lack of a father. Shoving those thoughts to the side, he glanced around the room lit only by the moonlight filtering in through the windows.

At night, in the dark, the house creaked occasionally, and he wondered about the original owners. *Did their spirits live on in their former house? Had they shaken at the audacity of the last owners who'd painted the rooms plum and dark blue, replaced the stair posts with metal, and hung modern light fixtures? Or had their spirits celebrated each new owner and their own personal spin on making the stately home their own?*

He scrubbed his hand over his face before lifting his soda bottle to his lips. Staying up late wasn't unheard of for him, but he'd rather be up late making Caitlyn cry out his name than sitting alone in a dark, empty house. Empty except for the building materials and equipment that had been left inside.

A noise was heard coming from the back of the house. Standing without making a sound, he moved out of sight of the hallway, standing near the mantle of the large fireplace. At another time he would have considered the design of the new mantle that would be built that would more closely resemble what was in the original house. But now, all he wanted to do was set eyes on who was entering the house through the kitchen near the back. Pressing against the wall further, he silently stepped into the dining room so that his presence would not be detected.

Nate had come to him with his suspicions, and Griffin had set things in motion. He'd decided which of their working residences would have materials available for an attempted theft and let Nate know the trap he was setting. It had been hard to believe that Russ was stealing from him after the gratitude the teen had expressed, but Nate was adamant he was sure Russ was up to something.

Barely breathing, he waited, wondering if the person now coming down the hall could hear his heartbeat. Footsteps accompanied the thin beam of light as it approached. Peeking around the corner, he waited as the shadowy figure of a man moved into the room, the beam of light landing on the two generators in the far corner. Knowing he could not expose his hand too quickly, he waited as the figure tucked his small penlight into his front pants pocket, hefted the portable generator onto a small dolly, and rolled it back down the hall. Crossing through the dining room, Griffin was able to watch as the figure moved through the kitchen and out the back door, the now-stolen generator moving along with him.

Fifteen minutes later, a repeat performance was taking place. Assuming the first generator had been secured onto someone's vehicle, the shadowy figure was removing the second portable generator in the same way. He waited until they were on the back porch before he flipped on the lights in the kitchen. The figure dressed in black whirled around, his mouth dropping open as they blinked in the bright light.

"Hello, Nate."

Nate stumbled, shock written clearly on his face. "Griff… uh… Griff…"

"Don't even try it, man." Griffin's fingers curled into fists that he forced to rest on his hips instead of planting into Nate's face. "Don't even try to lie your way out of this."

"Lie? No, Griff. Seriously, man, I—"

"Shut the fuck up, Nate. You thought I was going to be at the Anderson House, sitting around waiting for Russ to show up? Well, guess what, asshole? When Russ came to me with his suspicions, I believed him. Now, seeing the evidence, I still can't fuckin' believe that you've been stealing from me."

Nate lifted his hands, shaking his head quickly. "No, no, you got this wrong. Listen, don't turn me in, and I'll get your stuff back."

"Sorry, man. Too fuckin' late." Griffin nodded toward the door just as several armed police officers and two detectives walked in. As Nate was placed under arrest and read his rights, Griffin stepped to the side. "Thanks, Kyle. I know this wasn't your division, but I appreciate all your help."

Kyle grinned. "Hell, helping the department shut down one leg of what we know is an ongoing organized ring of construction site thefts was not a problem. Plus, I never could say no to Caitlyn."

Griffin stayed for another half hour, answering the

questions of the detectives and making sure his equipment was in his truck and secure. Turning back to Kyle as they both made sure the house was locked up, he said, "Caitlyn's the one that brought the young man, Russ, to me as a potential employee. He's been great. Caitlyn's also the one that brought him to me when he had a feeling Nate was the one stealing but had received a message that if he said anything it would be pinned on him. As soon as Nate came to me trying to point the finger at Russ, I knew I was ready to take him down. And none of this would've happened if it hadn't been for Caitlyn's tenacity."

Kyle barked out a laugh. "Tenacity. What a fuckin' perfect word to describe my baby sister."

Griffin stood on the sidewalk and rubbed his chin. Holding the other man's gaze steady, he said, "You might as well know that I've got feelings for your baby sister. And while all you McBrides together can be pretty scary, I'm not going anywhere."

Kyle grinned, and Griffin had no problem imagining Kyle as an undercover drug cop, going after anyone he thought was guilty.

"Well, if you make it official, I'll be the first one to welcome you to the family," Kyle said. Then he leaned in closer and added, "But don't tell Caitlyn that. I'd like to make her sweat it out." Laughing, he clapped Griffin on the back before jogging over to his vehicle.

Three a.m. He should have been wiped out, but knowing Nate had finally been caught red-handed, he felt like he could breathe. As he drove home, he remembered Caitlyn had made him promise to come to her apartment no matter what time it was. Now, pressing on the accelerator, he grinned.

He entered her apartment quietly, closing the door behind him with a soft click. A lamp in the living room had been left on, providing a peaceful glow. Pulling off his boots and leaving them by the front door, he walked toward the main bedroom. Planning on sneaking quietly into bed, he was surprised to see Caitlyn sitting up, her back against the pillows, her e-reader resting on top of the bedspread. Her gaze hit him, and she gasped, throwing back the covers and flying across the room.

"Oh my gosh, are you okay? What happened? Did you catch him? Were the police there in time? Did he even show up tonight?"

Wrapping his arms around her, he lifted her feet from the floor as he chuckled just before planting a kiss on her lips, silencing her questions. Walking toward the bed, he leaned forward and gently set her on the mattress. "It's fine. I'm fine. Now, get back under the covers and stay warm. I'll be right there and tell you all about it." With a quick kiss, he headed into the bathroom where he got ready for bed after taking a quick shower. The boredom from earlier followed by the adrenaline rush was catching up to him. Pulling on boxers, he flipped off the bathroom light and walked back into the bedroom.

Caitlyn had slid down under the covers, her head resting on a pillow but her eyes pinned on him. He walked around to the far side of the bed, turned out the lamp, and climbed underneath the covers. She immediately rolled over and they met in the middle of the bed, their bodies pressed tightly together. "I know you're tired, but please, tell me how everything went down."

With his fingers threaded through her hair, he pushed the heavy tresses away from her face. The barest hint of moonlight filtered in through the window, giving just enough illumination that he could see her large blue eyes. "It went like clockwork," he assured. "About two o'clock, I heard a noise and did exactly what I'd been told. I stayed out of sight until Nate took the first generator and carried it all the way out to his truck. When he came back in, that's when I flipped on the light and stepped out. He tried to make an excuse, but I knew we had him. The police were right there to arrest him, even Kyle."

"I'm so glad Kyle was there."

"I have no doubt it was more for you than me since he's not a robbery detective, but I was grateful for his presence and assistance. The detective in charge told me that there's been an organized ring of construction site thefts, and they were hoping that Nate would give them the information they needed to shut it down."

She heaved a sigh of relief, her sweet breath brushing across his face. "Thank God, it's over, Griffin. I was so worried tonight."

"It's all good, babe. Now with that over with, I can focus more on my job and less on the thefts."

She snuggled closer, her legs sliding between his thighs. "Is your job the only thing you can focus more on?"

He thought he was exhausted, but he was instantly hard with her soft curves pressing in tightly. Sliding his hand from her back down to cup and squeeze her ass, he grinned. "Guess my job isn't the only thing."

She laughed just before he kissed her again, and he felt her mirth deep in his chest. Their lips melded together, tongues dancing. With a little wrangling and not much finesse, they managed to get their underwear off without much interruption to their kiss although a few more giggles and chuckles simply added to the way his body responded to her.

She twisted so that her back was pressed to his front, and with his hands cupping her breasts, he slid his cock into her slick sex. The tight warmth felt like coming home. He buried his nose in her shoulder, the scent of her silky hair mixed with the scent of their arousal filling the air.

Sliding one hand down her front, he circled her swollen bud as his cock plunged, the heat from their friction building. She'd become his everything, and suddenly, he needed to let her know with words and not just his body. "Caitlyn, do you have any idea what you mean to me?"

Her chest heaved with each heavy breath and her hands clung to his arms. Twisting her head, she kissed him, hard and wet, then mumbled, "Tell me."

"Everything. You in my life have become everything."

"What…" Her question died on her lips as he shifted his hips to thrust his cock into the hilt. She cried out his name, her fingernails digging crescents into his arm, the slight sting only serving to make him plunge harder.

As her inner sex gripped him, he shoved his face into

her neck and sucked on the delicate skin between her neck and shoulder where her pulse raced. Crashing over the edge after her, he continued to pulse until she'd drained every drop from him. With his arms wrapped tightly around her, pulling her into his chest, they stayed connected in the most intimate way until their breathing eased, their heartbeats slowed, and he slipped from her body. Nuzzling her neck again, he whispered, "I love you."

She twisted in his arms again, now pressing her front to his, her gaze searching his face before filling with tears. "I love you, too."

They soon fell asleep in each other's arms, Caitlyn first. As he lay listening to her steady breathing, he smiled. *A business that's growing and the woman I love in my arms. Yeah, things couldn't be more perfect.*

28

Caitlyn slipped out of the back of the auditorium and made a beeline for the ladies' room. One of her assigned duties was being at the high school on evenings when there was a band or chorus concert. She never minded her duties, enjoying the music, and was always interested in seeing the activities some of her students participated in.

Walking back into the lobby, she spied Barbara, Jamie, Renée, and Jon standing near the main staircase. Grinning, she walked over. "You guys need a break, also?"

"My duty is to keep an eye on the downstairs hallway going to the gym locker rooms to make sure nobody is sneaking around where they shouldn't," Jon said. He glanced over toward Renée, and his brow lowered. "Are you okay?"

Caitlyn peered closer at her friend, noticing Renée's fingers shake slightly as she rubbed her forehead.

"I've got a headache that I haven't been able to get rid of." Renée sighed. "I left my pain reliever up in my room today. I think I need to go get it."

"I'll go," Caitlyn volunteered. "You don't need to walk around, and quite frankly, I need to stretch my legs."

Renée nodded, then grimaced. Reaching into her purse, she pulled out her keys and handed them over. "I keep them locked in my desk."

"Thanks, Caitlyn," Jon said before turning back to Renée. "Let's go sit over here so you don't have to go back into the auditorium."

"I'll be back as soon as I can," Caitlyn said as she turned and jogged up the main staircase to the second floor. The science wing was at the far end of the building, and she tiptoe-walked as fast as she could down the dark hall, hating the sound of her clicking heels on the tiled floor. Making her way to Renée's classroom, she found the key to enter, then flipped the switch on the wall, blinking as the dark space quickly illuminated with the glare from the fluorescent lights.

Walking straight to Renée's desk, she unlocked the drawers, looking through each one with no success. Finally opening the large drawer, she spied a bottle of over-the-counter headache medicine. Reaching in, she noted a box decorated with the script T&B tea on the top. Knowing it would only take an extra moment to heat a mug of herbal tea in the teacher's lounge, she wondered if Renée would find that soothing.

Reaching into the drawer, she pulled out the box and

opened it. There, on top, were packets of tea, and she smiled, thinking of how many boxes she had packed over the past year of sharing the Victorian house and helping Terri and Bjorn with their business. The shredded paper stuffing around the tea bags seemed disturbed and she pushed it to the side. A large plastic bag with white powder was at the bottom of the box, smaller bags filled with powder shoved to the side.

Staring at the contents, she plopped into the desk chair, still bent over the drawer as she tried to discern what she was looking at. *Why is this packed into the bottom of the box of tea? Is it some of Renée's chemicals for her class? That can't be right... she'd never put chemicals near something she was going to drink.*

The inkling of an idea began to take shape, but Caitlyn shook her head slowly, her mind unwilling to follow the train of thought. With a shaking hand, she placed the box back into the drawer. Standing quickly, she stepped back as though the drawer now contained snakes ready to strike. *But Renée? Why does she have it here?*

"Oh, God," she whispered to the empty room as Russ' words came back to her. *"I got to the nearest men's room down the hall and pulled out the bag. There was a smaller bag of pills and four bags of white powder. I emptied all the bags into the toilet and flushed them away."*

None of what her eyes were seeing or the thoughts her mind was churning made sense. Clapping her fingers over her mouth, she swallowed deeply. *Is Renée receiving drugs and planting them here at school for the kids to deal with? And hiding them where all the mixture of scents will disguise what's here?*

No answers were going to be found, but she startled, realizing she had been gone several minutes and needed to get back to the lobby with Renée's meds. Snatching a tissue from the desk, she picked up a small bag of white powder and shoved it into her purse. Then, making sure the tea box looked just like she'd found it, she grabbed the bottle of headache pills and closed the drawer, locking it securely. Rushing out of the room, she looked back, determining it was as she found it, flipped off the light, and re-locked the outer door. Tiptoe-running back down the dark hall, she jumped when two people came out of one of the dark classrooms.

"Shit!" she cried out, throwing her hands up in front of her.

Barbara and Jamie cried out as well, all three staring at each other, wide eyes. Barbara's lips were slightly swollen and her hair a mess. Jamie grinned, wiping a pink gloss from his lips.

Slapping her hand over her pounding heart, she stared at the two of them, shaking her head. "Jesus, you two are worse than the teenagers slipping around up here to make out!" Inclining her head toward Jamie, she added, "You missed a little of her gloss on your face," and then toward Barbara, she said, "And you might want to smooth your hair back down."

Barbara, blushing furiously, glided her hands over her hair as Jamie continued to wipe gloss off his lips. "Sorry, Caitlyn. We didn't mean to scare you."

As her heartbeat slowed only a tad, she nodded. "It's okay. I need to get back down with Renée's medicine." Hurrying on past them, she made it back to the lobby where Jon was standing next to Renée with a soda in his hand.

Scowling, he asked, "What took you so long?"

"Sorry, I ran into Barbara and Jamie." She hoped her excuse would satisfy, and it seemed to work as he took the bottle from her, tapped out two tablets, and handed them to Renée along with a soda.

The bag of powder in her purse felt like a hot beacon, glaring out for all to see, and she was torn between wanting to get away from Renée and not wanting to draw undue attention to herself. Thankfully, the concert was soon finished, and as the attendees streamed out of the auditorium, she moved away from Renée and hurried out to the parking lot.

Continually looking over her shoulder, she didn't breathe easy until she pulled into her neighborhood. One of the houses down the street appeared to be hosting a party, and she had to circle the block to find a parking spot, grumbling that it wasn't near the Victorian where she usually parked.

Hustling down the sidewalk toward the back of the house, she noted how dark the windows were. Griffin was out at a birthday celebration for his brother. Terri and Bjorn had mentioned a concert near the harbor they planned on attending. And Margaretha was probably in bed or getting ready for it.

Slipping into the back door, she started toward the

stairs when she stopped and sucked in a deep breath. All the way home, she'd tried to decide what course of action made the most sense. Now, standing in the lit main hallway that led from the front door to the back with the wide staircase to the side, she let out a long, slow breath. Pulling out her phone, she dialed Kyle, but it went straight to voicemail. "Kyle, it's Caitlyn. I need you to come to my house as soon as possible. It's official. I'll explain when you get here." She knew her message would probably send her brother off the deep end, but she had to get rid of the bag of powder from her purse, and he'd know what to do with it. Next, she sent Griffin a text. **Come home as soon as you can. It's important. I found something at school and am having Kyle come look at it.**

She started toward the stairs, then halted, her mind still a tangled mess of thoughts. Renée was one of the people who had ordered something from T&B during the fair. *Are they involved also?* She stared at their door, her body halted in shock. *Is she getting drugs from Terri and Bjorn or just using their box to hide them in?*

Blowing out a breath, she tried to stop the pounding of her heartbeat. *Maybe Terri and Bjorn aren't involved. Maybe this has nothing to do with them. Maybe Renée just used the box to hide her own stash.*

Bringing her hands up to the side of her head, she rubbed her forehead, uncertainty filling her. Just like with Russ, she hated the idea of casting suspicion on someone completely innocent. Dropping her hands, she stared at Terri and Bjorn's front door and remembered she had a key to their apartment. Not long after she moved in, they had gone on vacation for a week, and she'd been given a key to water their plants. She'd forgotten about the key, and they must have also. Looking down at her keyring, she flipped through several until she found the one marked T&B.

They're not here. I could slip in and just take a look around for a couple of minutes. She'd spent plenty of time in their spare bedroom where they kept products, samples, supplies, packing boxes, labels, and a multitude of other items that she used when she helped them package their products to mail. She'd never seen anything suspicious there, and as many times as she'd been in that room, she couldn't imagine it was where they'd keep something illegal. She'd also been in their kitchen and living room numerous times. *But their bedroom. I've never spent any time in the bedroom.*

Moving quickly before she decided her idea was completely harebrained and ridiculous, she knocked on their front door just to make sure they weren't there, then unlocked it and stepped in. It was dark, with just a small night light in the hallway between the living room and kitchen that led to the bedrooms. Hurrying into the main bedroom, she flipped on the light switch which turned on a small lamp by the bed. Glancing around, she wasn't sure how she'd ever figure out what they might have. Besides the typical bedroom furniture, the room was crowded with more furniture, including two overstuffed chairs, a tall antique armoire, rugs of multiple colors, and two bookcases crammed full of books.

Feeling a bit claustrophobic, she raced into the

connecting bathroom and glanced inside the vanity cabinets and linen closet, finding nothing. She moved around the bedroom with just as much haste, finding nothing behind the books in the cases, nothing in the drawers although she didn't dig through them, finding that idea to be too distasteful even though she was searching in someone else's bedroom, and nothing in the armoire.

Kneeling on the soft rug near the bed, she spied several plastic storage boxes. Pulling one forward, she unsnapped the top but it was filled with knitting needles and skeins of yarn. *This is ridiculous! What the hell am I doing?* Angry that she'd allowed herself to suspect her neighbors even though she still had to deal with the knowledge that one of her friends and coworkers had drugs with them, she grabbed one last plastic box from under the bed and yanked it out. Unsnapping the lid, she peered down, and this time, her breath halted in her throat. *Oh, Jesus!*

Inside were several large plastic bags, each filled with smaller bags packed with white powder. Her hands shook as she stared down at the contents. And while she could not discern what the powder was, she felt for certain she wasn't looking at baby powder.

Snapping the lid back on, she pushed it back to where she found it. Not wanting to dally any longer, she stood, glanced around to make sure the room looked the way it should, and flipped off the light switch as she went back into the living room. Refusing to let her mind settle on the implications of everything she'd discovered this evening, she cracked open their front door and peeked out, ascertained all was clear, then went out and locked the door carefully behind her.

Tiptoeing toward the main staircase, she heard Terri and Bjorn on the front porch, approaching the front door. Whirling around, she raced to the back door and out onto the porch, pressing herself flat against the wall in the dark.

A grimace settled on her face as she realized she hadn't needed to run away. *I could've just kept walking as though I'd come in the back door and gone up the stairs to my apartment. They'd never know I'd been in their apartment! God, I'm such an idiot!* Standing on the back porch, she drew in a deep breath to steady her heartbeat and prepared to walk back through as though she'd just arrived home from school. Her hand was on the knob when she heard part of their conversation as they approached their front door.

"Renée said she wasn't sure."

"And why the fuck did she send her to her classroom?"

"She had a headache. She wasn't thinking straight."

"Wasn't Jon there? Why the hell didn't he think?"

"Don't be pissed at me! I have no idea!"

"What are we going to do about Caitlyn?"

"Jon's pissed we befriended her and used her since she works at their school."

"Well, we didn't know that when we first started using her. Anyway, she'd never suspect."

"At least not until now."

Their voices faded away as they moved into their apartment. Caitlyn remained, rooted to the new wooden floor of the back porch, her gaze moving over the beautiful spindles that Griffin had made and Russ had painted. His creative project. Her home. Margaretha's beloved Victorian. *The home to drug dealers transporting their drugs to high school students and who knows who else through their business.* More truth slammed into her. *They disguise with scents in potpourri, candles, tea, incense.* Her chest quaked as she squeezed her eyes tightly shut. *And I blissfully helped them.*

Desperate for the safety of her apartment, when it grew quiet in the hallway, she slipped through the back door, tiptoed past their front door, and hastened toward the stairs leading to the second floor. Just as her foot landed on the bottom step, an arm snatched out and banded around her. Emitting a squeal, the cold edge of a sharp object pressing into her neck sealed off any chance for her to cry out.

"No way, Caitlyn. I can't let you do this," Bjorn's voice whispered in her ear, barely heard over the pounding of her heart.

Terri darted out of the door, her eyes wide. "Bjorn, what are you doing?"

"I saw her reflection on the porch when we came in. She heard us and then looked like she was sneaking upstairs."

"Jesus, she's our friend! She was probably just going to her place!" Terri cried, her voice rising with each word, her gaze darting between Caitlyn and Bjorn.

Caitlyn struggled, but Bjorn's arms tightened and the blade dug into the skin. "We can't take a chance," he argued. "I'm not going to prison, Terri. Not happening. Now, get some tape so I can keep her quiet."

Terri hesitated then turned and bolted into their apartment.

Caitlyn's mind raced through the scenarios for defending herself that her brothers had taught, but with the blade so near her jugular, she remained still, her breathing making the sharp edge prick.

A noise at the back door of the house had both of them look up, seeing Griffin walking through the door with Kyle right behind. "Help!" she screamed, instantly bringing Griffin and Kyle racing forward.

"No!" Terri cried out, coming out of their apartment door just behind them as Bjorn shouted, "Move and she dies."

Griffin halted, growling, "Let her go, man. You gotta let her go." He looked over his shoulder toward Terri. "Tell him!"

Kyle stepped forward. "You do not want to do this. Right now, I've got no idea what your deal was, but you're looking at kidnapping, assault with a deadly weapon, and anything else I can throw at you, asshole."

Terri whimpered. "Bjorn, don't... this is messed up, babe. It was just supposed to be easy money. It was just peace, feeling good, making some money, and having fun. This... Bjorn, this isn't right."

"Shut up! I knew it was a mistake as soon as we found out she worked at the school with our people!" He jerked Caitlyn toward the front door. "Terri, get to the car... get it started. I'm going out with her, and we'll get away—"

A horrific crack sounded, knocking Bjorn into Caitlyn, and they jolted forward. She threw out her hands to catch the stair banister, feeling Bjorn slipping to the floor behind her. Whirling around, she spied Margaretha standing behind him, a cast iron frying pan in her hand, her chest heaving.

29

Griffin and Caitlyn crawled into bed at about six a.m., the adrenaline having worn off hours ago. Looking at each other, exhaustion mirrored on their faces, she began to giggle, and he wondered if she was finally reacting to the stress. "Babe?"

"God, I'm so tired, and all I can think is holy moly, what just happened?"

He slid down under the covers and pulled her closer. "Come on, crazy girl. Snuggle up with me." She immediately acquiesced and pressed tightly against him.

As a heavy sigh left her lungs, her sweet, minty breath blew over him and he smiled. Holding her gaze, he swept her hair back from her face. "You okay?"

She nodded, but he was worried.

"Babe, it's okay to say that you're not."

She pressed her lips together, rolling them in for a moment, then sighed again. "No, really, Griffin, I'm good. I mean, my head hasn't quite wrapped around everything yet, but you're safe, I'm safe, a huge drug ring that affected my workplace and a lot of kids has been taken care of."

"Yeah, but that involved four friends of yours, two as coworkers and two as neighbors. That's a lot to take in."

She sucked in another ragged breath before letting it out. "Yeah, that's going to take some getting used to." Her face contorted. "And the kids. The kids they used as carriers. It all makes me sick to my stomach and mad as hell!"

As soon as Margaretha hit Bjorn over the head, Kyle had jumped into action, kicking the knife away from Caitlyn, pulling out zip ties to secure Bjorn while Griffin grabbed Terri. Kyle called into the station, and soon his partner and other officers showed up. And that started the rest of the night.

Kyle reported that Carter and his partner had headed to the school to search Renée's room and Jon's office in the locker room, finding drugs in both places.

Tara, finding out what Carter was doing, had called in the rest of the family, and soon they all descended onto the Victorian. Margaretha was hailed a hero, and while she perched on her sofa, the detectives interviewed Caitlyn. Tara, Kimberly, Rory and Sandy, Erin and Torin, and Sean and Harper had filled the room, all checking on Caitlyn. Soon, Colm and Sharon made their way in as well, wanting to make sure their daughter was all right. Margaretha was going to make tea, but the McBrides had insisted she stay put and fixed tea for everyone.

More calls had come in from the Kings and various

McBrides had fielded those, letting their friends know what was happening.

Considering the crowd, Griffin was sure the officers were glad everyone was in another apartment so they could search Terri and Bjorn's place but assumed Kyle and Carter's detective partners were used to the McBrides' sense of family first.

As everyone had trickled back to their homes, Kyle let them know that the investigation would be ongoing, but what they had was a huge bonus to the department who'd been trying to crack some of the drug traffic going in and out of the high schools. "Right now, Renée is talking. It seems that Terri and Bjorn supplied the heroin and there was an out-of-state supplier of Fentanyl that Renée cut into the heroin. Jon made arrangements for kids who he could coerce to be their carriers and dealers. They tried to keep the operation contained but learned quickly that dealing with teens was difficult. They were in the process of pulling back and only using adult dealers, but Caitlyn stumbled into their operation before they had a chance to pull it out of the school completely."

Caitlyn had slumped against Griffin, her stunned expression hitting him in the gut. She'd shaken her head slowly as her hand squeezed his. "I can't believe it. Even when I saw the evidence in Renée's room, I couldn't believe what I was seeing. And Jon? Oh, my God." Bending forward, she'd placed her elbows on her knees and pressed her head in her hands. "All these people I know. How could I have been so blind?"

"Babe, they hid this part of their lives from you."

She'd twisted her head around, holding his gaze before finally nodding.

After shaking Griffin's hand, Kyle had bent to kiss Caitlyn's head, saying, "Good work, sis. Love you."

After everyone had left, he sat with Caitlyn and Margaretha. His mind hadn't processed everything but wanted to make sure they felt safe. He didn't need to worry... Margaretha brought out the wine, and even though it was almost three a.m., they drank toasts to catching *reprobates,* as Margaretha called them.

"I'm disappointed," Margaretha had admitted. "I thought I was a good judge of character."

"Hey, I used to help them with their business, not having any idea that part of their business was drug dealing!" Caitlyn had slammed back another glass of wine. "I wish I had them back here and *I'd* hit them with a frying pan."

Chuckling, he'd pulled the empty glass from Caitlyn's hand as Margaretha laughed. "Who knew a frying pan could be such a weapon?"

"I know!" Caitlyn had nodded emphatically.

After chatting a few more minutes, they'd hugged Margaretha tightly, Caitlyn tearing up as the reality of the night finally settled over her. As they left their landlady's apartment, he'd swept Caitlyn into his arms and carried her up the staircase and into her apartment.

And now, lying in bed, safely tucked together, he said, "It'll take some time to process, babe, and who knows how much more will come out with the investigation, but just know this: you did something amazing. You've made the world a little safer for those kids in your school, and that's huge." A tear slid down her cheek and he leaned forward to kiss it away. "I love you, Caitlyn," he vowed.

Her lips curved and she let out another cleansing breath. "And I love you back."

As she finally drifted off to sleep, he breathed her in, letting his soul settle. A future with her would never be boring... and it was all he wanted. Smiling, he followed her in slumber.

30

SIX MONTHS LATER

"We're almost there." Caitlyn had her arm looped through Margaretha's with Griffin on the other side. Caitlyn couldn't help but bounce a little as they stopped on the front walk in front of the large Victorian home that Griffin and his crew had finally finished. It was the house that had a view of the North Central High School's stadium from the back deck. Now, painted a soft blue with white trim, the house was a perfect mix of historical replication, just waiting for a new family.

The owners that had hired Griffin had had a change of plans halfway through his restorations. A new job in a new city meant they needed to find a new owner. Willing to sell for less considering the work wasn't complete, Griffin decided to purchase the house. His crew could finish the work and sell it for a profit, or if things went the way he hoped, he'd keep it himself.

He'd involved Caitlyn in all aspects, keeping the new ownership a secret. She'd excitedly helped him choose paint colors, floor patterns, tiles, seeming to enjoy the research necessary to bring the restoration into modern times.

And when he'd dropped to one knee in the middle of the living room and proposed, she'd flung her arms around his neck and cried as he slipped the ring onto her finger. Claiming she couldn't imagine being happier, he grinned, surprising her once more. Telling her that the house they'd lovingly restored together was theirs made the marriage proposal even more exciting.

When the house was finally complete, they moved in. Their families had helped with the move, and at the end of the day, as he looked around at the mass of people in the house, he'd grinned. Combining their two large families simply meant there was that much more love to go around.

Now, he and Caitlyn had a surprise of their own to share. After Terri and Bjorn had been arrested, their apartment searched, and their drug business dismantled, Margaretha had decided she no longer wanted to be responsible for a large house with renters. She wasn't sure what to do but was ready to have fewer responsibilities. "I enjoyed being a landlady, but now, I think it's time to step back." She'd shrugged, adding, "But I have no idea what to do or where to go."

"Then sell this place and come live with us when we move," Caitlyn had blurted.

As soon as she spoke, her gaze sought his, and he'd grinned. His impulsive beauty had come up with the perfect solution. And now, they were ready to show Margaretha their surprise.

"Here we are," Caitlyn said, her eyes bright with

excitement as she gently pulled the blindfold from Margaretha's eyes. "This is home."

Margaretha blinked her eyes, then gasped, clasping her hands together over her heart. "Oh, my!" She twisted around and looked up at Griffin, her smile wide as tears filled her eyes. "It's magnificent! If the inside is anywhere near as beautiful as the outside, you've outdone yourself."

His heart filled with pride mixed with the joy of being able to share their house with her. "Come on, ladies. Let's go in."

The next hour was filled with wandering through each room, Caitlyn showing off each part of the restoration and Margaretha clucking with delight. The first floor held not only the living room, dining room, large kitchen, and family room but two rooms that had been a sitting room and office. Griffin had created a large bedroom, smaller sitting room, and full bathroom, just perfect for Margaretha. While Caitlyn had taken her out that morning for a leisurely brunch, he'd brought in his crew to help move her furniture into the new house.

As soon as she spied her beloved furnishings in her new rooms, she threw her arms around both of them, hugging them tightly.

The wide staircase led to the second floor complete with four large bedrooms and two full bathrooms. A smaller staircase led to the third floor for part of the attic had been finished into a large room, perfect for what he hoped would one day be a playroom for their children.

As they finished their tour, they once again wrapped their arms around each other, hugging tightly. He knew he was lucky. He not only had the love of his family but now his tribe had expanded to all of the McBrides, and by proxy, all of the Kings and now had the delight of bringing Margaretha into their fold, as well.

Looking up, Caitlyn declared, "We're all going to be so happy here!"

He had no doubt she was right.

Six Months Later

Sharon McBride ran through the house after kicking off her shoes as soon as she entered the front door. The wedding at the church was over and the family photographs had been taken, and now it was time for everyone to descend on her backyard for the full reception. Even though the caterers were already here, Hannah was overseeing everything, and the setup was complete with tables, chairs, a portable dance floor, the DJ, and more tables laden with food and beverages, she was in a full-blown tizzy.

Before she made it to the kitchen, Colm caught up with her and gently grabbed her arm, pulling her in close as he wrapped her in his embrace. "Breathe," he ordered softly, kissing the top of her head.

She did as he said and felt her shoulders relax ever

so slightly. Mumbling against his tux-covered chest, she asked, "Why did I think it was a good idea to host the reception here?"

"Because Caitlyn's our baby. Because we've spent the past almost forty years in this house celebrating every milestone. And because we're lucky enough that when we asked her where she'd like her reception to be, she answered quickly that she wanted it to be here, surrounded by everyone she loved. And because of all of those reasons, we are blessed."

She closed her eyes and tightened her grip around his trim waist. This man was her rock and had been for many years. Leaning back, she stared into his handsome face and smiled. "You're right. Let's go throw a party, sweetheart."

He laughed, a sound she never wanted to end, and they walked together into the backyard. Thirty minutes later, with family and friends gathered, they turned and watched as the back door opened and Rory announced loudly, "Give a great big welcome to the newlyweds, Caitlyn and Griffin Capella!"

The gathering erupted into cheers as Caitlyn and Griffin walked into the yard. The evening passed quicker than Sharon could have imagined, and before she knew it, she watched as Colm led Caitlyn onto the dance floor for the father-daughter dance. Hannah and Chauncey King flanked her, providing her with their loyal support.

All around the edge of the dance floor were family. Sean and Harper. Kyle and Kimberly. Tara and Carter. Rory and Sandy. Erin and Torin. And their extended family, the Kings. Brock and Kallie. Brody and Amber. Brianna and Ryker. Blayze and Dawn. Bekki and Killian.

Smiling as Colm handed Caitlyn off to Griffin, she held out her hand, and he led her onto the dance floor, quickly joined by all the others. She tried to keep the tears at bay, but they fell unheeded. It didn't matter; after all, they were tears of joy.

The DJ and caterers had cleaned, packed up, and left. The dance floor, tables, and chairs had been hauled away. Their sons, daughters, sons-in-law, daughters-in-law, and grandchildren had all gone home. Caitlyn and Griffin had thanked and hugged everyone before leaving for their honeymoon.

And now, late at night in the large backyard, two couples sat in the Adirondack chairs, staring up into the starry sky. Sharon was settled on Colm's lap, Hannah on Chauncey's.

"It's hard to believe that we've sat in these yards for the better part of the past forty years," Colm said.

"Thanks for making me feel old," Hannah laughed, taking another sip of wine before leaning her head on her husband's shoulder and looking upward.

"Do you remember when we both moved in next to each other, just a few months apart when Sean and Brock were toddlers? We were both pregnant and so excited to have neighbors that we could become friends with." Sharon reached over and squeezed Hannah's hand.

"Who knew we'd keep having babies, raising them all together?" Hannah said, sighing. "And now, they're all married and out on their own."

Sharon waved her hand around. "And now we have this big yard for all our grandkids to come to play in."

"I figure the grandkids will keep the path between our two houses worn down just like our kids did," Chauncey said. "Less grass for me to mow."

As the four fell into silence, Sharon was sure that their thoughts, like hers, were reminiscing over the years. Finally, she turned to Colm, seeing him staring into the sky. "What constellation do you see tonight?"

Colm was quiet for a moment, but she waited patiently, knowing he would choose just the right words at just the right time.

"Ara."

Blinking, she glanced up and then back to him. "Ara?"

Colm grinned as Chauncey chuckled, both men nodding.

"Well, you're going to have to explain that one," Hannah said, twisting to look at both men.

"Ara... the altar. It's a southern hemisphere constellation, described by Ptolemy. It was the altar where the gods first formed an alliance before defeating the Titans. Chauncey and I found it years ago and remarked then that it reminded us of this yard... these houses. The alliance between the McBrides and the Kings."

Settling deeper on her husband's lap, Sharon

grinned, thinking of her family and friends in Hope City.

Perfect.

This ends this installment of the Hope City series by myself and Kris Michaels... we have had so much fun bringing the McBrides and Kings to you!

For those of you who read each of my releases, here are the next two!
Protecting Her Heart *(Baytown Boys)*
And
Josh *(Lighthouse Security Investigations)*

If you've never read my Baytown Boys series, it's small-town romantic suspense... full of friends, family, love, and happily ever after for our heroes!
Click here for the first book in that series is
Coming Home

Keep reading to discover all my books!
Thank you readers!

ALSO BY MARYANN JORDAN

Don't miss other Maryann Jordan books!
Lots more Baytown stories to enjoy and more to come!
Baytown Boys (small town, military romantic suspense)

Coming Home

Just One More Chance

Clues of the Heart

Finding Peace

Picking Up the Pieces

Sunset Flames

Waiting for Sunrise

Hear My Heart

Guarding Your Heart

Sweet Rose

Our Time

Count On Me

Shielding You

To Love Someone

Sea Glass Hearts

Protecting Her Heart

For all of Miss Ethel's boys:
Heroes at Heart (Military Romance)

Zander

Rafe

Cael

Jaxon

Jayden

Asher

Zeke

Cas

Lighthouse Security Investigations

Mace

Rank

Walker

Drew

Blake

Tate

Levi

Clay

Cobb

Bray

Josh

Long Road Home

Military Romantic Suspense

Home to Stay (a Lighthouse Security Investigation crossover novel)

Hope City (romantic suspense series co-developed with Kris Michaels

Brock book 1

Sean book 2

Carter book 3

Brody book 4

Kyle book 5

Ryker book 6

Rory book 7

Killian book 8

Torin book 9

Blayze book 10

Griffin book 11

Saints Protection & Investigations

(an elite group, assigned to the cases no one else wants…or can solve)

Serial Love

Healing Love

Revealing Love

Seeing Love

Honor Love

Sacrifice Love

Protecting Love

Remember Love

Discover Love

Surviving Love

Celebrating Love

Searching Love

Follow the exciting spin-off series:

Alvarez Security (military romantic suspense)

Gabe

Tony

Vinny

Jobe

SEALs

Thin Ice (Sleeper SEAL)

SEAL Together (Silver SEAL)

Undercover Groom (Hot SEAL)

Also for a Hope City Crossover Novel / Hot SEAL…

A Forever Dad

Long Road Home

Military Romantic Suspense

Home to Stay (a Lighthouse Security Investigation crossover novel)

Letters From Home (military romance)

Class of Love

Freedom of Love

Bond of Love

The Love's Series (detectives)

Love's Taming

Love's Tempting

Love's Trusting

The Fairfield Series (small town detectives)

Emma's Home

Laurie's Time

Carol's Image

Fireworks Over Fairfield

Please take the time to leave a review of this book. Feel free to contact me, especially if you enjoyed my book. I love to hear from readers!

Facebook

Email

Website

ABOUT THE AUTHOR

I am an avid reader of romance novels, often joking that I cut my teeth on the historical romances. I have been reading and reviewing for years. In 2013, I finally gave into the characters in my head, screaming for their story to be told. From these musings, my first novel, Emma's Home, The Fairfield Series was born.

I was a high school counselor having worked in education for thirty years. I live in Virginia, having also lived in four states and two foreign countries. I have been married to a wonderfully patient man for forty years. When writing, my dog or one of my four cats can generally be found in the same room if not on my lap.

Please take the time to leave a review of this book. Feel free to contact me, especially if you enjoyed my book. I love to hear from readers!

Facebook
Email
Website

Made in the USA
Coppell, TX
18 December 2021